He's a theif who would st

SAVAGE
GRACE

New York Times & *USA Today* Bestselling Author

TERESA MUMMERT

Table of Contents

I'm embarrassed to admit I don't live up to my name – *Grace Savage.*

I am neither refined nor fierce.

But my future stepbrother was both. Born with a silver spoon in his mouth and willing to wield it as a weapon – it was no surprise that he was revered at Hidden Hills High.

Ryatt *"Handsome"* Ransom was as beautiful as he is brutal. And when he decided I was a problem, there was no escaping his wrath. He vowed to ruin me. And he would have, had I not stumbled upon one of his many secrets.

Just when I thought I'd gained some semblance of control, I realized Ryatt doesn't play fair. There is no honor among thieves, and *Handsome Ransom* would steal my heart to spite me, no matter the cost.

To the girls whose touch makes a man's heart soft and his cock hard.

PRAISE FOR THE AUTHOR'S PREVIOUS WORK

"If there's one thing I can always count on with Teresa Mummert, it's her ability to craft a story so compelling that it leaves you pleading for more. She has a way of making you feel like you're living out each scene, every struggle, and each kiss. It truly is storytelling at its finest." - *Author Brandy Lynn*

"Hands down one of the BEST books that I have EVER read!!" - *For the Love of Books*

"One of the most AMAZING novels I have ever read!!!" - *Flirty and Dirty Book Blog*

"This book was so incredible, I cried A LOT, I smiled, I loved, and I devoured this book." - *Swoon Worthy Books*

"I truly loved it!! It was captivating and emotional. It tugged at my heart and soul—such an amazing story!" - *Author Kim Karr (Connections series)*

"I think this is my favorite Teresa Mummert book to date." - *Author Jules Snow (Devoured series)*

"It is such a different book and plot. I just loved how unexpected it was." - *Author Debra Anastasia (Poughkeepsie series)*

"Teresa Mummert has a gift, one that many don't possess. It's the gift of being able to suck in a reader so far they don't see the twist in the story coming." - *Author S.K. Hartley (Bad Boys series)*

"SO D*MN GOOD!!!!!!!!!!! I Loved it!!!! Incredible writing!" - *Author Kathryn Perez (Therapy)*

"Every word captured me, and every sentence made me ache for the main characters in this beautiful story." - *Author Amanda Bennett (Broken series)*

"This book was perfect. Flawed characters and a very real, dark past...interwoven perfectly into a web of lies and an amazing ending." - *Author K. Pinson (Mirrored series)*

"It's a beautifully written, riveting story that grabs you from the beginning and keeps you guessing how it's going to unfold until the very end." - *Author Sophie Monroe (Battle Scars series)*

"It's soooooooo good. I honestly loved it!!!!" - *Author Tijan (Fallen Crest series)*

"I think what I loved most was the originality of the story. Teresa nailed this one!" - *Author Maureen Mayer (Second Chance series)*

"I truly believe this to be a masterpiece story and one that will live in my heart for a long time and that Teresa needs to write a sequel and soon!" - *Author Vicki Green (My Savior Forever)*

"He's more myself than I am.

Whatever our souls are made of, his and mine are the same."

— Emily Brontë, Wuthering Heights

PLAYLIST

Closer – Kings of Leon

Addicted to Love – Florence and the Machine

You Should See Me in a Crown – Billie Eilish

Take Me to Church – Hozier

Never Say Never – The Fray

Bad Guy – Billie Eilish

Ready for It – Taylor Swift

Way Down We Go – Kaleo

Sex is on Fire – Kings of Leon

Outside – Staind

Look What You Made Me Do – Taylor Swift

Heathens – Twenty One Pilots

Pillowtalk – Zayn

If You Could Only See – Tonic

Power – Isak Danielson

PROLOGUE

RYATT

"Are you ready to come home now?" My father's voice grated my nerves, and my heart began to thud against my sternum. He wasn't asking. Not really. This was a taunt. He had the power to keep me away for as long as he pleased. And nothing brought my father more joy than to inflict pain upon his only son.

"Things will be different this time," he added.

I rolled my eyes, resting my elbows on my knees. "What's changed?" I rasped, genuinely curious if he had something important to tell me.

"You've become hard. *Unpleasant*," he bit out. "Normally it would please me to know you were finally living up to your name. But your priorities have shifted."

"They haven't." It was the truth. I'd only ever had one goal, to destroy the man who created me.

My father let out a humorless chuckle. "You think I don't see what is happening? You thought you had the smoking gun, but you've only handed me more ammunition."

"Take your best shot," I bit out.

***

1

GRACE

I sank down at my desk, my fingers gripping the edge of my notebook. I was the new girl. *Fresh meat.* I'd heard murmurs and whispers in the hallway about me as I passed. This school was exclusive. A nepo baby playground.

I didn't belong here. They knew it, and I knew it. I blew a long chestnut strand of hair from my face as I popped in my earbuds to drown out the sound of chatter while I waited for class to start.

Pulling my novel from my messenger bag, I began to flip through the pages, wanting to get another chapter in. The love interest was just realizing he'd inadvertently put the woman he'd fallen for in danger, threatening their happily ever after. I sighed, my eyes scanning the page, skimming the words.

A hand slammed on my desk startling me. I glanced up over the slate gray slacks, to a crisp white button down, that hugged its owner's muscles like it was tailored for him, to take in the boy with anger marring his perfectly sculpted face. He was rolling up the Oxford sleeves to his elbows, the top few buttons undone, revealing swirls of dark ink across his flesh. I gasped, yanking out my earbud when I realized he was talking to me.

"Who the fuck are you?" he asked, his thick eyebrows drawn together over narrowed cerulean eyes.

"Ryatt, I am trying to teach a lesson. If you could take a seat, I would greatly appreciate it. Tomorrow let's try to get to class on time," Ms. Bane scolded him, but her tone wasn't unfriendly. Not like *his*.

"My flight was delayed."

"Don't you have a private jet?" someone from behind me called out.

His lips twisted in a sadistic smirk. "Are you deaf?" He asked me.

I shook my head. His lip curled further. "Mute?"

I shook my head again, swallowing against the lump forming in my throat. He bent lower, hovering over me, his voice menacing. "Are you fucking *stupid*?"

"N-no," I bit out, my heart jackhammering in my chest. I could feel everyone's eyes locked on our exchange. This wasn't the first impression I wanted to make at my new school.

"Are you sure? Because you're in *my* seat."

"Oh," my lips popped open as I began to gather my things.

"Ryatt, it would have been your seat had you managed to make it to class on time," the teacher droned, her hand planted on her hip.

The boy ran his fingers through his dark hair, causing it to stick up haphazardly, somehow it still managed to look perfect. He turned, looking over his shoulder at the teacher, his eyes assessing her. I wished I had the guts to tell him to go screw himself. She didn't deserve this bullshit. Neither did I for that matter.

"I asked her a question. I'll move when I get a response."

It was a glimmer of hope. "What q-question?" I asked, my fingers going to my locket, fidgeting with it nervously. His gaze landed on mine, his smile more playful now like he was enjoying this humiliation or the fact that I was playing along.

"What is your name," he bit out the words slowly.

"Grace Savage. *You*?"

His eyes narrowed as he drew back to his full height. He must have been over six foot, towering above me like he was deciding whether to pick the entire desk with me and toss me aside.

"I'm the guy who is going to make your senior year a living hell if you don't move. *Now*."

His eyes locked on mine as he gripped the edge of my desk. We stared each other down, and honestly, I was afraid I would burst into tears if I moved.

"That's enough. Principal's office," the teacher barked. "Now."

But the boy didn't move, didn't flinch. He just watched me, nostrils flaring. "We'll finish this later," he promised, grabbing my novel before turning and stalking out of the class, slamming the door behind him.

As the room filled with the excited chatter of the other students, Ms. Bane yelled over them, struggling to regain control. I let my long hair hang like a curtain beside my face to block their view.

"He's such a prick," the girl in front of me whispered.

"I noticed," I deadpanned.

"His name is Ryatt Ransom, but everyone calls him *Handsome Ransom*, because obviously," she giggled. "But you don't ever want to get on his bad side."

Ransom. As in Enzo Ransom. As in my mother's fiancé. We'd moved into his sprawling estate two weeks ago, but his son was nowhere to be found. Enzo said '*his boy*' was spending time with his mother in Paris, soaking up the last days of summer. "I think it's too late for that."

The girl sucked air between her teeth. "At least he pays attention to you. I'm invisible."

I let out a small laugh. "I think you may need professional help."

"Oh, come on. Tell me you can't see it. He's like James Dean but with more tattoos."

"He also happens to be unstable."

"Aren't we all?" She shrugged. "I bet it makes for a fun time in bed."

I felt my cheeks heat. I wouldn't know what a fun time in bed even was. I'd gone to an all-girls school up to this point.

"I'm Mattie Carmichael," she whispered, scrunching up her freckled nose. "I'm not a trust fund baby. I'm a charity case." she rolled her eyes. "I'm sponsored by Joel Hamilton's dad. It's kind of like those commercials," she held up her hands making finger quotes, *"For just seventy-six cents a day, you can feed a poor teenager in private school or something."*

"Grace," I replied. "I'm not rich either."

"Let me see your schedule. We might have more classes together."

I dug the paper from my binder and handed it to her. The boy beside her snatched it from her fingers, balling it up and tossing it to another kid three seats away. *Perfect.* At least I'd have a few minutes after class to go to the office and have another one printed.

"Sorry," she mouthed, and I shrugged in return. It seemed there were only a select few who had any power in this school, and Mattie and I didn't make the cut.

***

I slipped out of the class, wanting nothing more than to run down the hall and straight out of an emergency exit. Unfortunately, I wouldn't know where to go from there. I was a long way from my home. My *real* home. And there was nothing left for me there anyway.

I traipsed to the front desk and had a new schedule printed, dragging my feet until the halls were empty.

The second I left the office, passing the threshold of the door, my shoulders were being shoved inside a single stall faculty restroom. The angry boy who'd accosted me in class was glaring down at me as he twisted the lock on the door behind him.

"What are you doing?" I asked as he stalked toward me, and I stepped backward until my back hit the wall. Ryatt closed the gap between us, pressing a hand on either side of my head to cage me in. He was so close I could see the flecks of gold in the aquamarine that circled his pupils.

"You know this is illegal, right? Kidnapping, harassment, stealing..." I bit out as he angled his head down at me, our faces nearly touching.

"Laws don't apply to me."

"Why, because your *daddy* can buy your way out of trouble?"

"I take it you figured out who I am."

I nodded, swallowing against the lump in my throat.

"You scared, Grace? Scream for help. I dare you," he challenged me, but my mouth snapped shut. I wanted to hash this out in private and not in front of an entire class of soulless leeches. "I don't know what that whore of a mother told you, but you've overstayed your welcome."

"I don't want to be here either," I seethed, tears springing to my eyes, and I pressed them closed, hoping to keep them from falling. I wasn't sad. I was *livid*. Unfortunately, my body responded to my anger by making me look like a frightened baby. "Your money doesn't impress me."

"That's not the only way I'm impressive," he shot back.

I rolled my eyes. "I'd rather be anywhere but here with you. Trust me."

"Good. Then there's no reason to tell everyone that we're family." His face went hard. "Because we *never* will be." His eyes narrowed to slits.

"Like I would want anyone to know anyway," I shot back, causing him to chuckle. His gaze flicked to my lips, his tongue running over his own.

"You're feisty. Like an angry little kitten." The back of his fingers trailed down my cheek. "You'll be fun to declaw."

2

RYATT

Grace shoved against my chest, and I let her push me backward until I was against the door.

"I want my book back." Her sea-green eyes narrowed at me with disgust, but her chin trembled like she was fighting off tears. I wanted to make them fall just so I could brush them away. I was sick like my father in that way. I liked to break my toys because they were replaceable.

I glared down at where her hands pressed against my chest, and she let her arms fall. "It was smut."

She scoffed, "It was a *romance*."

"Even worse."

Grace narrowed her eyes. "I had *two* chapters left."

"You're awfully brave now that we're alone, *Kitten*" I noted, pushing from the wall, causing her to take a half step backward.

"Yeah, well...I'm not a big fan of public humiliation."

"*I* enjoyed it." A slow smile spread across my face. "But if you prefer being degraded in *private*, I'm not completely unreasonable."

"I said I won't say anything. Can I go now?"

I stepped to the side, allowing her access to the door. She hurried around me, turning the lock before calling over her shoulder, "Keep the book. You need it more than I do," before she swung open the door and stomped down the hall.

I laughed, shaking my head before stepping out of the restroom.

"Well, if it isn't Handsome Ransom," a girl called out from behind me. I spun around to see Emma Withers, a new set of fake tits popping out over her uniform that was clearly from before she had a chest. "I didn't think you'd be doing senior year here."

I rubbed my palm against the back of my neck. "Me either. Change of plans."

Emma pulled her bleached barrel curls over her shoulder, pushing her chest out as she sauntered closer. "I missed you."

"I'm sure you did," I bit out, growing bored.

"Did you miss me?"

"I missed that mouth of yours," I shot back. It wasn't a lie. Emma had dead eyes and no personality, but she could suck like a fucking Hoover. "You coming to the bonfire tonight?"

"Only if you're *coming*," she purred.

"Why wait?" I asked, slipping back into the teacher's bathroom as she followed behind me.

I leaned my shoulders against the wall where I had Grace pinned moments before. My fingers deftly undid my slacks, freeing my aching cock from the confines of my boxer briefs.

"Jesus," Emma, giggled. "You're already so hard. I guess you really did miss me."

I rolled my eyes, biting back the fact that it wasn't her who had me stiff. Even when Grace was spitting venom at me, I couldn't help my physical reaction to her. I liked the fire in her eyes. She was one of very few people who dared challenge me, even if she was fighting back tears doing it.

Emma sucked the head of my cock into her mouth, and I hissed, gripping her hair as I leaned my head back against the wall.

"*Fuck*," I groaned as her head began to bob, taking my length down her throat. Few of the girls in my school could *actually* deep-throat ten inches. It was a talent that had kept Emma at the top of my rotation. She was almost as good as her mother.

I pulled out my phone, snapping a picture of the mayor's daughter on her knees for me, the heir to the Ransom fortune. Son of one of the most powerful and elite criminal organization leaders on the West Coast.

Allegedly.

Just because I was having a little fun, didn't mean I couldn't mix business with pleasure. Her daddy was causing problems and slowing our expansion South. Not to mention boosting rumors that several high-ranking government officials and law enforcement were in our pocket. Which was the truth, but it wasn't something we liked to brag about.

My father was a businessman. He derived his power from amassing fortune and using it to buy people off. But that isn't where true power lies. Some people don't fall victim to greed and couldn't be bought. *Self-righteous pricks on their moral high horse.* I had a better way. True power came from fear. I was building up my own portfolio, a wealth of *information.* Everyone had a secret or someone they loved that they would protect at all costs. And I was about to find out how far Mayor Withers would go for his precious, orally gifted Emma.

"Fuck," I growled, gripping her hair until my body stiffened. I pulled out of her mouth, coming all over her new tits.

"Ryatt," she squealed. "You soaked my shirt!" Emma bent over the sink. Desperately trying to scrub the come off her clothing.

"I thought that's why you bought them," I muttered.

There was a loud knocking on the door. "Is someone in there?"

I twisted the lock, pulling open the door to see Principal Sanders, his eyes going from mine to Emma's in shock.

"It's all yours," I shot him a wink as I patted him on the back and slid out into the hall.

Ryan nodded in my direction as he stood in front of the vending machines. "Hey, Ransom," he called out, flicking his blonde hair out of his face. "It's been a minute. Didn't catch you out on the waves."

"Vacation," I told him, pulling out my phone and scrolling through my apps.

"What's good?"

"As soon as payment is confirmed, it'll hit the cloud."

Ryan pulled out his phone and sent me two grand. "You're a legend."

"Got it." I scrolled through my videos and clicked on the thumbnail of Ms. Hart, an English teacher, going down on Lisa Armstrong, a junior. "Sent. Hope that takes care of your little problem." I clapped him on the shoulder.

"Appreciate it, man," he called after me as I made my way toward my next class, flipping through the security video from the last few weeks that Grace has occupied my home.

Sinking down at my desk, I clicked play, watching as she took in her new palatial home, her eyes dancing over the façade with disdain. The moment her mother was at her side, she forced a smile. *She's not a gold digger*. Further proving my point that *information* is the only route to true power. I flipped through the motion triggered thumbnail pictures, tracking her to her new room, where she pressed her back against the door, and slid to the floor, a single tear rolling over her cheek as she clutched her heart shaped necklace.

Scrolling further, I found that at three o'clock in the morning, every day, she would go out for a swim in the pool, or a soak in the jacuzzi, making good use of the jets.

"Ryatt," I voice boomed from in front of me. My head snapped up to take in Mr. Brooks looking like he was ready to quit on the first day back. "No phones, please."

***

3

GRACE

We sat at the lunch table near the door. I figured if anything were to happen, at least I could make a quick escape.

"I just don't get why he hates you," Mattie mumbled around her avocado toast.

"Who knows with people like that?" I rolled my eyes, taking a sip of my orange juice. "Maybe he wasn't hugged enough as I child. Or maybe he has a little *you-know-what*." I wagged my pinky finger at her. "So, he needs to pick on helpless little girls to make it feel bigger."

"Grace," Mattie made a choking sound, her cheeks nearly as red as her long tendrils.

"Screw him." I glanced at Mattie, whose eyes were now focused over my head.

"Is that an invitation? Because I don't fuck commoners," a gravelly voice spoke from above me. I pulled my eyebrows together, whipping around in my seat. My jaw went slack as I came face to crotch with Ryatt Ransom.

"You're not really a *helpless little girl*, are ya', *Savage*?" he asked, his voice low enough not to be heard over the hum of conversations at other tables. I was thankful this place was set up with smaller round café seating as opposed to the ones at my last school that fit forty people.

"N-no," I stuttered. *Why couldn't I stop stuttering?*

He sighed, looking up to the ceiling before back down at me. "Good. Then maybe you can tell me what a *you-know-what* is. Come on, Gracie, use your *big girl* words," he taunted.

His calling me Gracie threw me off guard. It is what my father had always called me, and my heart clenched at the memory.

My gaze flitted to the bulge concealed behind his dark pants, my eyes widening. He smiled down at me almost sweetly. It sent a shiver rocking its way down my spine. There was nothing sweet about him. He was a predator, getting ready to go in for the kill.

"You know what I meant," I bit out, feeling my face heat.

"I want to hear you say it." He reached between us, fingering the locket dangling from my neck. I flinched, worried he would rip the heart from my chest, but he just let it fall back against my skin.

"Penis," I whispered a little too loudly for my comfort.

That caused a low rumble in his chest, a genuine smile spreading on his face as he tilted his head to the side.

"It's my *cock*, and if you can't even say the words, you have no business talking about it."

"Why are you doing this to me?"

He was quiet a beat before replying, sinking down on his haunches to be eye level. His gaze was lethal, and I was breathless being this close to him. "Don't change the subject. I told you to say it. Now *say it.*"

"Cock," I whispered on an exhale, my skin growing clammy as I searched the fathomless depths of his ocean eyes, flanked by thick, inky lashes.

"Next time you question my manhood, I'm going to pull it out right here in front of everyone so you can tell them what you really think as you're choking on it." His voice was low, even.

My stomach churned. I wanted to bolt out the door, but this beautiful monster was blocking my escape route. "You want to know what I *really think*?"

That response caught him by surprise, his eyes widening fractionally at my challenge. "Tell me, Kitten."

I licked my lips, preparing to spew every curse word I could think of. But I also knew I was currently digging my own grave, and I didn't want to tie Mattie to my inevitable demise. She was an innocent bystander to the train wreck that was my life.

His eyes searched mine as he stared me down with rapt attention, rendering me mute. I swallowed back the words I wanted to say to him. "I don't think you play fair."

His lips curled into a devastating smile. "It's more fun this way," he shot back with a wink, leaning in fractionally closer before pushing to his feet. His attention turned to the boy who'd stolen my schedule. He stalked off toward him as they yelled something about an upcoming football game.

I spun back around to Mattie whose jaw was slack as she blinked at me. "That was so hot," she whispered, her voice coming out in a squeal.

"He is unhinged."

"Yeah, well, I *volunteer as tribute* if you're going to just ignore the way he was eye fucking you."

I screwed up my face in disgust. "He *literally* just threatened me with sexual assault and public humiliation."

"Yeah, but he did it with a smolder."

I choked out a laugh, but my insides were liquefied, churning at the thought of running into him again. "He... he wouldn't *really* do that, *would* he?"

"A girl can dream," she shot back, shaking her head before giggling. "Come on, Grace. I'm pretty sure not even *Handsome Ransom* could get away with that. He's just trying to scare you."

"It's kind of working."

"Are you going to the bonfire tonight?"

"What bonfire?"

Mattie rolled her eyes. "It's to kick off the new school year. Everyone goes. Even me."

"That doesn't really sound like such a good idea."

She waved away my worry. "Ransom will be busy. Trust me. He's been out of town for a while. He has to sleep with all the skanks to get himself reacquainted. Like a dog peeing on all the trees at the park."

I glanced across the cafeteria, just as Ransom looked up from the crumpled piece of paper in his hand, his eyes landing on mine.

"It'll just be a cesspool of sex, drugs, and underage drinking."

"Exactly," she chirped. "It'll be *so* much fun."

***

4

RYATT

Cara perched on my lap, holding a Jell-O shot as she talked animatedly to one of her friends. Her wheat ponytail swayed with every word. I couldn't remember the other chick's name, but we fucked a few months ago.

My eyes were already glazed over, and I was growing bored. But as a senior, I couldn't skip out on the festivities. Not that this was a school sanctioned event, but this is where people were made and broken. Our close-knit society was forged on the back of networking, and right now I was on top of the ladder, where I intended to stay. One day these teenagers would be running this town, and I would have them all in my back pocket.

"Oh my God. Isn't she *embarrassed*?" Cara hissed to her friend. My eyes searched in the direction they were looking, landing on Grace as she stumbled over a piece of driftwood, giggling with her fire crotch friend from first period. I smirked, finding it funny how little she cared. If she continued this way, I wouldn't have to do anything to help her ruin her reputation.

"Look at her clothes," her friend shot back.

"It's *Pink Floyd*," I pointed out, taking in her vintage t-shirt, growing irritated with their bullshit, hypocritical or not. "*You're* wearing a cocktail dress on the beach."

"Is that like a designer?" Cara asked, shaking her head at me.

"It's a band," I groaned.

"So, she's a *groupie*?" Cara shot back, cackling. I stood, dumping her off my lap and letting her ass land in the sand by my feet.

"I need a refill." I stepped around her and made my way to the keg, grabbing a bottle of liquor and filling up my solo cup.

"Oh, my God. Ransom!" Cara forced a giggle to cover her humiliation.

I couldn't help letting my eyes drift over the flames, watching Grace raise a glass to her lips, dribbles of liquid rolling down the sides of her mouth and staining her shirt. Maybe if she got wasted enough, we could strip her and leave her on the beach for the lifeguards to find in the morning.

"Hey, man," Jones grabbed my hand, pulling me in to bump shoulders. "Where the hell have you been? This summer was *lit*."

"Exploring the world," I replied, looking around for a new piece of ass who was less annoying.

"You mean exploring panties. Speaking of which, I wanted to ask you if you cared if I took a swing at that hot chick?"

"What *hot* chick?"

"The one you squared off with during first period," he replied. "Savage."

I smiled at the memory before shaking my head. "Nah. That one is a *special* project. But Cara is up for grabs."

"I can't believe she didn't move from your seat, man," he replied with a laugh. "She either has a death wish or you've finally met your match."

"It's definitely a death wish," I muttered, refilling my glass and wishing he'd shut the fuck up.

A group of people began to strip their clothes and run toward the water, screaming about a game of chicken. My eyes went back to Grace and her friend, watching as they stood from the log they were perched on and began to peel off their clothing.

Grace's eyes caught mine and she fumbled with her cut off jean shorts, like she wasn't sure she wanted to strip in front of me. So, I steeled my gaze, not looking away. Daring her to try to make herself at home with *my* friends in *my* town.

Her chin jutted up and she scowled, shoving them down over her hips with a little wiggle. She swayed, kicking them off her feet before gripping her shirt and ripping it over her head. Her eyebrow cocked, and I let my eyes drag down her body. *Fuck*. I shouldn't have enjoyed that as much as I did. Her bra was basic white with a thin line of lace around the edge. Her panties were bright yellow cotton with a Care Bear above her snatch. I smirked, and her mouth popped open as she looked down, through the haze of alcohol, remembering what she had on.

Her friend grabbed her hand and tugged her toward the water, and just that quickly, Grace had forgotten our standoff or the fact that when those panties hit the water, they would be completely see-through.

There was a very fine line of the pain I could inflict on her. And that level dropped to zero for anyone else. So, now I was stuck watching this girl who shouldn't be here, keeping her safe so I could get her home and torture her myself. I should call her mother. I should drag her out of the waves by her hair.

"Oh, my God. New girl was so eye fucking you," Cara slurred, tugging her slinky Dolce dress over her head. "Savage hearts Ransom," she giggled, drawing a heart in the air with her fingers like she was so fucking clever. "How *pathetic*."

"Aw, don't be jealous because the new girl is getting all the attention," Jones teased her, earning him a scowl and a backhand across his bare chest.

I rolled my eyes, my gaze drawn back to the water. "If you get wet, you aren't getting in my car," I warned, my gaze going to my black '67 Chevy SS that sat at the edge of the sand. It was the one vehicle I owned that I paid for with my own money, and had it restored. It took three years of work to get it pristine.

Cara rolled her eyes. "You treat that car better than you treat me."

"That's because I *love* the car. I tolerate you," I replied, causing Jones to spit out his drink as he laughed.

"You're so mean," she shot back before forcing a smile like I was teasing her. I *wasn't*.

And Cara didn't heed my warning, running down the beach and into the ocean.

Grace and her friend sat in the shallow water, letting the waves wash over their legs, not partaking in the drunken games unfolding around them.

"So, who is she?" Jones asked, his gaze following mine, staring at her like every other guy here.

I took another sip of my drink, trying to hide my annoyance. "Does it matter? She's untouchable," I warned, my eyes cutting to him.

"I got it man," he held his hands up in front of him. "I was just curious."

***

5

RYATT

Two hours later I was exhausted by all the mindless bullshit I'd had to endure mingling among my peers.

"You can't just abandon me," Cara whined like she actually cared about me. She was only using my dick like it was a rung in the social ladder she was so desperate to climb.

"You're confusing me with your father," I bit out, growing more annoyed. "I told you the rules. You broke them. Find a different way home."

"Come on, Ransom. You could always punish me," she suggested, cocking an eyebrow.

"You'd be torturing me with your presence." I rolled my eyes, turning away from her. "I'm a sadist not a masochist."

"I got her," Jones offered.

Her eyes narrowed. "Yeah, *Jones* will give me a *ride*."

I laughed, rubbing my palm against the back of my head. "Wear protection."

She stomped her foot in the sand before stalking off toward the parking lot. My eyes went back to the driftwood where Grace was hanging out with her friend. They looked exhausted, and barely able to function. I closed the gap between us. Grace nearly fell backward off the log when she glanced up to see who was next to her.

"Have fun?" I asked, assessing her.

Grace shrugged. "Not really," she replied, causing the redhead's eyes to go wide. "You?"

I shrugged. "Not really."

"Do you... *want* something?"

My eyes danced over her friend, annoyed she was still sitting there. "Let's go."

"Where?" she asked, pushing from the log before holding out a hand to help the ginger girl.

"You're drunk. I'm taking you home."

"No, you're *not*. I don't even *know* you."

"*She* knows me," I nodded toward her friend.

"She knows *of* you." Grace folded her arms over her chest. "What's her name? *Huh*? It's Mattie. Leave me alone, Ryatt. And I'll do the same, like we *agreed*."

I lowered my voice, "Grace, I'm not *asking* you."

She scoffed, looking around in disbelief. "Are you *stupid*?" she threw my insult back at me. "Here's a word you haven't heard enough as a child – *no*."

Mattie's eyes went wide in shock before she squeaked, "Um, maybe we should take him up on the offer."

I grabbed Grace's elbow, leaning in closer so the few stragglers on the beach didn't overhear our conversation. "Watch your fucking mouth when you talk to me." I bit out, struggling to keep my composure. "You're fucking *wasted*. I can't leave you here. It's not safe."

"I'll take my chances," she pulled from my grip and began stumbling toward the water.

"Grace," I bit out before stalking after her. I circled around her, dipping my should and grabbing her by the back of her bare thighs and lifting her so she folded over my shoulder, dripping all over me white tee.

"Put me down you asshole!" she seethed.

I stalked over to the passenger side of my car and lowered her to her feet as I caged her in against the door, my body pinning her in place. "You're going to get in the *fucking* car, or I will *throw* you in," I warned, my eyes searching hers.

"And they say chivalry is dead," she snapped.

"And if you don't listen, *you* will be too."

"If you touch me I'll –"

"*What*?" My gaze fell to her mouth as she licked her lips before drifting lower to her bra and panties. "What are you going to do if I touch you, Grace?"

31

She froze, her eyes locked on mine, daring me. "Do you always get your way?" she asked, breathless.

"Yes," I answered honestly. "Will you get in the car before someone calls the cops and I *really* get pissed off?"

She nodded. I followed the movement before taking a step back. "Good girl."

I grabbed the handle and pulled it open. Mattie slipped into the back before Grace slid her damp ass across the passenger seat.

I bit back a curse as I closed her door and rounded the front of the vehicle.

"Where do you live?" I asked the girl in the backseat, my eyes meeting hers in the rearview mirror.

"Milton Avenue, right after the ice cream place on Main."

I nodded, my eyes going to the road as I pulled out of the lot. I glanced over at Grace, watching as her hair dripped down over her skin, causing her to erupt in goosebumps. I switched off the air conditioner, shaking my head before turning up the radio. *Break on Through* by The Doors blared through the speakers and Grace began to mouth the words.

I tapped my fingers against the steering wheel as we pulled up out front of Mattie's house.

She got out and bounded away, giggling as she shouted her goodbyes to Grace, who had propped her feet against the dash. I scanned her long legs before meeting her wide-eyed stare.

My attention turned back to the road and took off toward our place. "You can't go in the house like that," I warned.

"Well, someone made me leave the beach without my clothes," she shot back.

"I think the words you're looking for are – *Thank you*."

She scoffed. "Oh, please. I was safer with the sharks than in here with *you*."

I stopped at the red light and tugged my t-shirt over my head before holding it out for her. "Put this on."

"No one is even going to be awake," she replied, shrugging it on over her head anyway. I hoped that was true. I didn't feel like dealing with my father's bullshit tonight.

"You could have drunk less, and it wouldn't be an issue."

Grace rolled her eyes, pushing a button on the radio and changing the station. "Excuse me for wanting to forget about my shitty existence."

I clenched my jaw, knowing she was referring to our interactions. "Right, life is so tough for you."

"What the hell would you know about *my* life? I wouldn't expect someone like you to understand. Not all of us were born with a silver spoon up our ass."

I whipped the car to the side of the road and slammed it into park before turning toward her. "Don't pretend you know my life either, *Kitten*. You have absolutely no idea who I am or what I could do to you. So, I'd suggest shutting your fucking mouth before you find out."

"Make me." Her bloodshot eyes narrowed before she twisted, fumbling with the handle.

"Grace," I barked as she unbuckled her belt and bolted out of the car, stomping angrily in her bare feet down the road illuminated by my headlights. "Fuck," I muttered, shoving open my door and stalking after her in nothing but my black board shorts.

"Get back in the car. Now."

She continued on, giving me the middle finger over her shoulder. I shook my head, closing the distance between us in three strides. I grabbed her damp hair, fisting it at the base of her skull.

She yelped. "You stupid –"

I tugged upward until she was forced on her tiptoes, her hands grasping mine and struggling to break free from my grip. I turned her, causing her back to arch, bending down so my face hovered over hers. "This is your one free pass because you're clearly drunk out of your *fucking* mind thinking you can disobey me. But if you don't march your ass back to that car now, I'll make sure you can't sit for the rest of the night."

"You're not in charge of me."

"Are you sure about that?" I asked her, my lips twisting in a smirk. "Say the word, Kitten. I'll show you."

Her mouth hung open, panting in frustration and shock before her face screwed up in anger. "Fuck you," she seethed.

"I was hoping you'd say that." I turned her around and began to stalk toward my car. I guided her to the center of the grill, pushing her down so she was bent over the hood. I shoved my shirt over her hips, exposing her still damp panties, leaving nothing to the imagination.

"W-what are y-you doing?" She tried to push herself up as my palm came down across her ass. She screeched, flattening against the hood.

"Are you done acting like a fucking brat, or do you need another?" I asked, leaning over her, ignoring how hard my cock was from taking in the view of her bent over my car.

"You're such an –"

My hand came down against her again, causing her to lurch forward with what sounded dangerously close to a moan, causing my cock to thicken more.

"I hate you," she bit out.

I shook my head leaning over her again, inhaling the smell of bonfire smoke that clung to her hair. "I don't think you *do*, Kitten. Because you haven't told me to stop, yet."

She gasped as my hand hit against her center. She cried out again, her cheeks flushed as she struggled to contain her breathing.

My stinging palm gripped her hip, my fingers flexing. "Again?"

Grace's tongue rolled out over her lips. "No," she whispered, and it felt like she was testing me to see if I really would stop.

"That's too bad." I released her hair, taking a step back from her, watching as she laid over the hood for a few more seconds before slowly pushing herself up, my shirt falling back over her ass to obscure my view. "Get in the car, Grace."

She did without protest, and we drove the rest of the way home in silence.

***

6

RYATT

Unfortunately, my father *was* still awake when we arrived at the house, his eyes dancing between Grace and I before she excused herself to go to bed.

"Fun night?" My father asked, before stalking toward his office. I bit back a curse as I followed after him, wishing I had forced her to leave the bonfire sooner.

He sank down behind his desk, eyeing me for a moment.

"I'd put a bullet between your eyes if I thought you actually had a brain," my father sneered. "How could you let her get drunk? What if something happened?" My father was an intimidating man. At six foot two, he was only an inch shorter than I was. But his hair was a thick inky black, a shade darker than mine. His eyebrows, the same color, were permanently stitched into a furrow. But I'd been dealing with him long enough that he no longer scared me. I wasn't the frightened little boy who hid behind his mother's skirt any longer. And it was only a matter of time before I proved that to him.

"Like what? Afraid I'll *spoil* her?" I asked. "I watched her. No one went anywhere near her."

"You better hope that's true, because Grace is special. I have big plans for her. If you fuck this up for me, your trust fund will be gone."

"Does she know about these *plans*?"

"You have a lot of balls coming into *my* office and questioning me."

I sighed, biting back an angry retort. "I won't let her out of my sight. You have my word." It sounded more like a threat than a promise.

He eyed me skeptically. "Don't disappoint me, son. I'd hate to have to *send flowers* to your mother."

I got the message loud and clear. If I fuck this up for him, I was as good as dead. I'd heard it hundreds of times.

"I didn't know you were so sentimental."

My father chuckled. "A woman's touch makes a man's heart soft and his cock hard."

"Inspirational. I take it we're talking about your *whore* now, and *not* my mother?"

He took a drink from his whiskey. "They're all the same in the end, aren't they? Compliant, obedient, docile," he scoffed. "It's a shame when they lose their fight... like your mother. Where is the fun in that?"

"I guess she didn't find you beating her into submission enjoyable foreplay." I exhaled, rolling my eyes. "Getting thrown away by you was the best thing that could have happened to her."

My father laughed, a deep hearty chuckle. "Your mother's departure was strategic. She coddled you, Ryatt. She was making you a pussy. I can't have you taking over my reign if you don't have the spine to do what needs to be done."

"You underestimate me."

He let that sink in before nodding. "Don't come for me, son, unless you have *nothing* to lose."

I thought of the men who lurked around my mother's home. They weren't there to protect her. They were there to keep *me* in line. To make sure I became the monster my father needed, without biting the hand that fed me. But she was merely a shell of a human now. My mother, the one I knew, was long gone.

"Heed your own advice," I hissed, storming out of my father's office. He followed me out into the hall, grabbing my shoulder and shoving me against the wall.

"I've tolerated your insubordinate behavior because you are my only son, but you threaten me again, I will cut out your heart and feed it to your precious catatonic mommy," he snapped.

"Always the romantic. Perhaps if you'd given her *your* heart, she would still love you."

"Woman don't want love. They want security."

"Like the eight men with weapons outside of her villa?"

"What the hell do you know about pleasing a woman?" he scoffed. "You've fucked anything that will split their legs in this town and look at you? *Alone.*"

"Because I choose to be. Loving someone is leverage against me. I'm not fucking stupid. Any one of those girls would be happy to be on my arm."

"That's not how this works," he bit back.

"I won't take an *offering*. I'll walk away," I warned, watching my father's eyes go hard.

"So you say," he taunted.

"Well, I haven't fucked *all* of them yet, have *I*, Dad?"

His icy blue eyes narrowed, his finger wagging in my face as his voice dropped low. "This is your only warning, Ryatt. Keep your fucking hands to yourself."

"Is this you playing the overprotective father, or are you trying to upgrade to the newer model?"

He cocked back, his fist connecting with my jaw and causing me to slam back against the wooden wall. The decorative molding was digging into my spine as the taste of copper filled my mouth. I turned my head to the left, rubbing my jaw when my eyes locked on to a wide emerald gaze peeking out from behind a pillar. *Fucking Grace.* She shouldn't be here.

I straightened, pushing off the wall, and looking down at my father. "Are you done?"

His eyes narrowed and he took a step back. "Keep your fucking hands off Grace or I will break every single one of your fingers myself. Then I'll throw you away and lose the key."

He turned on his heels, disappearing into his office. I stalked away in the opposite direction of Grace because if I followed her right now, I didn't know what I was capable of.

Instead, I slipped into the theater room, turning on the projector and flipping through videos in my phone, stopping on three seniors getting gangbanged by half the football team last year.

I pulled out my cock, stroking it, but it wouldn't get hard. I was too pissed about what had transpired. Now the little girl who'd already overstayed her welcome had listened in on a very private conversation. She's seen my father hit me. I turned off the video and switched to the security cameras, flipping through the different areas of the grounds before switching to her wing.

I glanced to the door before clicking on her room. She was on her bed, flipping through the movies on her television before stopping on some old chick flick.

Everything about her was fucking boring, and for some reason that fascinated me. She wasn't trying to impress me, or anyone for that matter.

I held up the keyboard, about to click to another room when her hand slid under her blanket.

"What the fuck?" I leaned forward, rubbing my palm against my jaw. Goody two shoes boring ass Grace was *fingering* herself, to a fucking Ryan Reynolds movie?

I pushed from the recliner and stalked across the sprawling estate. I didn't know if I was going to fight with her or fuck her. Either one would probably end up signing my death warrant, but right now, I didn't give a fuck.

7

GRACE

I pressed my eyes closed, flashes of ripped ink swirled abs rolling through my mind and the pads of my fingers slipped beneath the thin fabric of my cotton panties. The feel of his heavy palm against my ass caused pleasure to jolt though me. His hand gripped my hair painlessly but granted him complete control. And I let him have it, goading him on.

I began to work my sensitive bundle of nerves in small circles. Ryatt's angry scowl flashing across my subconscious. He was all I could smell, thanks to his shirt. My ass still throbbed from his earlier assault, even though the pain was a quick biting sting that long faded. I tried to ignore it, shuffling through my images of celebrities I found hot... but I saw Ryatt running his tongue over his lips, his angry glare locked on mine. My body shuddered, and I pressed back against my touch.

The door slamming open, bouncing off my wall registered a millisecond too late. I gasped, sitting myself up as I took in Ryatt's scowl in person. He stalked toward me, planting a hand on either side of my body and leaning over me. His mouth was only inches from mine when he bit out the words, "If you tell *any*one what you saw, I will fucking *ruin* you."

"I didn't see anything," I assured him. "And even if I *did*, I wouldn't say anything."

His eyes searched mine for understanding before they narrowed, his tongue running out over his lip and causing my core to pulse. I glanced to the cut on his swelling lower lip.

"You like to watch people, Grace? You get off on it? *Huh*? Is that why you're in here touching yourself?" he rasped.

Finally, my mind registered that he was taking in my face. My skin flushed, eyes hooded.

"N-no," I muttered, panic seizing my chest, throbbing between my thighs.

"Such a little liar." Ryatt grabbed my wrist from under the blanket, squeezing it painfully tight in his grip before dragging the blanket down my body slowly, exposing me.

"I like to watch too, Kitten." His eyes drifted lower, taking in my parted thighs, nostrils flaring before lifting my arm. With horror, I watched him raise my hand to his face, inhaling my scent from my fingers before shoving them into his mouth, slowly dragging his tongue over my digits. His eyes fell closed and I felt the vibration of a low groan as he sucked them clean of my juices.

My core pulsed, desperate for more of this pornographic display as his free hand slid into his pocket. Before I could register what was happening, he held up his phone snapping a picture.

"If you say one fucking word about what you saw, I'll send this pic of your wet panties to everyone in the fucking school." He bit out. I nodded, my head swimming.

His eyes fell again before he rasped, damn near against my mouth, "Did you finish, Grace?"

I inhaled sharply, my spine going stiff. "N-not yet." *Yet.* Why did I say that?

"Good." He smirked. His thumb rubbed over the pulse point of my wrist.

He turned and left, leaving me wishing he had.

***

8

RYATT

Why the *fuck* did I taste her? I raked my fingers through my hair as I paced my room, the flavor of Grace, mixed with the salty ocean water on her fingers still on my tongue. I shoved my hand inside of board shorts, pulling my swollen cock free as I leaned with a hand on my desk, jerking off while my eyes focused on my laptop screen.

Grace was in her bed, pouting after my intrusion. "Come on, Kitten," I muttered, fisting myself as I watched her readjust in her bed. After a beat, she slid her hand lower, and the view was no longer obstructed by her comforter. Her fingertips brushed over her panties. "That's a good girl," I rasped, squeezing my cock with a death grip. Grace bit down on her lip before her fingers slid under the thin fabric. She was rubbing her clit, her fingers not drifting lower.

Her eyes were closed, her brows pinched as she searched for her release. "That's it," I rasped.

Her back arched, her small tits tenting the fabric of my shirt that she still wore. She's so fucking close. I can't remember the last time I even cared if my partner came. Sex is nothing more than currency in this town. But I wanted to see her face, hear the tiny moans and whimpers that fall from her lips when she gets off. *What makes you come, Kitten?*

"Ryatt," she sighed. It's barely a whisper, but it slams against my chest, causing my release to rack through my body, coming all over my hand. I struggled to slow my breathing, looking down at the mess I made. But when my eyes went back to the screen, I saw her staring back at me, through the camera and I couldn't help but feel like she could *actually* see *me*.

***

The next morning, I sat at the table, trying desperately to ignore the stranger in my kitchen. "Ryatt, I'm so glad you were able to join us for the school year," Grace's mother Hope called from in front of the espresso maker. I gritted my teeth, hating that this woman was pretending this was *her* home and *I* was the outsider. "Do you have any classes with Grace?"

I relaxed my grip on my fork and knife, staring down at my steak and eggs. If I was going to be here, I needed to at least appear like I cared. My eyes met hers, and I realized how much Grace looked like her.

"A few," I bit out before sawing another bite of my steak, blood pooling beneath it on the plate.

"That's nice. I'm so glad she'll have a friend. Your father said you'd look after her."

I snorted as I looked up at her again. Her smile was sincere, and I couldn't figure out how the hell she was with someone like my dad.

"How *did* you and Enzo meet?"

Hope sank down in a seat across from me. "Your father had done some business with my late husband. He sent the most beautiful flowers after he passed away, made sure everything was taken care of. He's such a thoughtful man."

I dropped my silverware on my plate, leaning back in my chair, shaking my head. My father had killed Grace's dad and planned to marry the guy's fucking wife? "Yeah, that sounds like my dad. Real sweetheart." She flinched. She was quick to school her features, but I'd seen it, a flicker of pain.

Grace walked into the room, calling out a good morning to her mother before her eyes landed on me and her smile faltered. I drank back my orange juice as one of the staff took away my plate. My eyes fell to the back of her thighs. Her pleated skirt must have been rolled up on her waist half a dozen times. And somehow her knee highs made the look even more obscene.

"Would you like some breakfast, Gracie?" Hope asked. I watched Grace's face go hard. "Don't call me that."

"That's what I've always called you," Hope replied as Grace grabbed a bottle of water from the fridge.

"No." She spun around, leaning against the counter on her elbows. Causing her small perky tits to push against her fitted white Oxford. "That's what Dad called me." I didn't miss her eyes flitting to me. I'd called her Gracie and she didn't say anything about it. Not that I blamed her. But I wondered if it bothered her when I did it.

"Did you get the wrong size uniform?" her mother asked, finally taking in her daughter.

Grace scoffed, looking down over herself. "What's wrong with what I have on? It fits."

"Nothing. I just thought..." her voice trailed off. "Do you need a ride to school?" Hope asked.

"I'll take the bus," Kitten hissed before grabbing her bag and stalking out of the room. Moments later the front door slammed. Hope's eyes met mine before she looked down at the table, shaking her head.

"I'll keep an eye on her," I reassured her, causing her to smile, before I pushed to my feet and stalked after Grace, watching her hips sway as she crossed our driveway.

***

I made it to first period before Grace, slipping in and sinking down in the seat behind her new friend. When she entered the room, I saw her body tense before averting her gaze and trudging toward the back, sitting at the desk two rows behind me.

Class began and I pulled out my phone, doing a quick search for Grace's father, when I heard her giggle. My hand stilled and I glanced over my shoulder at Marcus Fuller as he leaned closer to her, showing her something on his kindle.

I ignored it, going back to trying to figure out how Grace ended up in my home in the first place. But her father was a mechanic. He had no record that I could find, and his death appeared to be accidental. It was rare anyone in my father's business made an example out of a killing, so that wasn't surprising. But it didn't explain why he was on my father's radar.

I scrolled thought the videos of her before I arrived, watching her spend hours lying on her bed, engrossed in her novel. Sometimes she'd touch herself to what she was reading. I zoomed in, taking note of the pages she was on before clicking on the next set of videos.

When she wasn't engrossed in a novel, she was on her phone.

I clicked on my Amazon app and ordered two kindles for same day delivery. It would be easier to track what she's into if we had synced devices tied to my account.

"I'm Marc," I heard him say.

"Grace," she whispered back.

"I'd ask you how you like it here, but..." his voice trailed off and she let out a small laugh, "your first day was kind of rough, huh?"

"Oh, you saw that?" she asked. "No big deal. People like that don't get under my skin."

People like that? I couldn't help but smirk.

"Are you sure? It looked pretty *intense*."

"I've met worse," she muttered, making me wonder who in her life had made her think that *I* was tame. "Besides, people who act that way only do it because they can't forge *real* relationships, so they control people with fear."

"I'm not really sure that's true with him," Marc replied, his voice barely audible now. "I just don't think he wants to get close to people."

"Must be nice not to have to worry about anyone but yourself."

"Probably because he spent so many years worrying about his mom."

I stiffened, rubbing palm along my jaw as my muscles tensed.

"What?" Grace asked. "What happened to his mom?"

"No one really knows," his words came out rushed. "My advice is don't try to figure out someone who doesn't want to be. There's emotionally unavailable and then there's *Ryatt*."

The bell rang and I pushed from my seat, stalking out of the room and down the hall.

***

9

GRACE

I'd learned a lot about Ryatt in the past three weeks that we'd been forced to cohabitate. There was hardly ever a time he wasn't entertaining women. When they weren't on their knees for him, they were trying to find ways to garner his attention. He didn't seem to care about any of them. Nevertheless, they were always there, lurking around the mansion. *Handsome Ransom* wasn't shy when it came to his debauchery.

You'd think that someone who had virtually anything they wanted wouldn't have a permanent scowl plastered on their face. He spent most of his time that he was alone in the theater room or swimming laps in the pool. He also worked out constantly, just beyond the pool house. I know that sounds kind of stalkerish but I'd learned his routine so I could avoid him as much as possible. Unfortunately, there were times I couldn't escape him, like at school.

As I watched him saunter toward me in the gym at the pep rally, I steeled my spine, not wanting to appear like an easy target. He sank down on the bench next to me, his eyes ahead of him, watching the cheerleaders perform as music blasted over the sound system.

"Why are you sitting near me?" I asked, causing his eyes to meet mine briefly.

"I can sit wherever the fuck I want. This is *my* gym." He nodded up to the letters on the wall that read *Ransom Gymnasium*.

"Of course," I snapped, rolling my eyes. "Are you going to the game tonight?"

He nodded. "I am. *You're* not."

"That's not really your decision."

His eyes met mine, narrowing as he lowered his voice. "Wanna find out, Kitten?" He punctuated his taunt with a wink.

"What is your *problem*?"

He leaned closer and I inhaled the smell of his cologne mixed with a hint of caramel from a candy he'd been eating. Before he could speak a brunette in a cheerleading outfit bounded over and sank down on his lap, her heavy floral scent overpowering his. He straightened; his attention now occupied as her slid his hand up her bare thigh.

I groaned, my eyes darting around the expansive space for Mattie. I found her standing by the door and I pushed to my feet, waving to her.

She smiled broadly when she saw me, bounding over to us. I scooted a little closer to Ryatt to make room for her to sit. My leg brushed against his, his arm moving against mine as he continued to rub the girl's thigh. It felt intentional. To be honest it kind of felt phenomenal, which solidified my suspicion that I am a masochist, because this was torture.

"Are you coming tonight?" Mattie asked.

"Umm... I don't know," I replied, trying to ignore the warmth of his arm against mine.

Ryatt cleared his throat as his companion whispered something in his ear.

"Actually, yes. I'm coming," I clarified. Ryatt's leg pushed against mine, but I just smiled, knowing there wasn't much he could do here. Thankfully we'd seemed to be past our public humiliation portion of our situation and have moved on to him making me uncomfortable in the confines of his mansion, where he was the only witness to his cruelty.

"It's gonna be so much fun," Mattie squealed. "They're going to announce the homecoming court at halftime. I mean, we all know who the winner will be," she rolled her eyes, glancing toward Ryatt.

I choked back a shocked laugh. "You're not serious."

She nodded, giggling. "It's always a huge deal. I mean, it is at every school, but all the parents put on a big fireworks show. They even do this video thing, like a real movie with all the people on the court. Dawson Gibb's dad is like a director or something. So, it's always insane."

"A movie?"

"Yeah. Well, it's like ten minutes, but it's so good."

"That sounds fun."

The cheerleader eating up Ryatt's attention skipped back out onto the court for another performance, but her stench lingered.

"Are you still going to the dance?" I asked her, wishing I could put some space between myself and Ryatt.

"Yeah. I don't have a date or anything. But I don't want to miss out. It's senior year, ya' know? I wish you'd come."

I thought that over. I didn't want to spend the entire year locked in my room, trying to avoid Ryatt. "Maybe we can just go together," I replied, shrugging.

"*Really*? Do you have a dress?"

My shoulders sagged. "No. It's probably too late. Maybe I can find a sundress or something. Would that be weird?"

Mattie shrugged. "It doesn't matter. No one even acts like they can see us anyway." I could feel Ryatt's gaze locked on me, and I wished that were true.

***

10

GRACE

An hour later I was climbing the stairs to my room, texting Mattie to reassure her that I would find something to wear for tonight. I pushed open my door, my jaw nearly unhinging as I took in my open closet door. Everything that I owned was gone, aside from school uniforms. "What the *hell*?" I threw my bag on the floor and rushed inside the walk-in.

"You really should listen to me, Kitten."

I spun around to see Ryatt, shirtless, gripping the top of my bedroom doorframe and causing his bicep to bulge. I folded my arms across my chest angrily. "Give me back my clothes, you psycho."

"Sorry. Can't. I threw them away."

"You *what*?" I stormed across the room, and he began to stalk toward me, causing me to stop in my tracks. Two strides and he was hovering over me, a hint of a smirk on his lips. "You are such a jerk," I bit out, noticing he must have showered and no longer lingered with the funk of desperate cheerleader.

"Are you *smelling* me, Grace?"

"What? No! I just thought I smelled something *rotten*." I inhaled sharply, making a face.

Ryatt chuckled, his eyes narrowing. "Is that so?"

"Yeah, it smells like white privilege and a decomposing soul."

He laughed deeply and the sound echoed off the walls in my room. I'd never heard him sound like he was genuinely enjoying himself before and it made me smile.

"Why are you smiling?" he asked, his eyes narrowing.

"Because you're too dumb to know I just insulted you."

"You need to learn when to shut your fucking mouth, Grace." Even when whispered with a smirk, his threats gave me chills. But I learned that this was just who Ryatt was, jaded and vulgar. He was used to getting his way. I wasn't, and something about that made me resent him, even if we were just victims of our circumstances.

"Make me."

His scowl fixed itself back in place. He took a step forward, and I countered, stepping back. He continued until the back of my legs hit my bed, and I fell onto the mattress. Slowly, Ryatt leaned over me, planting a hand on either side of my head and lowering himself until his face hovered over mine.

"*You're* too stupid to know that you're *prey*. And just because I enjoy playing with my food, doesn't mean you wont get eaten, Kitten."

"Eaten..." I rasped, my face turning red with the thought. His eyes searched mine like he could hear the question as it flitted through my subconscious.

"You do know I can read *every* thought... emotion...*desire*... that crosses your mind right on your face."

"If that were true, you would be protecting your groin."

He laughed again before one of his hands was on the side of my throat, his thumb tipping my chin up. "Keep acting like a little brat, and the next time I spank your ass I won't be as gentle."

"Like your father isn't gentle with you?"

His face went hard, the muscles in his jaw jumping under the taut skin. "Don't fucking compare me to him."

"I'm not scared of you."

The corner of his lip twisted up as he took in my expression. "There it is, Kitten... another lie."

"I'm going to the dance, even if I have to go naked."

"I guess I can throw away all your underwear then too."

"Go for it."

He thought that over before his fingers went to the buttons in the center of my chest.

"W-what are you doing?"

"We can start with the ones you're wearing." He deftly undid three of my buttons, revealing the lacy center of my bra that clasped in the front.

"My door is open," I warned, my words sounding breathy.

"I don't give a fuck," he replied, undoing the next button. I pressed my palms against his hot chest, his eyes meeting mine, waiting for me to push him away. I didn't. Instead, I ran my tongue over my lips, and he watched, doing the same before popping another button free. My chest was rising and falling rapidly now, my head spinning. Ryatt's eyes were on mine, and his hand stilled, eyebrows pinched.

"What?" I asked, wondering if he was repulsed by me. He'd probably seen hundreds of girls naked by now. I knew my body wasn't anything special. I certainly couldn't afford any *enhancements* like most of the people at my school.

"You're shaking." He raised himself up higher and I realized he was right. I was trembling and he wasn't even touching me.

"I am...I'm cold."

"You're really *that* stubborn that you're going to let me strip you?"

I nodded, because I absolutely was gritting my teeth and allowing it to continue. But it wasn't like I didn't *want* it to happen. I just had absolutely no idea what would come next, and that *terrified* me. I had no experience when it came to guys, and Ryatt was *intense* to say the least.

He pushed to his full height, towering over me. His eyes drifted over my body. "I have to go get ready to be crowned king." He walked backward a few steps. "Make good choices, Grace." He winked and turned, disappearing into the hallway.

***

I lay on my bed, staring at the ceiling in my room, wondering how I managed to humiliate myself at every turn. I wasn't used to men as fierce as Ryatt, but I knew bullies. And the one rule when it came to stopping them, was not to give in. The second he saw me as bowing down to him, he would just get more intense. It was all about being in control. *Power*. And I was too stubborn to give him any over me.

I pushed from my bed and shrugged out of my uniform, tugging Ryatt's t-shirt on he'd given me and a pair of sleep shorts that barely covered my ass. I gathered the hem of his shirt and twisted it into a knot above my hip. It was better than nothing for the game.

I shot Mattie a text and made my way across the property, slipping out of the gate and heading down the long winding road toward the rest of civilization.

By the time I reached the gas station I'd asked Mattie to pick me up at, I was exhausted. But I wasn't going to let someone like Ryatt tell me what to do.

"What are you wearing?" she asked with a laugh as she took in my brick red shorts.

"Long story," I huffed as I slipped into the passenger side of her car.

The parking lot at the school was overflowing, music blaring from every other car. Some people were already in their dance attire, the rest were in school colors. I'd inadvertently worn the opposing team's colors. "Shit," I muttered.

"No one will notice," Mattie replied.

***

We sat off to the side on the bleachers, surrounded mostly by parents. The game was boring, and I was questioning why I even put up so much of a fight to come. By the time halftime hit, I was ready to go home and call it a night.

"I'm gonna use the bathroom," I yelled over the chatter before climbing down the bleachers and making my way underneath of them to avoid the crowd.

I sidestepped a support brace when an arm shot out, gripping my waist and turning me around until my back was against the concrete pillar. Ryatt glared down at me. He was in all black, his sleeves rolled up his forearms.

"Nice outfit," I whispered.

His head cocked to the side, eyes narrowing as they dragged down my body. "I could say the same. You rooting for the other team?"

"Oh, you like it? Yeah, I wasn't given much of a choice, but if I can, I *always* try to cheer for the good guys."

"Your choice was to stay home or have to deal with me," he bit back. "And good guys tend not to have the balls to do what is necessary. That's why they finish last."

I laughed, shaking my head. "They finish last because they make sure their girl comes first."

"Did you learn about that in your little smut books?"

"You tell me? I know you've been following along, highlighting passages. I should have known there was a catch to your gift."

"There's always a catch." His eyes narrowed. "I told you not to come here tonight."

"So?"

"You're a glutton for punishment, aren't you, Kitten?" His palm slid around my throat as he stared me down.

"Maybe you don't get to decide what I do," I shot back, folding my arms across my chest.

The crowd cheered above us. The halftime show was about to begin.

"Aren't you going to be late for your adoring fans?" I asked as his fingers flexed against my neck and my arms dropped to my sides. "What about your queen?"

"I'm too busy playing with my pawn." His lips twisted up in a smirk before it fell. "Do you really think I give a fuck about what any of them think of me?"

I shrugged, swallowing against his palm. His eyes drifted down to where he gripped me. "I do. That's why you're afraid that someone will find out you know me."

"*Afraid*?" he laughed, shaking his head. He leaned closer, his nose skimming along my cheek until his lips brushed my ear. "Is that why you came here, wearing my shirt, smelling like *me*? You want them all to know who you belong to, Kitten?" He pulled back, his mouth dangerously close to mine. "You know, if I spanked you right now, your shorts wouldn't even cover my handprints across your ass. That would let everyone know." His free hand drifted down over the curve of my hip before gliding over the globe of my ass. His fingers traced the hem of my shorts, sliding toward my center from behind before rocking back toward my hips. My breathing hitched, my eyes locked on his, mesmerized. Off in the distance I heard *Ryatt Ransom is our Hidden Hills King* over the sound system. He didn't make a move to leave, didn't even blink.

His hand circled the front of my shorts, sliding the tips of his fingers under the waistband. "Let's go," he rasped.

"W-where?"

"I'm taking you home."

"I'm here with Mattie," I protested.

"Text her. Tell her you aren't feeling well, and you daddy is gonna give you a ride."

"You're sick, you know that?"

"I know." He smiled, genuinely as his hands fell from my body. "I think you might be too, Kitten."

11

RYATT

I grabbed Grace's wrist, guiding her under the bleachers, weaving through the pylons to a gate that ran along the back of the property. I hopped the fence before reaching over and gripping Grace by the waist and lifting her over as she let out a squeal.

"You're really going to leave and miss out on everyone fawning over you?"

"They always fawn over me," I shot back as we rounded the field.

"I want to go to the dance," she called out as I tugged her along.

"No."

She pulled her arm back and I stopped, turning to face her, but not loosening my grip. "What do you care?"

We reached my car, and I pulled open the passenger door, waiting for her to get in. She did and I slammed the door, my eyes scanning the lot before I got in the driver's side and pulled out of my spot.

I cranked up the radio as *Black Betty* by Ram Jam blared through the speakers.

"My dad loved this song," she called out over the noise.

"The mechanic?" I asked, causing her eyes to cut to mine.

"How do you know that?" She turned the knob, lowering the music to background noise.

I smirked, stepping on the gas as we made our way down the back roads. "I do my research."

"You're a *stalker*," she snapped, a hint of a smirk playing on her lips. "I know a little about you too."

"Really?" I asked. "Like what?"

"You like to swim, a lot. You spend most of your time in the theater room, when you're not entertaining *guests*."

I smirked. "What else?"

"You work out in that gym behind the pool house nearly every day."

We slowed to stop at a red light, and I let my eyes take in her toned thighs. "Tell me something else about myself."

She twisted her fingers together on her lap. "You never take anyone into your room."

"Why do you think that is?" I asked as we continued down the road.

"I dunno." She stared out of the passenger window, watching the town go by. "Maybe you like your privacy," she shrugged. "Maybe you're hiding something in there."

"Like what?"

"A body?"

I chuckled, turning down the road toward our house.

"Or... maybe that's the place where you feel like you can be yourself. And you don't want to share the real you with anyone else."

I gripped the steering wheel until my knuckles turned white.

"Maybe that's why you don't like me being in your house, because it puts me dangerously close to finding out who *Handsome Ransom* really is."

"I'm afraid there is no mystery there. What you see is what you get." I gave her a pointed stare before parking in front of the mansion. "Come on."

I got out of the car with Grace on my heels, making my way through the house toward my room.

"Where are we going?"

"My room. So, we can solve your little mystery."

When we reached my room, I typed in my code into the pin pad and shoved the door open. I stepped to the side, allowing Grace room to pass me, inhaling her scent as she brushed against my chest.

Her eyes danced over the bare space. There was a bed and a desk, but little else. She turned around, her eyebrows pinched together.

"I don't get it."

"Nothing to get," I shrugged. "It's not that deep." I took a step closer to her. "I'm not some tortured soul, hiding behind a mask of anger or whatever the fuck you're thinking to justify my behavior. I'm just not a good person, Grace. There's no excuse you can come up with in that pretty little head of yours to change that."

She exhaled, her eyes searching mine. "Fine."

"*Fine?*" I asked.

"Yeah, fine. You want to be the bad guy, then be the bad guy." She shrugged.

"Alright." I smirked, pushing the door closed behind me and locking us in the room, cloaked in darkness. I walked toward her, watching her eyes go wide before I stepped around her, clicking a few keys on my computer and causing music to echo in the nearly desolate space.

"What are you doing?" she asked, turning to face me. I sank down on my desk chair, legs splayed as I took her in illuminated by the light of the computer screen.

"You wanted to dance. *Dance.*"

Grace let out a nervous laugh. "*Here?*"

"Don't make me wait, Kitten."

Her cheeks turned pink, and she began to fumble with her necklace. "I-I don't know how."

"Sure, you do. You know if you went to homecoming, you'd be dancing for me anyway. You know I'd be watching you. So, let's cut the bullshit."

I pushed from my chair, reaching out and gripping her hips. I pulled her waist against mine and began to move slowly.

"You can touch me," I rasped. She lifted her hands and pressed them tentatively against my chest, sliding them up to my shoulders. My cock began to thicken against her. "Dancing is just like fucking. You need a compatible partner."

"I wouldn't know," she muttered.

"I think you do," I turned her around and grabbed her hips again, pulling her ass against me. "Just because you haven't done it before doesn't mean you don't know what makes your body feel good," I whispered against her ear as she ground herself against me. "Or what makes mine feel good." I tugged her backward. Sinking down in my chair and pulling her on top of me. "Now dance for me, like I asked you to." Her back pressed against my chest, and she rolled her hips, grinding against my length. I spread her thighs apart, my hands gliding up and down her silky skin.

"Like this?" she asked, her voice breathy and needy.

"Does it feel good?" I asked her, my lips against her ear.

"Yes." Her body began to shake under my touch. I slid my hand higher, rubbing the pads of my fingers against her center, causing her to whimper.

"Just like that, Kitten. Don't stop." I could feel how wet she was through her shorts. Her head turned to the side, her forehead against my cheek. She closed her eyes, her lips parted as she rocked against my hand. She was completely lost to my touch, just feeling, chasing the pleasure. "That's my fucking girl," I rasped as her body stilled and she cried out, my name falling from her lips as her pussy dripped for me.

"Oh my God," she whispered, struggling to slow her breathing.

"Go to bed, Kitten." I lifted her from my lap and made my way to the door, punching in the code and pulling it open for her. "I have to go get my crown. Don't wait up."

***

12

GRACE

I slid out of my room, glancing down the hallway to make sure the house was silent. I loved getting time alone and three in the morning was the magic hour. No servants lurked around corners and the family, Ryatt included, were fast asleep.

I tiptoed out of my room in my white bikini, excited to slip outside and take a dip in the pool. The stairs creaked, and I paused, glancing behind me. When I was sure no one was stirring, I continued my descent.

I practically ran across the formal dining room, squealing in delight as I yanked open the back door and followed the stone path toward the pool house. A low flicker inside caused me to stumble and duck as it cast shadows on the wall.

I crouched down, crawling my way to the window and peeking inside, nearly letting out a scream when I realized someone was sitting a few feet away, facing the opposite direction. *Handsome Ransom.* Devil in the flesh.

I sneered, squinting to see if I could figure out what he was looking at. It was an image of a woman, legs splayed. His head rolled to the side, the muscles in his arm pulling and stretching. And then I heard the panting of his labored breathing. *What the hell?*

I slipped around the shrubbery and perched myself at the next window. That's when I realized the picture he was staring at was the one he'd taken of me in bed. And the jerking motion he was making was because he was pleasuring himself. To me. Shame flooded my veins. Heat raced through my core. He made another sound, like a growl, before his velvety voice curled around my spine with his words.

"*Fuck*," he rasped.

The apex of my thighs pulsed with anticipation. And then I noticed something strange beneath his arm. A dark mass.

He clicked a button on his phone, causing mine to chirp in my hand. I fell backward, just as a woman lifted her head from his lap, wiping her hand across her mouth.

I pushed to my feet, sprinting across the lawn and ducking behind a massive oak tree. I held up my phone, clicking on the new message icon before turning down the screen brightness. There from an unknown number was the picture of me, legs splayed, with the message – *Are your panties wet again from watching me?*

I clutched my phone to my chest, squeezing my eyes closed as I heard the door to the pool house open and close. There was some muffled murmuring before footsteps retreated down the narrow path. I struggled to catch my breath, afraid to move.

"Such a naughty little kitten," Ryatt called out. "We have motion lights, sensors, cameras... as you're well aware." I could hear the smile in his tone. "Did you really think I wouldn't know you were watching me?" He paused a beat, but I didn't respond, frozen in fear, hoping he wouldn't waste any time looking for me.

"Or did you *want* me to catch you?"

I said nothing.

He sighed dramatically. "Fine, have it your way."

My phone chirped in my hand again with a message from Ryatt that read –*come out come out wherever you are*, giving away my location. I pushed from the tree, standing as I raised my hands in surrender. "I wasn't watching you," I called back to him, as his eyes raked down my body, taking in my bikini.

His eyebrow cocked. "Liar."

I pictured him, looking at the dirty image he'd snapped of me. But then I remembered the girl between his legs.

"Where's your friend?" I asked, folding my arms across my small chest, pushing my breasts up higher.

"I was done with her," he replied coolly as he sauntered closer.

"I knew you were no Prince Charming, but I'd thought you'd at least reciprocate."

"You thought about me eating you out, Kitten?" he asked, smirking only inches from my body. "*Interesting.*"

My face paled. "I just meant, I can't believe women go down on you, and you give them nothing in return."

"Why should I care? I got what I wanted."

I rolled my eyes, stepping around him and stalking toward the hot tub. "Spoken like a true fuckboy."

Ryatt's fingers circled my bicep, jerking me to a stop, his mouth next to my ear and fanning his hot breath across the surface, causing goosebumps in its wake. "Let's get one thing straight," he snapped. "I don't do anything I don't want to do. And neither do the girls I fuck. They suck my cock because they want to please *me*. That's enough for them. Just like when you sit your little ass in that jacuzzi and pretend that the jets pumping against your clit is my tongue, will have to be enough for you. Better get used to it, Gracie, because not a single guy within a hundred miles is going to touch you this year. As far as they're concerned, I *own* you. You're officially *off limits.*"

"You don't own me."

His eyes drifted over me before meeting my gaze. "You sure about that?"

I gasped, his fingers released me, and my knees nearly buckled as I watched him stalk off toward the main house.

***

After another sleepless night of tossing and turning, I walked into first period, groaning internally when I saw Ryatt in the seat I'd stolen from him on the first day. He was making it a point to actually be punctual, even if it was just to spite me. And the only other seat available was next to him.

I looked back at the door behind me, contemplating skipping class. Ryatt's eyes were locked on me, tracking me. There was a glint in his eye like he was daring me to make a run for it. And had Mattie not waved to me, I would have.

I sank down into the empty desk, giving her a small wave.

"Hey, I have to get a uniform for my new job. Wanna come to the mall with me?" she asked. "We can go after school on Thursday."

Ryatt pulled out his phone, scrolling away, but I knew he was listening to our every word.

"Um, yeah. That sounds like fun."

"Great," Mattie replied, gathering her long hair and twisting it into a messy bun. "I've been talking to this guy online. He's gonna meet us there, with his friend." She raised her eyebrow, suppressing a smirk.

"Oh, I dunno –"

"Come on, Grace. He's cute. And I can't meet this guy alone. He could be a serial killer or something."

"So, you want him to have *two* victims?"

Her shoulders fell, and she turned to face the teacher. "Forget it."

"Fine. Yeah, that could be fun," I conceded.

"You'll go?" she asked, twisting back to face me.

"Yes. I'll go."

"Great," Mattie squealed, doing an excited shimmy in her seat.

My phone buzzed and I pulled it out, clicking on a message from Ryatt, saved under the name *Rotten*. Loud moans rang out in the classroom as my eyes read over the message accompanying the video of him getting head last night. It read –*Since you like to watch me. I thought you might enjoy this angle better.*

"Oh, my God," I screeched, dropping my phone.

"Ms. Savage," the teacher barked.

I sank to the floor as Ryatt's foot kicked my phone further up the aisle. Another message popped up on the screen, of my ass from behind right now as I crawled in front of him. "Damn it," I yelled, finally gripping my phone and closing out of the messaging app. *So much for not humiliating me in public.*

"Principal's office," the teacher yelled over the laughter, and I turned to glare at Ryatt, wanting to strangle him, but the look in his eyes caused my words to die in my throat. "Now," the teacher barked.

I pushed to my feet and stalked angrily out of the room, my face feeling like it was on fire.

I slipped into the office, my hands still shaking from the embarrassment I'd endured.

13

GRACE

"Grace," a man called out when I stepped inside. His hair was thick and chocolate colored, the same as his eyes. He looked too young to be staff, but too old to be a student. "Grace Savage, correct?"

My brows pinched in confusion, and he held out his hand for me to shake. "I'm William Madden, guidance counselor. You're sponsored by Enzo Ransom. He's a good friend of our school."

"Y-yes."

"What brings you to my office? Been finding your way around okay?"

"Um, yeah. I just... I got sent to see the principal by the teacher."

"You don't peg me for a troublemaker." There was a glint in his deep coffee eyes.

I laughed, "I'm not. I swear. Trouble seems to find *me*."

He eyed me for a moment. "Want to talk about it? Principal Sanders is in a meeting, so he won't be able to see you." He took a step back, holding out his arm, showing me the way into his personal office. "I was meaning to meet with you soon. Introduce myself." I stepped inside the space, my eyes dancing around the room as he entered behind me, closing the door and muting the chatter of the secretaries.

"Please, have a seat," he offered as he circled his desk and sank down into his own tufted wingback chair.

I sank down in the seat, folding my hands together in my lap, my mouth feeling dry.

"What's going on?"

My eyes danced over the pictures on his desk, one of him in his graduation gown, another with what I assumed was his mother. And one of him on the beach with a woman. The surfboard in the image was propped against the wall behind him. "Someone sent me a message."

"Okay," his thick brows drew together as he leaned back in his seat, stretching his legs under his desk.

"It was... inappropriate, to say the least. But I was surprised and dropped my phone. So, it continued to play." I could feel my face burning, my eyes dancing everywhere but to him. "In front of everyone."

Mr. Madden rubbed his fingers along his tanned stubbled jaw. "Do you know who sent it to you?"

My eyes snapped to his before I sat up straighter, shaking my head. His gaze narrowed slightly.

"Grace, I'm well aware that some of the students here can be *intense* and even act like their wealth or power puts them above others. But it doesn't."

"I know it doesn't."

"But I can't help you if I don't know who they are."

I reached to my chest, fumbling with the necklace as silence stretched between us.

"Let me see it."

"What?"

"Let me see the message." He held out his large palm over the desk between us.

"I-I'm not sure you want to –"

"Grace, I promise you it's nothing I haven't seen before. And what we talk about in here is just between us."

I inhaled, my head feeling dizzy as I fumbled with my phone, pulling up the messages and placing it in his hand. His eyes flicked to me before he held the device up and clicked play. Immediately the sounds of moans filled the small space.

"*Jesus Christ*," he muttered, turning down the volume. His eyes met mine and I wanted to melt into a puddle on the floor. "That's not *you*, is it?" he asked. Then I saw his finger slide up, and I remembered the image of my ass as I was struggling to pick up the phone. His eyebrow rose.

I swallowed against the lump in my throat and shook my head as I took the device back from him. "Definitely not."

"So, I take it the..." he cleared his throat. "The male in the video is the person who sent it to you."

I shrugged.

"Your file shows the Ransom estate as your home of record. Why is that? No fixed address?"

"You've seen my file?"

He nodded, leaning back in his seat again. "You're the first student Enzo Ransom has ever sponsored. It piqued my curiosity."

"I live there."

"You *live* with Ryatt Ransom," he replied, not hiding the surprise from his voice.

"Oh good. You've heard of him," I deadpanned, causing the side of his mouth to curl up and a dimple to push deep into his cheek.

"That's very *interesting*," he replied.

"That's not the word I would use to describe it, Mr. Madden. Am I going to get in trouble for the video?"

"No," he shook his head, running his fingers through his hair that was a few inches long on top, and looked like it had been styled by the ocean breeze. "But you should delete it. If the other... *participant* is underage, you could get in trouble for having it."

"Oh, right," I started tapping on my screen, causing the video to autoplay again.

Mr. Madden rounded his desk, plucking it from my hand and quickly deleting it before handing it back to me and shoving his hands into the pockets of his slacks. He leaned back against the edge of his desk, next to my chair, looking down at me.

"How is it here? Besides the video," he asked.

"It's okay," I replied with a shrug, causing him to chuckle.

"That's not very convincing."

"It's just... different. I'm not used to this lifestyle."

"Well, look. I know I'm older, *but* I didn't grow up in this kind of place either. So, I mean it when I say I'm here to talk. There are also a few other sponsored students here that can relate to your experience."

"You're not that much older," I observed. "To be honest I thought maybe you were a student who failed a couple years."

That caused him to chuckle. "So, I look *stupid*. Great. I'm actually twenty-six, but *thanks*, I guess."

"I didn't mean it in a bad way."

"I know. It's not a big deal. I actually stopped shaving so people would take me seriously around here. To be fair, you don't look your age either."

"Really?" I asked, scrunching up my nose. "Compared to the other girls around here, I thought I looked like a little kid."

His eyes dipped below my face before locking back on mine. "Definitely not. And too smart to be hanging out with someone like Ryatt Ransom."

"It's not like I have a choice."

"Like I said, I'm here if you need to talk."

***

14

GRACE

After avoiding Ryatt for the last three days, Mattie and I spent four hours wandering around the Hidden Hills mall. It was so nice to be out of the house and not have to constantly look over my shoulder. It was the first time since moving here that I felt like I could let my guard down and be myself.

"I can't believe that boy gave me his number," I whispered, causing Mattie to giggle.

"He was hot too."

"The best part is he's new, so he's not some pretentious jerk under the Ransom spell." We stepped outside as the sun was sinking below the buildings. "I'm so tired," I whined as I looked up to take in Mattie's Honda Civic. I nearly tripped over my own feet when I noticed the sleek black classic car parked next to her. "Shit," I muttered.

"What?" Mattie glanced in the direction I was staring.

"That's got to be some random coincidence, right?" I asked, feeling like all my blood was leaving my body.

"Let's just get out of here before we have to deal with his cult of bitches."

I nodded, sliding into the passenger side of her car. She shoved the key into the ignition, turning it and... nothing.

"Does it do this a lot?" I asked. Mattie just shook her head. I let my eyes fall closed as I murmured a few curse words. My eyes drifted past Mattie to see Ryatt stalking across the lot, looking like he'd just stepped off a runway.

I got out of the car, glaring over at him.

"What's wrong, Kitten?" he asked, a ghost of a smirk on his lips.

"Mattie's car won't start."

"Pop the hood." He tapped on the hood and Mattie pulled the lever so it would release. He slid his hand in his pocket pulling out a small part and sliding it back into place. "Try it now," he barked loud enough for Mattie to hear.

"How do you know about cars? I didn't think people like you ever got their hands dirty."

"I can get *very* dirty," he muttered, almost bored.

My mouth hung open as I glared at him. "Why would you mess with her vehicle?"

"I had to make sure you were behaving yourself."

"Are you stalking me now?"

"*Now*?" he asked as if it wasn't obvious he had always been. He leaned forward, his voice gravelly next to my ear. "I'm always watching you, Grace." As he pulled back his eyes ran over my face.

"You're crazy."

"Certifiable." He slammed the hood before walking to his car and pausing before getting inside. "Erase that kid's number, or I'll erase his fucking face." He slipped inside of his car, the engine roaring to life.

I hurried up and got back to the passenger side of Mattie's old beater.

"What did he say?" she asked. I turned to take in Ryatt's profile, as he tapped something out on his phone.

"Just a dirty sparkplug," I muttered as my phone buzzed. It was a message from Ryatt that read –*Have her drop you off 24 Church Street.*

I hadn't even thought of where to tell her I lived. I looked back at him, meeting his gaze before nodding once.

"Where to?"

"Um... 24 Church Street."

Mattie typed the address in her phone, and we drove off toward the edge of town. We made plans to hang out again sometime soon as she pulled up out front of a small gray home with white trim and a red door, complete with a picket fence around the yard.

"Is this it?" Mattie asked and I shrugged.

"Um... yeah. Home sweet home." I opened the door, looking up and down the street for Ryatt's car but it was nowhere.

Reluctantly, I stepped out onto the street and waved her away, forcing a smile.

I watched as her taillights disappeared before yanking out my phone and typing out a message to Ryatt that said – *Where are you?*

He replied immediately –*Behind you.*

I spun around, my eyes landing on Ryatt standing in the doorway of the house. I opened the gate and trudged across the yard toward him.

"Where are we?" I asked as I reached him. He stepped aside, giving me room to enter. I did, walking past him and into what I assumed was a living room, but it was empty. I turned back toward him. "What is this place?"

"My home." He shoved his hands in his pockets. "I bought it with my own money."

"Seriously?" I asked, impressed. "Does your dad know?"

Ryatt clenched his jaw, shaking his head.

"I won't say anything."

"I know you won't. You're the only person I've ever met that can actually keep a secret." Ryatt took two large steps, closing the gap between us. My eyes were locked on his, uncertain of what he was going to do. I gasped when my phone was tugged from my hand.

"What are you doing?"

"Deleting that kid's number from your phone. Guys his age only think about one thing."

"Oh, yeah? What's that?" I asked as his thumb tapped away on my screen. "And how do you know my passcode?"

"*Fucking*," his eyes met mine. "I know *everything* about you, Kitten."

I scowled, holding out my hand. "Trevor is the same age as you," I pointed out.

Ryatt's eyes narrowed on the screen, his jaw clenching. "I know. I speak from experience."

"W-what's wrong?"

15

GRACE

Ryatt's eyes met mine, his face unreadable before they went back to the phone.

"Give me my phone back," my words came out in a rush as I reached for the device, but he turned, keeping me from being able to grab it. "Ryatt!"

"Who the fuck is Liam? You really *are* good at keeping secrets, aren't you?"

"J-just a friend."

"Just a friend," he repeated, his finger sliding against the screen to take in more of our conversation from the day. "Are you sure about that? He seems to have a crush on you."

"Can you blame him?" I joked, trying to ease the tension. That earned me a smirk before he went back to my device. "He doesn't. It's not like that," I clarified.

"No boys. It's against the rules."

"Since *when*?"

"Since you stepped foot into my house."

"Which house? This one or your father's prison?"

"Both."

I tried to grab it again, my hand closing around his. I almost got it free before my back was against the floor, Ryatt's heavy body on top of mine as my phone skidded across the hardwood.

"You're a jerk," I yelled, fighting to get a knee between his legs. But he was much larger and considerably stronger than I was. He used a leg to pry mine apart, settling between them as we struggled to control my arms. He grabbed my wrist, and I shoved my free hand against him, causing him to push all his weight against me. His thick length was now pressing back against a very sensitive area. I gasped, trying to raise my hips to push him off me, but it only caused more friction. To my absolute horror, a moan escaped my lips. Ransom's eyes darkened. He grabbed my other wrist without resistance, pushing my arms up on either side of my head. I was helpless and completely at his mercy. And worse, my body was aching for more.

"Keep fighting me, Kitten," he rasped. "I like it." I pushed back against him, and his hips rolled forward again, our bodies twisting together.

He was so hard, all muscle and attitude. He acted like a wild animal on most days, and even though I was pinned underneath him, I felt like, for this brief moment, I was making *him* lose control. Something he thrived on. I pushed up against him and he hissed, shoving back against me, painfully rough. His hand slid up my wrists, lacing our fingers together, keeping me locked in place. His hips rolled, and I widened my legs, granting him more access before I wrapped them around him, heels digging into the back of his thighs, now needing him to be impossibly close.

His face hovered over mine. I wanted him to kiss me so badly that my mouth was watering. His lips were open, his hot breath fanning over my face.

"*Ryatt...*"

"What do you want, Gracie?" he asked, his voice thick with lust.

"You can," I whispered, my gaze dropping to his mouth.

"I don't kiss."

"Anyone?" My voice wavered, worried he meant just me, like I wasn't worthy.

"No."

"Why?"

"Kissing is for people who love each other."

"And you've never loved anyone but yourself, right?" I sassed back, causing him to smirk.

"And you *hate* me, right?"

"Right," I agreed as his eyes searched my face.

"What is it you *really* want?" His hips pressed into me, and I gasped.

"More," I whimpered.

"Then beg me, Kitten."

"N-no," I snapped.

"*Beg* me," His lips brushed against the side of my neck, ghosting over my skin and causing goosebumps to trail after them.

I swallowed against the lump in my throat. "*Please...*"

To my absolute horror, he stilled a wicked grin on his lips. He lifted his body from mine, and I lay unmoving, splayed out before him as I struggled to catch my breath. He adjusted the hard length in his pants.

"Still think I don't own you, Gracie?" He grabbed my phone from the ground, snapping a picture. "Should we send this to *Liam*, show him how wet you get for me?"

"He isn't a student at Hidden Hills."

Ryatt shrugged, looking bored. "Doesn't matter."

"I thought that was the whole point. You don't want anyone who knows you to know we live together."

"Don't say it like that," he shot back.

"Like what?" I asked, pushing myself up to lean back on my hands.

"Like we're in some sort of secret relationship, living together."

I rolled my eyes. "Trust me, I would never want to be in a relationship with you."

His face went hard. "I meant that it wouldn't be a secret."

"What?" I asked, feeling like he was giving me whiplash from his volatile mood swings.

"If we *were* in a relationship, everyone would know. I wouldn't be ashamed of you," he clarified. He held out his hand for me to take and I did, allowing him to pull me to my feet. I nearly collided with his body, his eyes on mine before he held out my phone between us. I took it, muttering, "Thanks. That sounded dangerously close to a compliment."

"Just a fact." He shoved his hands in his pockets.

"So," I looked around the barren home. "Are you moving out of the big house?" *The big house* is what we called the mansion because it felt like a prison, and it was obviously massive.

"I can't." He shook his head and silence stretched between us. "The passcode to the door is your dad's birthday, since it's what you already use for your other devices."

I narrowed my eyes at him. "Why are you giving me the code?"

"You need a place for your little friend to pick you up from," he replied with a shrug.

"*Really*?" I asked, a wide grin spreading on my face. "What's the catch?"

"No catch."

"There's *always* a catch," I eyed him, wanting to know what he would get out of helping me.

"It's *convenient* for me."

"I don't know, it seems like you might *actually* be doing something *nice*. Maybe you're not as bad as I thought you were."

Ryatt smirked, sardonically. "I can promise you, Kitten, I'm much, much worse."

***

16

RYATT

I'd spent the last couple of weeks slowly furnishing my new place, even though I had no idea when I'd actually get to occupy it. We dubbed it the church because of the street, and it made it easier to talk about with our parents around. At least it was getting some use from Grace, who used it as a location for her friend Mattie to pick her up or drop her off from. They even on occasion used it as a place to study.

I grabbed my phone, sliding my finger across the screen when she sent me a message. A picture popped up of the note I'd left her that read *–Order pizza for you and your friend. - Daddy –*along with cash.

What is wrong with you? –she texted.

Just trying to make it look believable –I sent back. Then I added *–Did you eat?*

After a few seconds her reply came through *–Pizza.*

Good girl – I responded before looking up at my father who was droning on. This meeting had already gone on an hour longer than planned. My eyes scanned the other men in the room, giving him their undivided attention. The twins, Ryder and Ryker Cross who came down from Sacramento sat to my left, and Relic Grayson who was next in line to control Fresno was on my right, beside my father. Even with different dads, we all bore a striking resemblance thanks to our mother's strong genes, but that is where our similarities ended. And I wanted nothing to do with my siblings, even if it was business related.

I focused back on my phone – *Has Mattie left?*

Yeah. BTW, it doesn't cost $200 –Grace replied.

I know – I tapped out on the screen. – *Send a pic to show me where you are.*

You know where I am. There're cameras everywhere. – she sent back.

I'm waiting, Grace.

Like this? – Seconds later an image of Grace lying on a bed, her hair fanned around her head, popped up on my screen. *Or this* – Then another angled slightly downward, showing the top of her chest concealed beneath her uniform. *Maybe...* – The third showed her skirt, ridden up to the top of her milky thighs, her legs slightly parted and I had to adjust myself discreetly under the table. *Satisfied yet?* – The next image had her hand on her inner thigh.

Move your hand higher, Kitten – I texted.

She did, sending back an image of her uniform skirt around her waist, her fingers inside of her white cotton panties.

Are you wet? – I asked, staring down at my device. Instead of typing back a reply I received another image of her fingertips, glistening with her arousal.

"Ryatt," my father called out. All eyes were on me now. "Where is Grace? I'd like to introduce her."

"She's coming," I replied. "She was studying with a friend and it's running late." I had made sure she was out of the house because of this meeting. I wasn't about to subject Grace to more of our fucked-up Ransom business. The less she was involved, the better. And I didn't trust the twins around her.

My father nodded before muttering something about next time to my brothers. They all stood, shaking hands, and I used the opportunity to slip out of the room.

***

I stepped into the church, grabbing a slice of pizza from the box on the counter, and making my way toward the bedrooms. Grace's was the one on the left. It was much smaller than the master, but it was only set up as a place for her to hang out with Mattie. She'd never actually slept here. I haven't either.

I knocked against the hardwood before turning the knob and shoving the door open. Grace lay on her stomach across her bed, still in her school uniform, her feet in the air as her eyes scanned the pages of a novel. I couldn't help but wonder if she was still wearing her wet panties or if she'd changed.

"You ready?" I asked her.

"It's so peaceful here," She whined before turning the page with a sigh.

"Well, you *are* in the presence of a God."

Grace rolled her eyes. "So blasphemous. In *church* no less."

I shrugged. "Let's go, Kitten. I'll bring you back soon."

"I hate going back to the big house."

Taking another bite of my pizza, I leaned against the doorframe. "Speaking of which, my Halloween party is coming up."

That got her attention and she turned to look at me. "I know. It's all anyone has been talking about around school."

"You'll need to stay in your room."

"Why can't I stay *here*?"

"Because it'll be going all night. We need to be under the same roof."

"Then why can't I join the party? I can make a costume."

"Because it's not a place for someone like you."

"Like me?" she snapped, rolling her eyes. "Afraid my poverty will somehow rub off on you?"

"They'll be people there that aren't from our school. It won't be safe. It's not up for discussion." I'd already told my brothers that Grace would be off at a friend's house during the party. I couldn't imagine how badly things would go if they saw her.

"I don't have to listen to you, Ryatt." She turned her attention back to her book.

I sucked the sauce off my thumb as I watched her, knowing she was going to defy me. "It's for your *safety*."

"Your rules are to *control* me. I'm not one of your *Stepford* Hidden Hills whores. I can make my own decisions, thank you very much."

"Right now, you're under my roof, Grace."

"You mean the place you keep secret from everyone?"

"Everyone but you." I shoved the last bite of my slice in my mouth, knowing exactly where she was going with this.

"That gives me *power*, doesn't it?" she asked with a smirk.

"You've always had power over me, Grace. You just don't know how to *wield* it."

"Is that a euphemism?"

"It's a fact. Let's go."

She didn't budge and I blew out a heavy breath. "Fine. I'll give you an outfit." Slowly replacing Grace's wardrobe that

103

I'd stolen was really becoming a pain in the ass, but it gave me some leverage and times like now when she wanted to act like a brat, it made getting her to comply that much easier.

"Really?" she asked, beaming.

"But I get to choose what it is."

She rolled her eyes. "I don't need any more pink baby doll dresses and knee highs, thank you very much."

"Fine. Two outfits."

Grace sighed dramatically as she pushed from her bed.

***

17

GRACE

I was pouting, pacing my room, knowing that while my mother and Ryatt's father were out of town for a couple nights for a business meeting, Ryatt was hosting one of his infamous Villains and Vixens parties. I'd heard chatter about it around school for weeks. Of course, I was forbidden to step foot anywhere near the event. I was still invisible in our town. A ghost.

But if that were true, no one would even notice me lingering around the crowd. I could slip in, enjoy a fleeting moment of teenage rebellion, and Ryatt would be none the wiser. The dress code, or lack of dressing was simple enough. Wear as little as possible.

I decided on my white bra and panties, and a dress slip for modesty, topped with a feathery white eye mask and wings.

My heart raced as I made my way to the other side of the sprawling mansion, taking service hallways and slipping down stairwells that were only used by the help. My skin was clammy, and my mouth dry with anticipation as the steady pulsing of bass over an expansive surround sound system thudded in the distance.

I spotted the bar, an actual real hand-carved bar imported from an Irish Pub. People milled in and out of the room, lost in their own gossip and debauchery to spare me a second glance. It was almost too easy.

I grabbed a cup and filled it to the brim with some sort of sweet concoction labelled Jungle Juice in handwritten calligraphy.

I took a sip, puckering at the intense alcohol flavor. My eyes danced around, looking for the monster himself – *Handsome Ransom*. I slinked into the next room. Lights bounced and pulsed around me, and I could barely make out a single face in the gyrating crowd. It smelled of liquor and sweat. And somehow, I was the most dressed in the crowd. Girls were disposing of their tops, emboldened by drugs and anonymity. Guys wore only pants or boxer briefs. Their faces covered by masks or painted.

I continued on into the next hall, slipping into a sitting room, stopping as Ryatt came into view, perched upon a throne-like chair, his face painted like a skull. A black light bounced around him, and he glowed, looking even more menacing. But he wasn't the only one. There were three other chairs occupied by equally intimidating guys. It was like the four horsemen of the apocalypse decided to throw a party. I knew these are the outsiders he had warned me about, the reason I was supposed to avoid the festivities.

Ryatt's chest was bare, his coal-colored pants unbuckled, belt splayed. His hair was tousled like someone had run their fingers through it. I wondered who. Several girls were around him, orbiting him like he was the sun. And he was *the son* of the most powerful man on the West Coast. My eyes drifted lower, taking in the ridges and valleys of his muscular tatted stomach. His eyes were half-mast, focused on his phone in his hand before his gaze searched the crowd, nodding and giving a courteous grin to those who captured his attention.

I took another sip of my drink, watching him from the fringes of his flock. They all seemed to worship and fear him, desperate to earn his approval, like their entire identity was contingent on his approval.

I sneered, leaning back against the wall, taking another healthy swig as one of the blondes sank down on his lap, handing him a cup. He shoved his arm in the air to toast, "Here's to power. Here's to honor. If you can't come in her, come on her!" The crowd around him erupted as he gulped down the drink, throwing the cup on the floor. He whispered something in the girl's ear. She bit down on her lip, giggling at whatever he'd said. He grabbed something from a bucket beside him and handed it to her. *Party favors?* I watched her open whatever it was and hold it to her nose, inhaling some sort of powder. She pushed to her feet, and he smacked her ass before another girl sank down on their knees between his legs. This lucky guest received a pill that Ryatt placed on her tongue himself. This routine repeated about three more times before he looked at me. Our eyes locked, causing me to sway from the alcohol. He pointed before crooking two fingers and beckoning me to him.

I forced myself forward, ignoring the looks of people around me. Ryatt leaned back in his seat, watching me. He patted his thigh, and I hesitated before sinking down on his leg. He grabbed my hips, pulling my ass down center on his lap. His lips were at my ear. "How long were you going to stand there watching me?"

"I haven't spoken to anyone."

"You don't know how to listen, Kitten," he rasped. His fingers gripping me tighter.

"I'm wearing a mask. No one knows who I am."

"That's not what I'm worried about, Grace. My friends are heathens."

"What does that make you?" I felt him thicken beneath my bottom, and his fingers flexed against my flesh.

"I'm a God."

"You're drunk." I rolled my eyes and made a move to stand but he tugged me back against him, causing his length to rub between my legs, and I gasped at the size of him.

"I'm your God too, Grace. You just haven't gotten on your knees to worship me yet."

I scoffed. "Like all these *other* girls?"

He laughed. "What's wrong, Kitten? You think you're *special... different*?"

"Yes. I have standards."

"*Do* you?" he asked, amused, rocking my hips back against his length.

"Can't imagine what more you could want than wealthy, good looking, charming..."

"Cocky," I shot back.

"Very, *very* cocky," he rasped, pushing his hips up so his length grinded hard against me. "As much as I'd like to show you, I have guests to entertain." His hips continued their assault, slowly, methodically. "Be a good girl and go to bed, Grace."

I finished my beverage before pushing from his lap and returned to the bar for a refill, wanting to drown in my self-loathing and a few shots of tequila.

***

I took a small sip from my solo cup, perched on the stairs, well after midnight with my mask in my hand. I was tired of Ryatt bossing me around. This was my home too. Even if it was only temporary.

"Ransom invited *you*?" Some boy called up the stairwell to me, his face covered in a red and black devil mask. He wasn't being rude. He was genuinely shocked. I would be too. And since no one knew I would soon be his sister, I got it. He pulled off his disguise, offering me a grin.

I shook my head, taking another long sip of the jungle juice punch concoction that was more liquor than fruit. "Crashing," I lied. His smile grew.

"That's pretty cool."

I let my eyes rake him in. My vision was beginning to blur so I squinted, tilting my head. He looked cute. His dark hair was shorn close, his skin was a light olive. I was pretty sure he played football. I'd seen him sporting a jersey in the hallway. I struggled to remember the name emblazoned on the back.

"Johnson?" I asked.

"Jones," he corrected, crushing his empty cup in his palm.

"I'm Grace," I replied.

"I know."

That caused me to smirk. "You know who I *am*?"

"Everyone knows who you are. If we come within six feet of you, we're six feet down." He shrugged. "At first, I thought Ransom wanted you for himself. But I guess he just really needed a new victim."

"New victim?" I asked. "Who was the last one?"

Jones laughed, shaking his head. "I could make you a list, but it would probably be easier to name the people he hasn't targeted."

Taking another drink, I let that sink in. He'll grow bored and find someone else to torture soon enough. But this was our senior year, and I wasn't going to miss my first chance at a normal school to figure out who I am. I wanted to kiss boys and go on first dates. "So, why are you talking to me? Aren't you worried Ryatt will find out?" I asked him, chewing my lower lip.

"I've known Ransom since the fourth grade. I'm not scared of him. Wanna go for a walk?" he asked.

I thought it over. Most of the people here were in the other wing of the house. "Want to explore instead?" I asked. "I found some cool rooms up here." I motioned behind me.

Jones smiled wickedly, taking the steps two by two to join me. We quickly hurried up further into the darkness as we made our way toward the rooms. "That's a library," I pointed to my left. "I checked it out earlier.

"Let's see what's in there." There was a mischievous glint in his bronze eyes.

"Spoiler alert. It's books." I grabbed the handle, twisting it and shoving it open. Jones gasped when he took in the room. I couldn't blame him. I did the same when I first saw it. Rich mahogany and dark leather covered nearly every surface. The thick scent of pricey cigars hung heavy in the air. The drapes were drawn. Making the space virtually black, aside from the light filtering through the old stained-glass windows above salvaged from an old church in Europe. They threw streak of gold and crimson across the space giving it a magical feel.

"This place is dope," he whispered, grabbing my hand and turning me to face him.

"Do you read?"

"Not really." He stepped closer and I instinctively took one back, bumping against a bookshelf. Jones closed the gap between us, pressing his lips hard against mine. My stomach revolted and I pushed against his chest, but he was too strong.

"What are you doing?"

"Having a little fun," he slurred against my mouth.

After a moment. The sound of zipper teeth separating caused my heart to race. "No, I think you should go back to the party." I shoved harder. "Stop!"

"Don't be such a cocktease." Jones's fingers grasped my hair, tugging me down to my knees and caging me between his muscular legs.

"Jones," I squealed.

There was a loud thud, and Jones was knocked to the ground in front of me. I peeked up through my hands to see Ryatt, his eyes blazing as he looked from me to Jones.

18

GRACE

"What the fuck are you doing in here?" he asked, his voice eerily calm. I knew he was talking to me. I was the banished one. I stood, my legs shaking as my knees threatened to buckle.

"You don't own me."

"*Don't* I?" He glanced back over his shoulder before his foot connected with Jones' ribs. He let out a guttural groan, his arms wrapping around himself.

"Now is not really the time –"

"Now is the *perfect* fucking time," he snapped, glaring down at me. "Are you trying to piss me off? Huh? You want to act like a little slut?"

"That's rich coming from you. It's none of your business."

"You *are* my business, Grace," he scoffed. "Did you think he wanted to discuss fucking *literature*?" His voice echoed in the expansive room. But I knew no one would hear him, not with the music pumping and everyone gathered in an entirely different wing. "The only spine he was going to run his fingers down was yours."

"You sound jealous," I shot back.

"Don't mistake me finding you *fuckable* for catching feelings." His jaw tensed, his muscles jumping under the skin as he placed his hand around my throat. "You're a possession. A *toy*. I just don't like to share." He didn't tighten his grip, just backed me up a step away from where Jones still lay on the floor. His eyes flitted to where he gripped me, and I knew he could feel my pulse thrumming under his touch.

"You're spoiled," I seethed.

"I am. *Rotten*," he agreed.

My body was practically levitating with my adrenaline rush.

"You knew if you went off with him, it would piss me off. You *both* knew."

"I should go," Jones made an effort to stand, but Ransom twisted around and plowed his fist into the side of his face, causing him to collapse on the floor with a pained groan.

I squealed, covering my face with my hands.

"Say it," Ryatt commanded.

"Say *what*?" I asked, swinging my arms out at my side.

"That you knew going off with him was against the *rules*."

"You don't make the rules," I spat.

"You *knew* what you were doing."

"Oh, I *wanted* it?" I snapped. "Did you really just say that? So, I deserved to have him try to *force* himself on me?"

114

Ryatt's eyes went wide, blazing with anger as he glanced at Jones and back to me. "He was *forcing* himself on you?"

"He –" I couldn't speak, choking on the truth. He *was*. The reality of what was going on through the fog of alcohol hit me like a punch in the gut. Ryatt read the truth written all over my face.

I'd seen him angry before, but now he looked absolutely feral. "Get on your fucking knees," Ryatt growled. I leaned back against the shelf, causing the books to slide against each other. "Not you."

"W-what?" I whispered.

"Jones. Get on your fucking knees. *Now.*"

"What are you doing?" I asked, panic causing my chest to feel like it would fracture from how hard my heart was beating.

"He earned this, Gracie." Ryatt reached behind the desk and pulled open a drawer, sliding his hand inside. The sound of a gun being cocked caused me to gasp.

Jones pushed himself to all fours before holding his hands up in front of his chest. "I was just playing around with her. I wasn't gonna hurt her."

My stomach rolled as I took a tentative step closer.

"Well, now *I'm* playing with *you*."

Jones was mouthing "*Please*," to me over and over, desperate for me to be his savior. The power dynamic had flipped so quickly it felt like I had whiplash.

"*Hey*," Ransom snapped his fingers in Jones's face. "Don't look at her. Look at *me*."

"I promise –"

Before he could get the words out, Ransom shoved forward, the barrel of the gun filling Jones's mouth and causing him to gag. But Ryatt grabbed his head, so he couldn't back away. Couldn't move. Jones's face was red as tears rolled down his cheeks. Ryatt slowly pumped the weapon in and out of his mouth.

"He can't breathe," I cried out.

"Good," Ryatt snapped, holding stock still. "Doesn't feel so fucking good when you're on the receiving end of it, does it? Relax your throat and take it."

"Ryatt!"

Ryatt's gaze slid to me, his eyes raking down my body before going back to Jones. "She's *mine*. Got it?" Ryatt tugged the weapon free, and Jones fell to his hands, dry heaving.

"You're crazy," Jones sputtered, blood, tears, and saliva coating his face. One of his eyes was nearly swollen shut.

Ryatt sat the gun on the desk, his eyes narrowed. "I'll show you fucking crazy," he barked, and then the sound of another zipper lowering caused my body to tremble. He pulled himself free from the confines of his pants and I gasped as I took in the length of him. "Keep making those sexy little noises, Kitten. You're making me hard."

Jones looked to me, his eyes pleading for help going back to Ryatt. "I'm s-sorry, Ransom. You don't even like her."

"She's the one you should be apologizing to," Ryatt rasped.

"I'm sorry, Grace. I was just having fun. I'm drunk. I didn't mean it."

"What do you think, Gracie? Do you think he's really sorry?" Ryatt looked to me, his eyes taking me in as he slowly stroked his length. *Jesus Christ how was he able to look so terrifying and sexy at the same time?* Then I remembered that Lucifer was once an angel. I'm sure he had been just as pleasing the eye, and only half as cruel as Ryatt.

I licked my lips, my eyes dancing between them, realizing how close I'd become to being another statistic. *Fun?* This was going to be *fun* for Jones? It wouldn't hurt to let Ryatt scare him so he didn't do it to someone else. And for once, it felt like the monster was in *my* corner. I wanted to keep him there. I felt a sliver of power, and now I understood why everyone in this town was desperate to get their hands on it like a junkie looking for a fix. It was intoxicating. I shook my head slowly, biting the inside of my cheek.

Ryatt's mouth curled into a wicked smirk as his attention went back to Jones. "Open your mouth."

"N-no," Jones whimpered, tears rolling down his face as he sobbed.

Ryatt watched him cry at his feet for what felt like an eternity, before taking a step back from him. "You think you can come into our house and disrespect her?"

Our house.

"Please, Ransom," he begged.

"Get the fuck out," Ryatt ordered. It only took a second for him to scurry out of the room, leaving me standing in the dark with *Handsome Ransom*, his very prominent member in hand, and now his attention was devoted to me.

Shit. Shit. Shit.

My hand went to my chest to fidget with my locket. When I noticed it was gone.

"My necklace," I croaked, dropping to my hands and knees as I searched the floor.

"We'll get you a new one" Ryatt groaned, causing me to still.

"It's *important* to me." Tears clouded my vision. I crawled across the floor in front of him, sliding my hands along the wood. "My dad gave it to me."

"Get off your knees, Grace," he bit out as I glanced up at him, noticing that his cock was larger now, easily twice the size it had been, jutting out of his hand. I'd never actually seen one this close, but I was pretty certain this is what Ryatt was referring to when he said he was impressive in other ways. "Better yet, stay down there." His hand slowly stroked his length as he watched me watching him. I swallowed hard, and his attention fell to my throat, his fist moving faster. "Do that again."

"What?"

"Swallow," he rasped. And I did, without a thought, his command sending a bolt of excitement through my belly.

"Be careful what you wish for," he rasped. "You wanted my full attention." His gaze dropped to his thick length. "It's yours."

"I didn't..."

"Have you ever sucked a cock before, kitten? Or do you just like to watch other girls get what you want?"

I thought back to him in the pool house, and how it seared my gut when I realized he wasn't alone. I shook my head.

"Big girl words, Gracie. I want to hear you say it."

"N-no. I've never... s-sucked a cock before."

He groaned, his hand moving faster over himself.

"Why?" My mouth was suddenly parched.

His tongue ran over his lower lip and my core pulsed, wetness pooling in my panties. "Open your mouth for me,

Kitten," he groaned. "I'll be gentle. I promise," But his words sounded taunting.

"I don't trust you," I admitted, causing him to smirk.

19

RYATT

The way she was staring at me, at my cock, with a hungry look in her eyes, still swimming with unshed tears, made my dick throb. To be honest I didn't think I'd get the tip past her lips before blowing my fucking load if given the chance.

How she was still kneeling before me and didn't run from the room, screaming for help was beyond me. And it was the only reason I could get my dick semi-hard when I went after Jones. It was always rock fucking solid when Gracie was around. I hated her for it. I didn't like to not be in control. Especially when it came to the *one* person I couldn't fuck.

I knew what I just did was fucking *crazy*. *She* makes me fucking crazy. And that prick needed to be taught a lesson. If Grace wasn't distracting me, I would have ended his fucking life. My father was right – *soft hearts, hard cocks* and all of that bullshit.

Gracie watched me, her tongue running out over her plump lips, and *fuck me*, I wanted to shove my dick inside of her mouth and fuck her face senseless. But I wouldn't do that. Not *today*, at least. But I could help erase the bad memory of his aggression with a more *palatable* one.

She shuddered like the realization of the danger she'd been in just hit her. "He was going to hurt me," she whispered, her eyes meeting mine.

"And I hurt *him* because I protect what's *mine*," I rasped, glancing up at the camera behind her. They were everywhere. I wouldn't let these assholes roam my home with free rein. And I kept an eye on Gracie. She was too innocent. That's why I enjoyed fucking with her. There was something so tempting about the one girl I couldn't have; the girl who didn't want me. But I couldn't trust anyone else not to hurt her. Case in point, that shithead Jones. From the time it took me to cross the house, he'd already tried to force himself on her. It was too close, and it was taking all I had in me not to hunt him down and end his fucking life. "You don't have to trust me, Grace. It doesn't hurt my feelings. In fact, I'd think less of you if you did. You're smarter than that."

She scoffed, "That's because you're a sociopath."

"Are you wet for me?"

"*What?*"

"Is your pussy *wet* for me?"

Grace slowly nodded; her cheeks flushed.

I groaned, the air was thick between us. How I'd gone from taking shots off Wren Cross's stomach to stroking my dick to Grace is a muddled blur. But I was here now. And I was *so* fucking close.

"What do you want me to do?" She asked.

That was a loaded fucking question and the possibilities filtered through my brain.

"Crawl to me, Kitten," I ordered, stroking myself as she watched, her eyes flitting between my cock and my face. She did, closing the gap between us on her hands and knees. "I want you to open your mouth for me, Gracie. Nice and wide. And stick your tongue out like a good girl." I was crossing a line. Fuck that, I was vaulting a canyon. But if I didn't *touch* her, I would hang on to some semblance of control. I was testing myself as much as I was testing her. *How far would she let me go? How far could I push her?*

Her lips parted, her pink tongue peeking out over her lower one. *Jesus fucking Christ.* She was going to be the death of me, literally, if I get caught corrupting her. But I couldn't just walk away now. I gripped myself tighter, pumping as her eyes locked on mine. "I'm going to come in your pretty little mouth," I warned. I thought of taking a picture of her at the angle, but I knew I could never erase the image of her submitting to me from my mind.

She blinked up at me as I stepped closer to her, a pearl of excitement beading on my head. I brushed it across the tip of her tongue and shuddered, coating her mouth with come. She sat there, patiently waiting as every ounce of pleasure was wrung from my body.

"Fuck that's beautiful," I rasped. As soon as I finished, I tucked my cock away and pressed my hand under her chin to close her mouth before sliding it down to her throat, helping guide her to her feet. I gripped it tighter, our eyes locking. "Swallow." My hand stroked her neck, coaxing her to take every last drop. Her neck bobbed, and I groaned, knowing she did just what I wanted.

"That's my girl," I praised, pulling back from her. "Let's go."

"Where are we going?" she asked as she followed me from the library.

"To your bedroom."

She sucked in a ragged breath, and I knew she was thinking about what we would be doing. I didn't say anything as I stalked down the hall and slipped inside her room. Grace followed, her fingers ringing together in front of her.

I watched her face, as I reached up, sliding the strap of her wings from her shoulder before she turned around, allowing me to pull them off. "Lay down," I ordered, my lips brushing the shell of her ear. She turned back around, her eyes meeting mine before the column of her throat bobbed. Taking two steps, she climbed onto her bed, perched on her hip.

I closed the gap between us, looking down at her in her silky slip. She laid back, resting her head on her pillow. I climbed over her, straddling her hips before leaning forward, and reaching between the gap between the headboard and mattress.

"What are you doing?" she asked as I pulled a silver chain into view.

My free hand circled her arm, raising it above her head. "Chaining you to your bed," I explained, clasping a cuff around her wrist.

"W-what?" Her hips rose, and I sank my weight down on her before fighting to push her other arm above her head. After securing it, I sat up straight, watching as she struggled to free herself. "Why?" When she noticed the way I was looking at her, she stilled, her eyes wide with fear.

It didn't help that my cock was rock hard and straining against my pants.

"Are you going to hurt me?" Her voice was so small, wavering under the weight of her words.

"Would you like me to?"

She licked her lips before shaking her head.

I climbed off her, adjusting my cock in my pants. "I'll be back in a few hours, Kitten. Get some sleep."

"You can't just leave me like this."

"You should know by now, I can do whatever the fuck I want."

"Ryatt," she pleaded.

I paused, turning to take one last look at her sprawled out on her bed. "I knew you'd be on your knees for me like every other girl in this town."

She drew back as if I'd slapped her before I closed the door behind me. But this changed nothing between us.

***

I stalked down the hall as I flipped through the different cameras on the property. The party was still in full swing, bass thumping. I grabbed a shirt and tugged it on, not bothering to button it before shrugging on my leather shoulder holster. I sent a quick text to Antonio, one of my father's personal guards, and slipped out front into the muggy air.

Relic stood on the porch, a cigarette between his fingers as he leaned against a pillar. We were the same height, but he was wide with thick bulky muscles. His hair was to his shoulders, and he'd grown out a beard over the summer. He looked like he should be wielding an ax and wearing plaid, not a two-thousand-dollar designer suit. "Ditching your own party, little brother?" he asked, a drunken smirk on his painted face.

"I have some business to handle," I replied, my eyes scanning the lot.

Relic flicked his cigarette to the cobblestone below. "Let's fucking go."

A few minutes later a sleek black car pulled up and Antonio got out, circling the vehicle before pulling open the back door.

"Where?" he asked as his eyes met mine thought the rearview mirror.

"Won't be far," I replied as the car lurched forward and made its way down the winding private drive, lined with trees. Just outside of the property was a figure, stumbling their way down the road. "Pull over."

The car came to a stop and I rolled down my window as Jones glanced over at me. His eyes went wide with recognition. "I don't want any smoke, man. I'm leaving. I promise."

"I'll give you a ride."

He shook his head, swaying on his feet. "I-I'm fine. I can make it."

The driver's door opened and slammed closed, and I watched Jones's face twist in fear as Antonio made his way toward him. I couldn't blame him. He was a big motherfucker. I watched Jones shake, wondering if he was going to piss himself before Antonio grabbed the door handle and pulled it open, gesturing for him to get in.

I barked out a laugh. "Man, you should see your fucking face."

Jones chuckled nervously.

"Get in. We need to talk."

He eyed me before nodding and sliding in beside me, rubbing his palms against his thighs. "Listen –"

I held up my hand before speaking to Antonio. "Take us to Cent City."

"Central City East? As in *Skid Row*?" Jones asked, his voice wavering.

"I need to restock a few things," I explained. I wasn't one to use but I liked to keep party favors around. They came in handy for guests, or for when you need to make something look like an accident. But that wasn't what this venture was about.

"I kinda just want to go home," Jones pleaded.

"It's too late for that."

His bloodshot eyes met mine and I smiled.

"Come on, Jones. You know I can't just let you walk away."

He swallowed hard, the column of his throat bobbing. "I'm not going to talk to her or even look at her again."

"I know."

"I won't say a word about anything," he continued.

"I *know*."

The car slowed, causing Jones's voice to raise an octave. "I'll do whatever you want, Ransom."

"But you didn't."

"What?"

"This is the good part," Relic rasped with a hint of amusement.

I tried my best to blend in with my peers. But sometimes they reminded me that we were from different worlds. A simple fuck up in theirs meant a fist fight or a nasty rumor. In mine it was kill or be killed. "I told you not to touch her."

"I didn't think you were serious."

"Do you think I'm serious *now*?" I asked. "Who the fuck *am* I?"

"You're Ryatt...Ransom, my *friend*."

"No," I corrected him. "I'm Ryatt Ransom. I'm the guy who's going to ruin you."

"What? Ryatt, please –"

"Get out of the car," I bit out as just as Antonio yanked the door open.

"You're going to hurt me?"

"You were going to hurt *her*."

"I'm sorry."

I didn't look at him, didn't respond as I pulled out my phone to check the cameras in my house. Grace was still on her bed, staring up at the ceiling, and I pushed her to the recesses of my mind.

Antonio grabbed Jones's arm and pulled him from the vehicle, I followed after him. This type of job was Antonio's specialty, but this felt personal. It shouldn't. This was what we did. Jones wasn't stupid. He crossed me, and I had been a few minutes later, he would have taken advantage of Grace.

I cracked my neck, as murderous thoughts, the image of her on her knees before him flooded my mind. I closed my eyes inhaling sharply before I hit him. And hit him. And hit him. The skin of my knuckles split, the bones bruised.

Relic stepped beside me with a baseball bat and made sure his legs and arms would be little use to him this football season. We didn't stop until he was on the ground, unmoving. And then *I*, Ryatt *fucking* Ransom, hit him again for good measure.

I stared down at him, waiting for any signs of life, any feeling from my chest of guilt or remorse. He gasped for air, his hands shaking. "Stay the fuck away from Grace," I ordered before nodding to Antonio and slipping back into the car, covered in Jones's blood. *My heart was still hard*, I thought idly. But so was my cock at just the thought of Grace chained to her bed.

"Grace," Relic began as the car made its way back to the mansion.

"Don't," I warned him.

Relic shrugged. "You should introduce us. Especially since we practically killed that kid for her."

"You didn't do it for *her*. You did it for *me*."

"You can't keep her from us forever," he warned.

***

After running through the shower to wash away Jones's blood, I slipped back into the party, mingling with my guests before heading outback to watch a few girls skinny dip and call my father.

The phone rang three times against my ear before his gruff voice answered. "This better be fucking important."

"I'm gonna need you to send flowers to Danny Jones's mother. He's probably going to have a lengthy stay in the hospital."

"What happened?" he asked, his voice sounding much more alert.

"You told me to protect Grace. I am."

He was silent for a moment before clearing his throat. "I'll make a few calls." The line went dead. I slid my phone back in my pocket and focused my attention back on the girls splashing in the water.

***

20

GRACE

I tossed and turned throughout the night, only succumbing to sleep when the sun began to crest over the trees. My arms were twisted uncomfortably over my head. I groaned, blinking open my eyes, gasping when I saw Ryatt sitting in my vanity chair, watching me.

"What are you doing?"

"Admiring the view," he rasped before pushing to his feet and stalking toward me. I rolled on my side, away from him. "Don't pout, Kitten."

The bed dipped, a palm snaking its way over my hip. I gasped, jerking away from his touch when he chuckled, tugging my hip and causing me to fall on my back as he perched over me on his knees.

"You're a jerk, you know that?" I asked as he looked down at my chest. I knew my nipples were peaked. Pulling his phone from his pocket, he snapped a picture of me tied down beneath him.

"Parties over. Come help clean up." He shoved his phone in his pocket and freed one of my wrists.

My brows pulled together. "The party I wasn't allowed to attend? No, thank you. You do it."

"I don't do manual labor," he quipped. "That's for people like *you*." He undid the other cuff, and I immediately began rubbing my wrists.

"Have your *servants* do it."

"I remember you partaking in a few activities last night. Now let's go before I drag you downstairs, kicking and screaming." He climbed off the bed and grabbed my arm to tug me to my feet, but I yanked back, freeing my hand.

"I'm not cleaning up after your mess."

"Really? Because I remember you swallowing every drop of *my mess* a few hours ago."

"Lapse of judgment." I threw my pillow at his chest. "Let me guess, you'll show the entire school that pic if I don't get up and clean up after you."

He shook his head, his expression unreadable as he tossed the pillow back. "No. This is just for me."

With that, he turned, and stalked out of my room. I closed my eyes, replaying his last words in my mind as I slid my hand down over my stomach, slipping the tips of my fingers beneath the fabric. My lips popped open with a sigh, my back arching from the bed as I rubbed myself in slow, deliberate circles.

I could still feel the weight of his body against me, the way he looked at me as if he wanted to touch me. I bit into my lower lip to stifle a moan as my hips rocked against my hand. My own fingers didn't do him justice.

I flipped over, shoving my pillow beneath me and riding it. I wondered if I had been on top of him, would he have pushed me off or let me take control? It was a stupid question because Ransom thrived on being the one with all the power.

I gasped, my hips rocking faster as stars sparkled behind my eyes, and waves of euphoria crashed over me.

"*Fuck*, that was hot, Kitten."

My eyes shot open, taking in Ryatt as he leaned casually against my door frame.

"Get out," I barked, pushing from the bed and swiping my hair from my face. His gaze fell to my soaked panties.

My flower covered pillow was clutched in my fist, and I threw it at him again. He didn't toss it back. Instead, he raised it to his face, inhaling the fabric. My skin grew hot, and my core clenched.

"I think I'll keep this. I like the idea of falling asleep and waking up to the smell of your pussy."

I shivered; my words lodged in my throat as my heart hammered inside of my body.

He shook his head, his eyes going from the pillow to my face. "I think you're the one who doesn't play fair, Grace," he threw my words from the cafeteria back at me.

I steeled my spine, jutting my chin in the air. It was the first time he'd admitted that I was a formidable opponent. It was a crack in his dominating façade. Even if it was wrong. I hadn't lured him back. I was just too wound up to think clearly. Ryatt had that effect on me.

"You know what I think?" I asked, folding my arms across my chest.

He fought against a smirk, taking a step closer so I'd have to crane my neck up to meet his gaze. "Tell me."

"I think you *want* me."

That caused him to bark out a laugh. "*That's* what you think?" he asked, amused.

"Yeah. I do. I think you want me." I cocked an eyebrow, trying to appear like I was as calm as he was, but I could feel my fingers trembling.

"That's funny," he scratched his eyebrow with his thumbnail. "Because I already *have* you, Grace. And if I wanted to do anything with you, I would. And you'd let me. Because *you* want *me*."

"You're delusional."

"And you're a *liar*," he bit back, his face nearly touching mine.

"You came into *my* room, remember? You sought *me* out."

"You're in my *house*, remember?" His playful tone had evaporated, no longer hiding behind teasing banter.

"You mean your Daddy's house. The *church,* where you like to cosplay as the middle class is *your* home," I seethed. "And how could I forget? You remind me every chance you get."

Ryatt rolled his eyes, the muscles in his angular jaw jumped under his skin. "Take the hint. *Leave.*"

"Where am I supposed to go?"

He shrugged. "You're eighteen. Move into the church."

"*What?* You can't be serious." My heart lurched at the proposition and for a brief second, I entertained the idea. But I couldn't leave my mother. Not yet.

"Why not? I would still be able to keep an eye on you."

My chest deflated. "Move from one cage to another?"

His face went hard. "Don't compare me to my father."

"Why don't *you* just leave? You have a place to go. You hate your dad, my mom, and me," I added. "It seems like you're the common denominator in this problem."

"I can't leave, until you do."

"What? *Why?*" I asked, my face screwing up in confusion.

He shook his head, regretting what he'd said. "Forget it. Get a shower and get dressed. I need your help."

"You have a funny way of asking," I scoffed, my eyes narrowed.

His voice lowered, his lips going to my ear. "You need a shower because you just got done fucking yourself. I like being the only one who knows your *scent*," he bit out. "And I *wasn't* asking. You're *going* to help me. If you think I wasn't playing fair before, you have no idea what I'm capable of."

I chill rolled through me, covering my skin in goosebumps. I'd seen the feral side of Ryatt, and I didn't want to be on the receiving end of that kind of wrath. His eyes met mine, making sure I knew he was serious before he turned, stalking out of my room with my pillow clenched in his fist.

***

The weekend dragged on and by the time our parents got back home, Ryatt and I were barely speaking.

"Maybe Ryatt can take you," my mother suggested.

My eyes met hers over the dining room table. I hadn't heard a word she said because I was watching Ryatt smiling down at something on his phone, wondering if he was talking to someone.

"Take me where?" I asked.

"Shopping," she replied, brushing her dark hair over her shoulder. "We really do need to get you your own car."

"We have drivers," Enzo replied before taking a sip of his wine.

"I'd rather walk," I muttered.

"I'll take her. I need a few things anyway. We can go on Wednesday." Ryatt's tone was flat and he never looked up from his phone screen.

"Fine. It's settled," Enzo added. "Now to more pressing matters. I have a meeting coming up in a few weeks with Gio, and I think we should all go, have a nice family vacation."

Ryatt's gaze snapped to his father. "In Naples?"

"Florida?" I asked.

"Italy," Ryatt replied, his eyes never leaving his father.

"Oh, that sounds lovely," Grace's mother Hope chimed in.

"You remember his son Luca," Enzo folded his hands together, propping his elbows on the table.

Ryatt's gaze flicked to mine. "Yeah, I remember him."

"He's looking forward to seeing you again."

21

RYATT

How the fuck could I forget Luca Rossi? The first time I'd met him he'd dumped a man in a wheelchair into a giant fountain and laughed as he drowned. He was eleven at the time.

My father never included me in his Rossi bullshit. They were a family of fucking psychopaths. And it was just good business for my father to keep the heir to his throne in a separate location. So why drag me into their mess now?

"Are you sure that's a good idea?" I asked, my eyes flitting to Grace.

"Are you questioning me?" my father snapped back at me, his expression hard. "You'll be there to protect Grace. That's your job. And I trust you can handle it."

Grace's eyes widened at my father's words. I leaned back in my seat, taking a drink of my wine. "You know I can," I confirmed.

"Good. Then I'll make arrangements."

***

The loudspeaker crackled to life and the lunchroom noise faded to a dull murmur as the vice principal spoke. "Attention students. We will be hosting a fundraiser for one of our own this Friday," her voice wavered. "Danny Jones, a star athlete with a promising future in our community, was viciously attacked over the weekend. All proceeds raised will go toward his medical bills. guidance counselors will be available to all students needing someone to talk to."

Her voice droned on but all I could focus on was Grace. Her gaze was locked on mine as the room erupted around us. Fear and confusion twisted her features. I pushed from my seat, stalking toward her and slipping out of the exit. Her footsteps soon followed, and she hurried to my side.

"Ryatt," she whispered.

"Not here," I replied, continuing outside, slipping around the corner away from prying eyes.

"Did you..."

My eyes met hers in warning and she gasped, shaking her head, looking at me as if she could finally see me for the first time.

"What did you do, Ryatt?" Her words were a rushed whisper.

"What I had to." I took a step toward her until her back was against the wall. I pressed my palm to the stone, leaning in closer.

"He was your friend."

"He was a *danger* to you."

Her tongue ran over her lips, and I glanced down, watching it roll over her pink skin before our eyes met again.

"Is that what your father meant by you protecting me?"

I clenched my jaw, wishing he'd never divulged that information. "What exactly is it you think my father *does* for a living?"

"H-he owns a lot of lucrative businesses around the world."

"You're not that naive." I watched the column of her throat move as she swallowed. "He owns a lot of very important *people*." I corrected her. "*We're*... not who you think we are, Grace."

"What does that mean?"

"It means... that if anyone touches you, *hurts* you, I will fucking *destroy* them."

"You'd do that?"

"I already have."

Her mouth popped open, drawing my attention back to her lips. We were a hair's breadth apart and I could smell the coconut scent that clung to her skin. It was intoxicating and I realized I could distract her from all of these revelations.

"Aren't you going to run away from me now, Kitten?"

Her eyes narrowed. "I'm not scared of you. I know that you won't hurt me."

"Won't or *can't*?" I smirked, tilting my head to get even closer. "There are many ways I can torture you without inflicting physical pain," I whispered, my fingertips slowly dragging up the inside of her thigh, under the material of her pleated skirt, causing her breath to hitch.

"So, no one can touch me but *you*?"

I brushed my knuckle over the damp cotton of her panties as my lips went to her ear. "No one but me, Grace," I rasped, sliding her panties to the side and pressing the pads of my fingers against her clit. Her hips pushed back against my touch.

"Is that a *rule*?" she asked, her voice thick with lust.

"The most important one," I groaned, pulling back so I could watch her rub herself against me. In awe of how she trusts me, using the very hand I'd used to assault someone for her, to bring her pleasure. Her chest rose, brushing against mine.

The bell rang out. Our lunch period was over, and it should have snapped me back to reality. But I didn't stop. My eyes stayed locked on Grace's as I worked against her methodically.

"Someone could come out here," she breathed. She was soaked, and I knew she was close.

"Let them watch."

Grace whimpered, her teeth pushing into her bottom lip. "We can't get caught, Ryatt. I-I heard your father threaten you not to touch me."

"You're worried about *my* safety?"

She nodded, infinitesimally and it caused a visceral reaction inside of me. I can't remember the last time someone cared what happened to me.

My jaw clenched, knowing she was right. I shouldn't be doing this. But I was desperate to watch her unravel from my touch. "You think you can be quiet for me?" I asked as her body quivered. She shook her head, and I couldn't help my smirk as I covered her mouth with my heavy palm, muffling her moans.

"That's it, Grace." *Give yourself to me.*

My fingers were dripping as her body shook from my touch. After the last rapture of her release rolled through her, I let my hand fall from her mouth as she struggled to slow her breathing. She watched me with hooded eyes, her cheeks flushed pink as I licked my fingers clean. Something passed over her features, something *more* than just satisfaction. It was unnerving and I took a step back from her, creating some physical distance between us.

"We're late for class," I rasped.

"Hey," a gruff voice called from beside us. "Grace, are you okay?" Mr. Madden's eyes flitted between us, taking a step closer.

"She's fine," I snapped.

"I'd like to hear *her* say it," he replied.

My eyes were locked on Grace's as the column in her throat moved. "I'm fine, Mr. Madden," she reassured him with a smile. I sure as fuck didn't like *that*. *What the fuck?*

"Get to class," he ordered, his eyes on me.

"Go on, Grace," I spoke low, watching her eyes go back to him before nodding.

"You too, Ryatt," he added.

I watched as Grace slipped around the corner and back inside the building before giving him my attention. "I see you're acquainted with Grace."

"We've spoken."

"Have you? She didn't mention it."

Mr. Madden smiled, sliding his hands in the pockets of his slacks. "Just part of her orientation. It's my job to make sure she's acclimated."

"I've seen how you welcome new students. *Help* the less fortunate," I bit out, stepping closer to him.

"I don't know what you're talking about, Ryatt."

"Don't you? You're not the William Madden that was suspected of an inappropriate relationship with a student during your internship?"

"It was an unfounded rumor. One I'm sure you knew something about."

"There were pictures," I corrected him. "I'm warning you. Stay away from her."

"I didn't cross any lines, Ryatt. Look, I'm not sure what your deal is with Grace, but I *do* know, she's a good kid who doesn't need to have her high school career derailed by someone who won't remember her name in a month."

"I appreciate your concern, but Grace is *my* responsibility. I got it from here," I warned before stalking off toward my next class.

***

22

GRACE

"Have you seen Ryatt?" I asked Lucia as she cleared my lunch plate from the table. He was supposed to take me to the store to get a few things, but he'd been MIA since we'd gotten home from school. She shook her head, but her eyes flitted behind me in the direction of the theater. I thanked her for the food before making my way down the south hall, my steps echoing loudly against the marble.

I grabbed the handle of the door, and shoved it open, nearly falling over my feet when I saw Ryatt with a brunette perched on his lap. Ryatt glanced over at me, looking bored. "Need something?"

"Who are you?" The girl asked, and I didn't miss the hint of jealousy in her tone.

"That's my little sister," he replied, his thumb sliding across her thigh. My eyes went wide, not believing he actually admitted that to someone. "Give us a minute, Marie?"

She straightened her top and got up from his lap. I took in his bare chest and how his slacks were undone.

I waited until she was in the hall before closing the door. "I'm your sister now, huh?"

He chuckled, rubbing his palm along his jaw. "She goes to Cedar Point. It's like an hour from here."

I nodded, chewing on my lip.

"What's wrong, Kitten? You look upset."

I narrowed my eyes, but my stomach was rolling. Was *I* jealous? "For a guy who likes to say I belong to him, you sure do get around."

His lips twisted in a heart-stopping grin as he adjusted himself beneath his pants. "You belong to *me*. I don't belong to *you*. But if you want to take her place," he began, gripping his thick length inside the confines of his pants and slowly stroking himself, "I'd be willing to let you swallow my come again. *If* you beg me for it."

I scoffed, shaking my head, *hating him*. "I'm going to have to politely decline, *big brother*. I thought we had plans today, but you've clearly double-booked your schedule. I'll find my own way," I bit out as I yanked open the door to the soundproof room, my eyes assessing the girl in front of me. "Enjoy your imitation," I called over my shoulder before shoving past her, the sound of his laughter made me livid.

I crossed back toward the house's front entrance, wanting to go outside and get some fresh air, when my eyes landed on the table in the foyer. Ryatt's keys to his car sat tossed in the center.

I chewed my cheek, hearing Ryatt's voice in the distance as he approached, muttering something to her about a previous engagement.

A grabbed the keychain and darted out the front door before he could stop me. With purpose, I stalked toward the sleek black car with fire in my veins.

When I reached the vehicle, my eyes went back to the front door, second-guessing myself. Then I remembered what he was off to do and who he was going to do it with.

"Screw you," I muttered under my breath, yanking open the driver's side door and sliding inside. I gripped the wheel until my knuckles turned white. He's going to be pissed. He's going to retaliate against me. I shoved the key into the ignition, twisting it, and the car roared to life.

"You can do this," I whispered. I knew how to drive, but I'd never been behind the wheel of such a large car. I moved the vehicle into drive just as Ryatt flew out of the front door, still shirtless. His eyes were wide, and he was yelling something I couldn't hear over the sound of the car. I narrowed my eyes, flipping him off as I pulled out, taking off down the driveway.

My phone began to ring almost instantly. "Can I help you?"

"Turn around now, and I will forget about this little tantrum," he seethed.

"Hmm..." I pretended to consider his offer. "No thanks. I need to get some shopping done."

"Grace, if you don't bring your little ass back here right now, the things I am going to do to you will go against the Geneva Convention."

"Oh, so big and scary," I taunted him. "You have to catch me first."

"You know I have tracking on everything I own, including my vehicles, right?"

"Vehicles? As in *plural*?"

He let out a throaty laugh. "I own twelve," he replied, the sound of an engine revving in the background. "As well as three motorcycles, two boats, a handful of all-terrain vehicles..." he droned on.

"I get it. You're spoiled." I swallowed hard, my eyes flitting to the rearview mirror.

"*Rotten*," he confirmed. "I'm warning you, Kitten," he bit out as the sound of a motorcycle flying up the road behind me caused me to gasp, dropping my phone. I quickly felt around, kicking it with my feet before bending to grab it. I could hear him yelling through the device as I went to lift it to my ear, my eyes landing on the tree I was hurtling toward.

A scream ripped from my throat as I collided with it, the sound of metal crunching and tires squealing filled the air.

The door was pulled open within seconds, and my seatbelt was taken off. I was yanked free from the wreckage. "Gracie?" Ryatt asked, gripping my shoulders. "Are you hurt?"

My eyes met his, dazed.

"Grace?" He gripped my jaw tight in his large hand, forcing my face toward his as he inspected me. "Say something, Sweetheart."

Sweetheart? Did I have a concussion? "I-I think I'm okay," I replied.

"What the *fuck* were you thinking? You could have killed yourself."

"At least you would have been off the hook then, right?"

"*What?*" He drew back as if I'd slapped him. "You think I *wanted* you to wreck? You think I wanted you to get hurt?"

"It would save *you* the trouble of hurting me, and you wouldn't have to keep an eye on me anymore. Free up your *schedule*," I replied, the thought of that girl sitting in his lap churning my stomach.

"You jealous of that girl, Kitten?" he asked, the ghost of a smirk playing on his lips.

"No," I shot back as another car pulled off the road behind us. Suddenly, lights flashed on the dashboard and in the grill of the vehicle. It was an undercover cop.

Ryatt's jaw clenched before he turned toward the man, putting himself in front of me.

"You alright, Ransom?" the officer asked. It shouldn't have surprised me that he knew him by name.

"Yeah, took a turn a little too fast, Baker," he replied coolly.

The cop looked back at his motorcycle before his eyes landed on us, eyebrow raised. "You were driving?"

Ryatt's hand rubbed over the back of his neck, and I couldn't help but let my gaze drop over his bare, muscular back. "No one drives my car but me," he replied.

"You okay?" the cop asked, looking around Ryatt to me.

"She's fine," Ryatt spoke for me. "I'll call for a tow truck. I'll have this moved right away."

The officer nodded, not bothering to ask any further questions as he retreated to his car.

Ryatt turned to face me, and I flinched at his severe expression. "Any last words?" he asked.

23

RYATT

Grace's body was shaking. "It was a nice car," she admitted, causing me to laugh sardonically.

"Yeah, it was," I ran my hand along the fender before turning my attention back to her.

"I'm sorry."

I nodded, rubbing my palm roughly along my jaw. "It's too late for that, Kitten."

"I-I'll find a way to pay for the damage."

I chuckled, shaking my head. "I don't need your money."

"I know you don't," her voice was low, defeated. "You really loved that car."

"It's just a car," I shrugged as I pulled my phone from my pocket and sent a message to the body shop I used to restore my old vehicles. "Nelson will bring a rollback out to get the car. Let's go," I nodded toward my bike, stalking over to it and grabbing my helmet off the ground that I had thrown when I saw she'd wrecked.

"You're not going to yell at me?"

"What good would that do *now*, Grace?" I asked, looking back at her.

"You know, you could have just taken me shopping like you promised."

"I know," I admitted, thinking about how she nearly lost her life because I was acting like a selfish prick. I knew she was going to be looking for me. I wanted to get a rise out of her, maybe take me up on the offer to take the girl's place. But I hadn't expected her to steal my fucking car. "Let's go."

"I'm not getting on that thing."

"You are," I placed the helmet on her head, buckling the strap under her chin.

"Ryatt, I'm scared."

"Of *me* or the bike?" I smirked, causing her to smile.

"Both," she answered honestly.

"We have bigger problems to worry about." I swung my leg over my motorcycle. "Get on, Kitten."

Grace only hesitated for a second before sliding on the back of my bike, wrapping her arms around my waist. I tried to ignore how her body felt pressed against mine. She was trusting me to keep her safe, and I wasn't sure I would be able to.

The ride to my home only took a few minutes. We were barely off the sprawling property. And I knew Baker had already contacted my father. He was part of his personal security force. A man like my dad had lots of enemies, always

156

lurking around every corner. So his private henchmen always had eyes on us when we left the estate.

I could only hope he'd grant me the small mercy of not telling him that Grace had been the one driving. My father was his boss, but he also knew I would be signing his paychecks one day.

I pulled into the garage, hesitating. Not wanting to get off the motorcycle. But I didn't have a choice. I had to face him. There was nowhere I could drive far enough away to escape his reach.

I unbuckled Grace's helmet and brushed her hair back from her face.

Her eyebrows were pinched together. "I am really sorry –"

I pressed my finger against her lips to stop her from talking. "Go straight to your room," I told her.

"You're worrying me."

I forced a smile. "For once, just do as you're told," I pleaded.

She nodded, swallowing hard as her tongue ran out over her lips.

My fingers wrapped around Gracie's necklace in my pocket. I'd found it a few days ago after scouring the library and took it to have the chain repaired. I was going to give it back to her today before my entire world imploded. "Here," I rasped, pulling it from my pocket. Her eyes lit up, and she gasped.

"You found it!" Her arms looped around my neck and she threw herself against me. I let my palm slide along her back before I stiffened, grabbing her sides and forcing her off me.

"I had to have it fixed." I unclasped the chain and she turned around, allowing me to loop it around her neck and secure it in place. She turned back around, her cheeks tinged pink.

"Thank you."

I swallowed hard. "Let's go." I stalked toward the garage entrance into the main home with Grace on my heels. I was on edge, waiting for someone to be lurking around every corner. Every little fuck up could have detrimental consequences. I'd learned that at a very early age. My father wasn't a kind man. He wasn't one who could be reasoned with. He thought in terms of loss or gain – whether it be about power, money, or property. I fell under the property branch of his control. I was an object, a trophy from one of his previous conquests.

I inhaled sharply as I noticed Wagner, the head of his security team, at the end of the hallway.

"Your father is requesting you," he called out.

I bit back a curse. "Gracie, go to your room," I ordered her.

"He would like you *both* to come," Wagner clarified.

I wanted to protest but knew it wouldn't do us any good. The best way to deal with my father was to give him what he wanted.

"Don't make a sound unless he asks you something directly," I warned.

We followed Wagner through the maze of halls before reaching my father's office. He rapped his knuckles against the door. We waited for a beat before I heard my father call for us to enter.

He held up a hand as he continued threatening whoever was receiving his phone call before slamming the small device on his desk. His lips twisted up in a smile as his eyes went to Grace.

"How have you been, Grace? Finding the accommodations to your liking?"

Grace's gaze slid to me before she cleared her throat. "Y-yes," her hand went to her chest, instinctively fumbling with her locket like she'd done before when she was nervous, offering herself some semblance of comfort. "You have a very nice home."

My father scoffed, waving his arms out wide. "A home is for a poor man who doesn't know what's *really* important in life. This, my dear Grace, is an *empire*."

I forced myself not to roll my eyes at his theatrics.

His smirk fell as his eyes landed on me. "I trust you've found it welcoming," he continued to speak to her, his eyes narrowing on mine.

"Y-yes," she stuttered, and I wished she wouldn't appear so weak in front of him, but I couldn't defend her. It would only make whatever was coming that much worse.

My father pushed from his chair and made his way around the front of the desk, his hands shoved in the pockets of his slacks.

Without thinking, I took a step in front of Grace. The move didn't go unnoticed, and I saw my father's jaw tense. *What the fuck did he expect?* He told me to protect her, and I would follow that order, even if he was the one I needed to protect her from.

"Slipping into the big brother roll," he seethed. "Little late for that after nearly killing her today."

I was thankful Baker had spared Grace the wrath of my father. The longer she remained on his good side and appeared to be compliant and malleable, the safer she would be.

"There was a deer," I lied.

"So, you swerved to spare its life, putting Grace's in jeopardy?"

"I didn't want it coming through the windshield."

He nodded. "What do you think, Grace?" he asked her. "Do you think my son did what he could to protect you?"

"Yes," Grace replied, and I could see her nod out of my peripheral vision.

"Do you think he'd protect you *now*?" he asked, his eyebrow cocked.

"Um..." I could tell she didn't know the right answer, and I steeled my spine, waiting for what was coming next. "Yes," she finally answered. *Fuck.*

My father's lips twisted into a deviant smirk. "Let's find out." His fist connected with my jaw, and I stumbled a step to my left. His next blow hit my stomach, and I doubled over, feeling like one of my ribs may have been clipped. He grabbed my shirt, holding me up as he leaned in closer.

"Who was driving the car, Ryatt?"

I looked up at him as blood pooled in my mouth, a smirk twisting up the left corner of my mouth. "*I* was."

His fist came down from above, hitting my eye and causing the skin to split over my brow. A drop of blood began to roll down my eyelid.

"Stop," Grace yelled.

"Shut the fuck up, Grace," I bit out, warning her. My father hit me again, this time from the left, and the force sent me to the ground. He leaned over me, swinging his foot into my ribs and causing me to sputter as Grace tried to stifle her cries.

"I don't want to have this talk with you again," He warned before stepping over me and disappearing into the corridor.

Grace dropped to her knees, assessing the damage, her fingers brushing over my cuts and bruises. Her brows furrowed like she could feel the pain with each pass of her fingertips.

"I'm so sorry," she whispered, her voice sounding muffled as my ears rang.

"I'm fine," I pushed myself to my feet.

"You didn't have to lie –"

"I didn't," I cut her off, my eyes locked on hers. She nodded, sniffling.

"Let's get you cleaned up," she offered.

***

I leaned back against the bar, drinking my whiskey as Grace tended to my wounds with the first aid kit she'd gotten from one of the kitchen staff.

Her fingers slid over my brow, sticking the butterfly stitches over the swollen cut. I didn't miss how her hands were shaking, her teeth pressing into her lip as she tried to concentrate. I wasn't used to anyone worrying over me like this. Even the staff would look the other way when I showed up bruised and bloodied. My father paid them well for discretion. In our line of work it was a necessity.

"How do I look?" I asked as her eyes assessed me.

"Like you got your ass kicked," she replied, struggling against a smirk.

"Feels that way." I held out my glass to her, and she took a tentative sip, her face puckering at the taste.

"That's gross."

"You get used to it," I shrugged, draining the contents before refilling it.

I watched as her chest rose and fell in quick puffs. She was nervous. Her hot palm sliding across my bruised ribs caused me to hiss. Her eyes met mine before going back to inspecting my skin.

"Where's it hurt the most?"

"My chest."

"Here?" Her palm pressed over one of my pecs. I grabbed her, sliding her palm to my sternum before taking another drink.

"What's the prognosis?" I asked as her fingers dragged lower, causing my cock to thicken.

"I think you need to defend yourself or you're going to end up dead."

I barked out a sardonic laugh, shaking my head. "If he wanted to kill me, I would be gone, Grace. He wanted to show you he is the one in charge."

"Why didn't you at least protect yourself?" she asked as I turned toward the bar, refilling my glass.

"Because I was protecting *you*," I replied. "That's my job."

Her hand fell to her side. "Why?"

"Why *what*?" I asked, turning back to face her.

"Why do I need protected? And from who?"

"It's a scary world out there, Kitten."

"There's something you're not telling me." Her eyes searched mine. But I didn't have the answers she needed. I knew something big was coming. I just didn't know what. Whatever it was, Grace didn't deserve it. But if she was unwilling to leave her mother's side, then I would stay too.

"You're safe with me, Grace," I replied, hoping that was true.

"Because it's *your job*," she threw my reason back at me, and I didn't correct her. The truth was, I liked having someone in these walls who saw me, who cared. Even if she did drive me fucking crazy. But the thought of me enjoying her presence was unnerving. It was dangerous, and I needed to remember that there is a reason she is here, and it doesn't include me.

I took another drink as silence stretched between us. "You know I'm going to have to find a way to punish you for what you did."

"I know."

***

24

GRACE

Punishment wasn't the term I'd use for what happened the next night. It was more like torture. And I had no choice but to endure every excruciating moment, pretending I didn't care. I shouldn't.

Ryatt tossed my book that he'd stolen from me onto my lap.

"What's this for?" I asked, flipping through the dog-eared pages and noticing handwritten notes in the margins. My heart began to flutter like a hummingbird's wings against my sternum. Somehow knowing he'd read the words I had, seen what I'd fantasized about, felt intimate.

"Chapter fifteen," he replied. "Read it."

I quickly flipped open the book and my eyes began to skim the page. June and Brody were in a cabin in the woods. Her stalker was outside of the bedroom window, watching as he took her from behind.

"Out loud," he clarified.

I felt my face grow hot, glancing up at him. "June arched her back, exposing herself to B-Brody who stood behind her, his thick length in his palm." I cleared my throat, hating how my voice wavered. "She knew her voyeur was out there watching, waiting to see what naughty things she'd do for him." My eyes met his.

"More."

I scanned the page, finding where I left off. "She was slick with need – the desire to be wanted, and the urge to be taken." I licked my dry lips, my tongue feeling thick in my mouth. "Brody entered her with a long, slow thrust, filling her, and stretching her. She moaned, as he gripped her hips, hard enough to bruise, wondering if the person watching would fill her the same way. If he would be gentle or fierce when he took her. If he would be disgusted or pleased by how wet she was at the thought of it all."

"You read absolute *filth*, Kitten," Ryatt chided, holding my gaze for a moment before he pulled open the back door and slipped outside.

My heart sank to my stomach, and I swallowed back the bile rising in my throat as I pushed to my feet and trudged outside after him.

The pool house was lit up and my feet moved on their own accord as I made my way to the row of open windows. There, my eyes locked on Ryatt's before drifting down over his bare tatted chest. His hand pumped his thick length. I ignored the brunette bent over in front of him wearing nothing but a white tee, like the one he'd given me after the bonfire. My cheeks burned as I watched him push forward, sinking inside of her. His palm was on her back, pushing her face into a pillow. *My* pillow with pink and yellow flowers on the case. I wondered if she could smell me on it... and if that was the point. He grabbed her hips, rocking into her, his eyes never looking away from me. I should have turned away, but my body felt like it was glued in place, unable to move until he released me from his gaze.

The whimpers and moans she made with every thrust assaulted me. I hated and envied her at the same time.

"*Fuck*, Kitten," he growled, causing my breath to get caught in my throat. The girl beneath him made a noise of approval, but he wasn't talking to her. He was speaking directly to me as he slowly rocked into her. My skin felt like it was burning hot. "You like that?" he asked, and I realized my eyes had drifted, watching his length slowly move in and out of her body. I was frozen for what felt like an eternity until her cries pulled me from my daze. She was coming hard. I blinked, wishing I could make myself leave. I turned to glance over my shoulder when he barked, "Don't move."

He withdrew from her body, his hand gripping his thick length as he pumped it a few more times before thick ropes of come coated her back.

The second he finished it was if the spell was broken, and I turned running back inside the main house and directly to my room, where I stayed the rest of the night, ignoring how wet my panties were as I reread my book, taking in all his notes and thoughts scrawled across the pages in blue ink.

***

It had been three days of Ryatt barely saying a word to me, driving me crazy. After the display he'd put on in the pool house, you would have thought it would be me avoiding him, not the other way around. Even though I shouldn't care what he did and who he did it with. It bothered me watching him act out a fantasy of us that couldn't come to fruition.

I twisted the handle to the theater room, blowing out a shaky breath as I shoved it open. It was two in the morning, but sure enough, Ryatt sat in the back row on a double wide recliner, a glass of dark liquor in his hand, his knees splayed as he stared unfocused at the screen. He never glanced in my direction as he spoke, "You lost, Grace?" he slurred, drinking back his beverage before setting it on a stand beside him.

"I couldn't sleep."

"Guilty conscience?"

I sighed, shoving my messy long hair back over my shoulder. "I didn't mean to wreck your car."

"You've wrecked my life," he shot back, but his tone was more exhausted than resentful. I took that as a sign that, for once, he was too tired to fight with me.

I padded over to him, sinking down beside him on the large seat, pulling my legs up to my chest. I was in Ryatt's tee he'd given me after the bonfire and panties. His eyes roamed over my bare legs before going back to the screen.

"Why can't you sleep?" he asked, clicking on a folder icon on the screen.

"Nightmare."

"Tell me, Grace. What is it that scares you when you don't have enough sense to be frightened of your current situation?" His eyes were on me now, waiting for a reply. But he wouldn't get one. I knew telling Ryatt my fears was only handing him more power. And I was desperate to hang on to the little bit I possessed.

"I'm not scared of you," I mumbled, resting my chin on my knees. Even if Ryatt hated me, I knew it was his job to keep me safe from him and the rest of the world.

"I wasn't talking about me."

My thoughts went to his Enzo and how he'd hit Ryatt in front of me. Ryatt never even tried to defend himself. Just took whatever punishment his father saw fit to dole out. I wondered why he didn't at least protect himself from the blows. "Is your father what scares *you*?"

His eyes narrowed, face going hard as he made a few more clicks. "You might want to leave now, unless you're planning to watch. I know you enjoy that."

"Watch what?" I asked just as the sound of moans filled the air. My head snapped toward the screen, settling on two girls going at it on the floor of a gym. The noise was deafening in the soundproof room. I recognized the giant hawk emblazoned on the shiny wood. This was filmed at our school. My cheeks began to burn as I took in Ryatt's profile. His eyes studied the screen, the muscles in his jaw jumping as the column of his throat bobbed. I let my gaze drop lower, taking in the hard planes of his bare chest, sliding down over the ridges and valleys of his abs before landing on his gray sweatpants. His very prominent length was outlined below the soft fabric, and it caused me to shiver.

I looked back to his face, inhaling as I noticed his eyes on me, watching me take him in. He looked back to the screen, his teeth running over his lower lip before his tongue slid out to wet them. I watched the girls who now wore only their panties, grinding themselves against each other at the direction of someone off-screen. I recognized the low, commanding voice of Ryatt.

I adjusted in the seat, hating that his words sent a pulse directly to my core.

"*That's it. Just like that*," he rasped in the video. "*Good girl.*"

"That's the vise principal's daughter with Pastor Rothchild's niece," he pointed out. This wasn't just homemade pornography. This was ammunition.

He clicked another video and there was Mr. Madden standing suspiciously close to a younger female, brushing her hair back from her face as his eyes studied her.

I swallowed against the lump in my throat. *Why was he sharing this information with me?* He clicked to another video, and my eyes went wide, taking in a large muscular man screwing someone bent over their desk. It took a moment to recognize their voice, but it was soon confirmed as he glanced toward the direction of the camera that it was Enzo Ransom, my soon-to-be stepfather. But the person under him was not my mother. I was pretty sure they weren't of legal age. And then it hit me, the short mousy hair and wide brown eyes. It was a girl who sat two seats in front of me in Geometry.

"Your dad," I whispered.

"Annalise is sixteen. She skipped a grade," Ryatt noted.

"Why don't you turn him in for this?" I asked. "You wouldn't have to put up with –"

"I'd lose everything if I turned him in."

"You put *money* over your safety?"

Ryatt laughed sardonically. "Everything includes *you*, Grace," he admitted before his eyes went back to the display, changing the video again. My heart began to stutter in my chest as I wondered what exactly he meant by that. "You can't trust the police here," he added in a warning. I nodded, thinking about the cop after my accident. He didn't even ask for paperwork.

The sound of Ryan Reynolds pulled me from my thoughts as I turned back to the movie. It was a shot of my bedroom. There I was, flashing across the wall, as I slid my hand under my blanket.

"That's the security camera, not your phone," I whispered, confirming what I already knew. Ryatt had been watching me. His eyes met mine, but no guilt marred his features. He simply nodded once.

"It's not on the main server. I remove all your videos," he assured me.

"But you kept it... as *blackmail*?"

"I kept it for *personal* use," his eyebrow rose as his hand slid under the thick fabric of his sweatpants, slowly pumping his length, concealed from my view. "Seems we both like to look at things we shouldn't."

My skin burnt with embarrassment. I watched him as he watched the recording, the pleasure on his face unmistakable.

His voice drew my attention as a replay of him threatening me before he gripped my wrist, slowly sucking my fingers into his mouth played out. I exhaled, remembering how good it felt to have his tongue on my skin.

He groaned. "I love those little noises you make."

His words caused the apex of my thighs to pulse, and I squirmed in the seat. He looked at my legs.

"Are you wet for me now, Gracie?" he asked, wrapping his long fingers around my ankle and pulling my legs apart so he could see my panties. I offered no resistance. "*Fuck*," he groaned, and I didn't need to look down to know the thin cotton was soaked. I slinked my hand lower to cover myself, but just the slight brush of contact sent a bolt of pleasure through me.

The video switched again, it was me on my knees, watching him as he stroked his cock in the library. His attention was still on me.

"Who do you think about when you touch yourself? When no one is supposed to be watching?"

My skin felt hot. "I-I don't –"

"You think about me, Grace." It wasn't a question. "I have thousands of videos. *Yours* are my favorite."

I shuddered, my fingers sliding over the damp fabric, remembering how much I wanted him that night, not caring about the consequences.

The muscles in his arm corded and stretched as he continued to pleasure himself at an excruciatingly slow pace.

"I didn't like watching you in the pool house," I whispered.

"No? *Which* time?"

Jesus, how many times had *I watched him?* The shame of that realization didn't curb my arousal.

The video switched, and I was again assaulted by images of myself in my bed, but this time, it was through his laptop as he stood over it, watching me from the privacy of his bedroom, stroking his impressive length, desperate to watch me come.

"I want to see you. Take them off."

Looping my shaky fingers around the edges of my panties, I raised my hips, slowly pulling them down my legs. Ryatt took them from my hand, pulling himself free from the confines of his pants, and wrapping them around his cock as he continued to stroke himself.

"Spread your legs wider," he rasped. I did what he ordered without thought, turning so one of my feet slipped behind his back, angling to give him a better view of my splayed thighs, bent at the knees. He turned toward me as well, a pearl of excitement beaded at his tip, and I licked my lips, thinking of the night I'd tasted the thick salty flavor.

"Has anyone else seen your pussy before, Kitten?"

"No. Just you."

"So beautiful," he groaned.

I slid my hand back between my thighs, gasping at how sensitive I was now, touching my bare flesh. The pad of my finger found my clit, rubbing myself in small circles as I watched him use my underwear to please himself. His breathing was raspy now, filling the small room as sounds of some other depraved scene played in the background. But my attention was only on Ryatt.

My own mouth hung open, gasping with each pass of my finger, wishing it was his. Better yet, the head of his thick length. I bit down on my lip, nearly drawing blood as I began to rock against myself. I was so close that my muscles began to coil, preparing for the onslaught of pleasure to rock through me.

"Are you going to come for me, kitten?"

I nodded, rubbing faster.

"Big girl words," he rasped.

"I'm going to come for you, Ryatt," I panted.

His eyes were on mine, holding my gaze as pleasure washed through me, coming hard against my hand as Ryatt's tongue rolled over his lips. He looked down between my legs, admiring the mess I'd made before his grip tightened on his own length, stroking it a few more times. The groans and heavy pants that fell from his lips vibrated through me, causing me to shiver. He came, coating my panties he held against him. His hand continued to move pumping himself a few more times, wringing every last drop of his come from his cock.

"I think that concludes our lesson for today." He tucked his length away, grabbing my ankle and sliding my panties back on me. Dragging his sticky mess up my legs. I lifted my hips for him, allowing his to pull them up over my ass. The look of satisfaction in his gaze would be something I would fantasize about forever. "Sweet dreams, Kitten."

***

25

RYATT

I sat eating my fruit parfait as Grace slipped into the kitchen, pouring herself a coffee into her thermos before loading it full of vanilla syrup, flitting around the room like a bee.

"In a hurry?" I asked her, watching as her body stiffened.

"I'm going to miss the bus."

"Take a car service," I replied, scrolling through social media posts on my phone.

"With what money?" she asked, taking a sip from her beverage and wincing as it burnt her lip. An errant thought of me sucking that lip into my mouth to soothe her ache passed across my subconscious, and my cock twitched.

"We're filthy fucking rich, Kitten."

She glanced around, worried that someone had heard my nickname for her, but we were alone. "*You're* rich. Not me. *Remember*?"

I grabbed the money clip from my pocket, pulling out a few hundred dollars and tossing it on the table. Her eyes narrowed as a noise escaped her throat.

"What? Not enough?" I asked, pulling a few more bills out and tossing them on the pile.

"I'm not taking that," she shook her head with a look of annoyance.

"Why not?"

"I don't want your daddy's money."

"It's not his. It's mine."

"I'm not a prostitute."

I leaned back in my seat, stretching my long legs under the table, unable to hide my smirk. "And I haven't *fucked* you yet. So, this clearly isn't payment for services rendered."

Her eyes went wide, her cheeks darkening at my words, and I realized what I'd said. *Yet.*

"I'll walk," she replied, gathering her things and hurrying out of the kitchen, forgetting her thermos. Moments later, I heard the front door slam behind her.

I pushed from my seat, gathered the money and grabbed her drink before following her outside and getting in my classic '72 hemi orange charger. The engine roared as I turned it on and hurried toward the edge of the driveway.

"Get in," I barked out the window.

Grace glanced over at me, rolling her eyes. "I don't want to ruin your reputation."

I pressed the brakes, and she stopped beside me. "It's not about that."

"What's it about then, huh?" she asked, leaning on the window ledge, giving me a perfect view down her top.

"You don't want to be associated with us."

"No kidding." She reached her full height and began stalking down the road again.

"Grace," I barked, but she continued on. "Grace!"

I slammed the car into park and shoved open my door, following after her. Grabbing her elbow, I spun her to face me. "Get in the fucking car."

"No."

"I'm not *asking* you. Get in the car before I make you."

"You could have offered me a ride in the first place. You could have been taking me this whole time," she shouted, waving her arms around. That's what this was about. I hurt her feelings, and now she was going to throw a tantrum. Her eyes narrowed in a challenge. I grabbed her ass, and she yelped as I lifted her in the air. Her palms gripped my shoulders, and her legs curved around my back, putting my straining cock right between her thighs.

"Put me down, prick," she seethed as I pulled open the door, and lowered her onto the tan bench seat, pressing my body against hers. She pushed against my chest, sliding herself further inside to escape me. "Aren't you afraid your friends will see us together?" she asked, her hips rising in protest, pushing herself hard against my length.

"There are very few things I'm afraid of, Grace," I shot back, rocking forward. "Those vapid cunts don't make the list."

"You seemed to care an awful lot when you found out who I was."

I tangled my fingers in her hair and gripped it in my fist, stilling her movements. "I don't care if the entire fucking town is watching. If you don't stop with your little attitude, I will *fuck* it out of you."

Her body stilled, eyes blazing as she blinked up at me, processing my words.

"No, you won't," she whispered, daring me.

"Try me." My breathing was ragged, and my mouth pooled with saliva. I was aching to taste her again since that first night, to *actually* feel her come against my tongue. My control was slipping.

Her eyes searched mine before licking her lips and pushing against my chest again. "We're going to be late. Let's go," she replied, finally agreeing to let me take her.

I reluctantly peeled myself off her, adjusting my cock in my pants before rounding the car to drive us to school.

***

I placed my palm on Grace's bare thigh just below the edge of her uniform skirt, as if she may bolt out of the vehicle at one of the stop signs on the way. Her skin was so fucking soft,

I couldn't stop my thumb from rubbing lazy circles against her flesh.

When I pulled into my usual spot, my eyes landed on Cara and a few of her friends with half the football team. I didn't show my trepidation. I told Grace I didn't care. Even though I knew showing up with her wasn't a good idea. For either of us.

I turned off the ignition, looking over at Grace, my eyes dancing over her profile. "Ready?"

Her eyes met mine, and I could practically feel her anxiousness radiating off her in waves.

"Are you sure about this?" she asked. I shoved open the door and rounded the car, opening the passenger side. Grace smiled nervously as she pushed to her feet, her body nearly against mine. I took a step back and her gaze followed mine to the crowd of my friends, gaping at us. I pressed my palm against the small of her back, urging her forward.

26

GRACE

"Let them stare. They're just jealous," he whispered.

I glanced up at him as we continued across the lot. "Can't blame them. You're *Handsome Ransom*," I mocked playfully, but my heart was hammering in my chest.

"I meant of *me*," he corrected with a panty-melting smirk. I felt my cheeks heat and cleared my throat, ignoring the lump forming.

The girl who had spent most of the bonfire on Ryatt's lap sneered at me. "You're joking," she muttered, folding her arms across her chest.

We stepped inside the building, cold air blowing down on us from the air conditioning. "I'm going to use the bathroom," I told him.

"I'll see you in class. I have some things to handle."

I nodded, watching as he began to stalk down the hall before shaking my head and making my way to the bathroom closest to our first period.

I slinked inside, giving a polite smile to the girl who had just finished washing her hands. I stepped in front of the mirror, finger-combing my long hair. I knew it must have looked wild after Ryatt had it tangled in his fist.

The door opened, and a high-pitched voice echoed in the small space. "You *can't* be serious."

I glanced over at the blonde from the bonfire. "Do you need something?" I asked as her two friends flanked her, sneering at me.

"You think you can just come here and take what's mine?"

I let out a little chuckle. I didn't know who this girl thought she was, but she *definitely* wasn't anyone important to Ryatt. "What is it that I took from you?" I asked, taking a step closer.

Her friend scoffed, "Cara's boyfriend."

The bell rang, signaling the start of class, but the girls didn't move.

"You're kidding, right?" I asked, my eyes dancing between them. "Oh, my God. You're not. You really thought you were dating him."

Cara's face turned beet red. "What would you know about it, *skank*?"

I smiled; I couldn't help it. I'd gone to an all-girls school my entire life, and I knew how catty they could be, traveling in little cliques. If you didn't stand up to them, they would become relentless. "I know he wasn't moaning *your* name last night."

Cara gasped, and without warning her friend's arms shot out, shoving me backward. My shoulders collided with the wall and I let out a grunt before pushing off it and lunging at the person who'd assaulted me. I grabbed her silvery blue hair, yanking her down to her knees as someone grabbed my shirt, tugging the neck and popping two of the buttons.

I raised my knee, colliding with Cara's stomach. She doubled over as she clawed at me with her hot pink talons, scratching me across my chest.

"You stupid bitch," one of them yelled and a palm collided with my face. Blinding white heat flooded my skin. I grabbed Cara's head in both hands, slamming her back against the wall with a loud thumping sound.

She slid down, sinking to the floor, groaning in pain as I cradled my own face in my palm.

"This isn't over," one of the girls warned before they opened the door, sliding back into the hallway.

I winced, blinking several times as I worked my jaw. My eyes collided with my reflection, and I winced. My skin was welted, flaming an angry pink. A single tear rolled down over the wound, causing me to flinch as the door to the bathroom slammed open, bouncing off the wall.

Ryatt's eyes assessed me before he closed the gap between us, taking my face between his large palms and inspecting the damage. "Who did this to you?"

"Apparently, it was your girlfriend."

His eyes narrowed in confusion.

"Cara and two of her bitchy friends," I clarified.

His jaw muscles jumped under his taut skin as he wiped the wayward tear from my cheek. My chin wobbled as anger flooded me. "Whatever is going through your head, whatever you're feeling, you need to shut it off."

"How am I supposed to just –"

"Think of it as a game. A mission. They can't see that they've hurt you."

"It's written all over my *face*," I gestured to the large handprint emblazoned on my skin.

"Doesn't matter. Never let them see that they affected you or this will only be the beginning."

I thought back to his father beating the hell out of him. He never showed emotion, never shed a tear even though he must have been in agonizing pain. I tried my best to straighten my spine, closing my eyes and taking a deep breath.

"Better," he replied before leaning down and I wanted to kiss him but didn't have the nerve. My palms slid against his chest, melting into him before he pulled back, leaving me breathless. "Let's go out there and show them why they shouldn't fuck with us."

Us.

My chest clenched at his words, and I followed him out into the hall toward our classroom. Ryatt's fingers entwined with mine as he pushed open the door. Seventeen sets of eyes watched as we walked inside together. I knew he was just making a point, but my skin was on fire where we touched, reducing the injury on my face to a dull buzz that I could easily ignore. I made sure my expression was unreadable as he stopped at the desk I'd taken from him on the first day, and held out his arm, gesturing for me to sit as our other hands separated.

I gave him a small thankful smile and slid into my seat as Mattie stared at me with her jaw practically on the floor. Ryatt sat at the seat directly behind me, and I could feel his eyes on me.

"*Oh my God*," Mattie mouthed, and I couldn't help the little laugh that escaped me.

"As I was saying," Ms. Bane called over the chatter. The class quieted down, and she continued her lesson.

***

After first period was over, Ryatt and I went to the office, and he had his schedule changed so we were in all the same classes. I didn't object. I was grateful I wouldn't have to navigate these halls by myself anymore. But I wondered what information he used against the secretary to have her do so without protest. I ignored the way Mr. Madden watched us, taking in my marred face, and the way Ryatt wouldn't leave my side. I turned away from him, hoping this wouldn't cause any trouble for Ryatt.

I knew it was his job to protect me, on his father's order. But now we'd muddied the waters. After what I'd told Cara and her friends, no one could find out I was living in his home. Although, I'm not sure who would believe her anyway. She was clearly delusional if she thought Ryatt was her boyfriend. But I couldn't take chances and screw things up for him. He was laying everything on the line for me.

Even through lunch, he was at my side, busy doing whatever it was he did on his phone. Mattie stared at him, unable to look away as she shoveled chips into her mouth.

"Mattie," I whisper-yelled at her to draw her attention away from him. "You're being weird."

"Sorry, but would you care to explain what's going on?"

Ryatt looked over at me, smirking as he waited to hear what I was going to say.

I swallowed, feeling my face heat. "We've called a truce." Ryatt went back to what he was doing, seemingly satisfied with my response.

Mattie's brows pulled together. "That's it? That's all you're going to give me?"

I shrugged, grabbing one of her chips and shoving it in my mouth.

"And your face?" Her eyes darted between me and Ryatt.

"I like to play rough," he replied, his voice low, not looking up from his screen and I felt my skin go red as Mattie made a choking sound.

Thankfully, his reply was enough to stop her from inquiring further.

The loudspeaker echoed in the expansive room. "Reminder to all seniors, we have an assembly in fifteen minutes in the Ransom Theater. Attendance is mandatory."

"I'm sitting with you," Mattie called out as she began to gather up her trash.

My eyes went to Ryatt. His gaze met mine, and he shrugged. "You have two sides," he replied, and I was thankful I wouldn't be forced to sit with his crowd. I stood, collecting the few things he and I had to toss before following Mattie to the trashcans.

"Maybe we should just skip," Mattie mumbled.

I yelped as I turned around and nearly ran into Ryatt, who towered over me.

"You're a bad influence," he pointed to my friend and a wicked grin spread across her face. "We need to go. It's a *rule*," he replied with a wink.

"Since when do *you* follow the rules?" I asked as we began to file out of the cafeteria.

"I never fuck around when it comes to school, Kitten. I have a 4.0 GPA."

That stopped me in my tracks. "You're kidding."

"I know. It's not fair. Good looks, brains, a *huge*... bank account," he deadpanned as he stepped aside, allowing Mattie and me to enter the auditorium before him. We decided on seats dead center in the expansive room. Mattie sat on one side of me, and Ryatt was on the other. He sank in his seat, his thighs splayed like he was already bored. His phone was in his hand, and he scrolled through different folders as we waited for the presentation to begin. All eyes seemed to be on me. News of the bathroom attack had spread fast.

My phone had been vibrating nonstop. And I've been discreetly checking my messages and texting my friends. Liam didn't believe the mark on my face was from Cara, and I honestly couldn't blame him for being suspicious.

Did he do that to you? – he messaged.

I glanced around before typing back – *I would tell you if he did. I promise that's not what happened.*

Tell me the truth – Liam sent back as Ryatt glanced over at me.

Later – I replied before shoving my phone in my bag.

I saw Cara and her friends a few rows ahead of us. She turned around, her eyes narrowing when she saw me next to Ryatt.

The lights dimmed, hiding my smirk as I focused on the stage ahead.

27

RYATT

Principal Sanders trudged out on the stage, clearing his throat into the microphone. He looked uncomfortable in front of the influential body of students.

"Thank you all for coming. We've gathered with you to help make sure you're all prepared for your graduation. There are a lot of things to go over, so let's just dive in." The giant projector screen lit up behind him. "Our student body president, Jenson Bloom, has put together a slide show detailing the events of that day and what we can do to be prepared. Thank you, Jenson."

About a third of the students gave a lackluster round of applause before the loading screen appeared, and we were hushed silent. After a few seconds, Cara was plastered across the oversized screen, wiping white powder from her nose as she sniffled. The camera pulled back, revealing her getting railed from behind by Trevor Rogers, a quarterback for the Hidden High Hawks. A few seconds later Jones was punishing her mouth with his cock. RIP scrolled over the video in comic sans, causing me to have to stifle a laugh.

The crowd gasped. Grace had her palm across her face, unable to suppress her shock. The video did one of those weird transitions where the picture swirls. I rolled my eyes at how Jenson edited the videos I'd given him. He wouldn't be winning any Oscar's but with short notice and only school computers to work with, he did the best he could.

Cara was now flashing across the screen, wasted at one of my parties, on her knees with a cock in each hand. Her two best friends on their knees as well, ready to race to see who could make their guy come the fastest. I glanced down a few rows in front of us as her head whipped around, her angry gaze landing on me as tears spilled down her cheeks.

I leaned over, my lips brushing the shell of Grace's ear, and whispered, "I figured, since you like to watch..."

She turned her head, her lips nearly colliding with mine as a wicked smile spread across her face.

"You did this for *me*?"

The realization of what I'd done slammed against my chest. I did this for *her*. I'd completely destroyed Cara for someone I shouldn't care about. I *couldn't* care about. My eyes searched hers, and I swallowed. This tightness in my chest felt suffocating. Grace's eyes narrowed, and I realized I'd let my mask slip. It was only for a moment, but she'd seen something in the way I was looking at her.

"Ryatt?" she whispered, her tongue running out over her plump lips. The room lit up, and the video feed was cut. I pulled back from Grace, rubbing my palm over my jaw as the principal's voice boomed over the speakers.

"I'm so sorry. Students, please head to your classes, and we will work to fix this error and find who is responsible."

Everyone pushed from their seats, the roar of their conversations deafening. We paused, watching Cara, Missy, and Sarah push their way through the crowd, desperate to get out of the room.

"Okay, that was the best assembly ever," Mattie laughed. Grace kept her face blank as we continued toward the exit. As soon as we slipped out into the blinding sun, Cara came into view, having a full breakdown as students circled her, holding up their phones to record or live stream her meltdown.

"You," she pointed at Grace, and I took a step around her, putting myself between them as she stalked closer. "You did this!"

Grace shrugged, her expression unreadable. "You did this to *yourself*," she replied, her voice sounding bored.

Cara's angry gaze snapped to mine. "Why are you protecting her?"

I rolled my eyes, shoving my hands in my pockets as I took a step closer to her. "Are you jealous?" Cara's palm came down across my cheek as the crowd gasped. I rubbed my hand over my face, a murderous smile twisting my lips as my eyes met hers. Those videos were only a tiny fraction of the ammunition I had on her, and I was already planning the sequel. Her gaze was wide, and she shook as the realization of who she'd just slapped hit her.

"Oh, my God. Ryatt, I'm so –"

Out of nowhere, Grace was in front of me, swinging a wild haymaker, hitting Cara in the nose. Blood spurted from her face as she fell onto her hip.

I wrapped my arms around Grace's waist, lifting her from the ground as she flailed in my arms, every expletive she could think of dripped from her lips like venom.

"Jesus *Christ*, Kitten," I chuckled as I held her against my chest, banding my arms around hers to keep her from getting free. "You really are a Ransom," I whispered against her ear.

"I'm going to sue you, you bitch," Cara screamed, blood running down her chin and dripping into her lap.

That comment stopped my laugh. My father was going to fucking kill me.

"You hit first. It was self-defense," I replied.

"I hit *you*," she spat back.

"So, you and your friends didn't corner Grace in the bathroom because you saw her with me?" I asked. Cara's mouth snapped shut, her tear-filled eyes looking around the crowd. "You're mad at *me*, Cara because *I* don't want you. Grace did nothing wrong."

Grace settled in my arms, finally giving up on trying to wrestle her way free, and I lowered her to the ground but kept my arms banded around her. The crowd was dead silent now, watching Cara fall from Grace – *literally*. You could practically see the prom queen title being ripped from her future.

"This isn't over," Cara barked as one of her friends helped her to her feet.

"Don't let your mouth write checks your ass can't cash," I replied before turning toward the building and dragging Grace back inside with me.

**

"How was school?" Hope asked. Grace's eyes met mine from across the table and a smirk tugged at the corner of her lips.

"Good," she muttered.

"That's not how I would describe it," my father growled as he approached the table, sinking down in his seat at the head. He sat his phone down on the table, replaying the video of Grace slapping Cara that was all over the internet. "Care to explain?"

"She cornered me in the bathroom. And when Ryatt confronted her about it, she h-hit him," Grace stuttered. "In front of everyone. And it wasn't like he could hit her back. And I couldn't just let her walk away from that."

Enzo raised an eyebrow, his lips curving into a grin. "Normally, I wouldn't condone such a public display. But she disrespected you and left you little recourse," he shrugged before raising his glass of wine. "Salut."

I raised my glass before drinking it down, thankful he wasn't pissed. I knew he would probably want more details later, but for now, at least, Grace and I were spared his wrath.

***

After we'd finished eating, I grabbed Grace, pulling her out to the garage.

"Where are we going?" she asked, hesitation in her voice.

"The mall. You can't keep walking around in the same few outfits and if I have to go shopping again for women's clothing, people are going to start asking questions," I quipped.

"Wouldn't want anyone to think you were doing something nice."

"First of all," I shot back. "There was nothing nice about me stealing all of your clothing and throwing them away."

She gasped. "Ryatt Ransom, did you just admit that you were wrong?"

"Definitely not admitting that," I replied, pulling open the passenger door of the charger for her and waiting for her to slip inside. I rounded the vehicle and slid in beside her. "But I fucking hate shopping, Kitten. Honestly, it's been more torture for me than I anticipated."

I laughed, shaking my head. "I'm sorry your own behavior inconvenienced you."

***

28

GRACE

After hours of shopping, we made our way to the church to celebrate. Ryatt opened a bottle of red wine, pouring a generous amount into two glasses.

"I hope you have a better toast than the one you did at the Halloween party," I teased, picking up my glass.

"May we get what we want. Never what we deserve," he held up his glass and winked before we both took a drink.

"You are enjoying this way too much. I was *assaulted*," I pointed to the fading welt on my face.

"And we *ruined* her, Kitten."

We.

"I'm not sure we should be proud of that," I replied, shaking my head before drinking another sip.

"Come on. Don't pretend you didn't enjoy it." There was a glint in his eye and my stomach fluttered. "We had fun together today."

"Maybe a little," I replied, holding up my thumb and forefinger a half inch apart.

"Just a little?" he asked, gulping down the rest of his drink before setting it on the island. There was a lightness about him tonight, like all the burdens that normally weighed him down didn't pass the threshold of the church. It felt like sacred ground.

"Are you hungry? You didn't eat much at dinner."

He shrugged. "Maybe for dessert." Grabbing his shirt at the back of his neck, he tugged it over his head. My eyes raked down over his muscular chest, taking in the inked tableau on his skin. I finished off my drink and set my glass next to his.

"What did you have in mind?" I asked, my voice sounding small. Ryatt walked by me, grabbing my wrist and tugging me behind him toward the main bedroom.

The master was much different from my room. The walls were matte black, same as the bedding. The furniture was dark ornately carved wood. It looked like something out of a castle, not a small home in the middle of suburbia. But there were other things, like metal rings installed in the ceiling that I didn't understand. There was also a projector and a screen that could lower from the roof in front of the bed, which wasn't surprising, considering how much he enjoyed watching his videos.

Ryatt walked around the bed, turning on the framed television. When the wall lit up, I was shocked to see an image of the bed. I glanced above the screen to see a camera. As my eyes scanned the perimeter, I noticed there were more embedded in each wall. Each work of art on the walls was a tv, each brightening and changing from some obscure painting until all four walls had their own view of the bed.

He clicked another remote and music began to play over the surround sound he had installed in the entire house.

His gaze turned to me, his eyes undressing me as they took in every inch of my body. "What do you think?" he asked.

I looked around before my nervous gaze met his. "It's... intimidating."

That caused him to laugh before he took a step toward me, his fingers playing with the hem of my skirt. "Wanna play, Kitten?"

I bit down on my lower lip, my body humming with anticipation as I nodded my head.

"Big girl words," he rasped.

"I wanna play."

His eyes stayed locked on mine as he slid his hands under my skirt, his fingers looping the edges of my panties and tugging them down my legs before I stepped out of them. Next, he removed each shoe and sock.

"Get on the bed," he ordered.

I climbed up, pushing myself to the center of the mattress, watching him. His length was thick and hard beneath his gray sweats. He palmed it over the fabric as he stared down at me.

"Spread your legs for me."

I did, slowly moving my legs wider until he was licking his lips.

"Touch yourself, Grace."

Propped on my elbow, I slinked my hands between my parted thighs, gasping as my fingers brushed my clit.

"Look at how beautiful you are," he rasped, his eyes going to one of the screens. I glanced up at the television, shocked at how rosy my cheeks were. How my eyes were hooded, filled with desire as Ryatt rubbed against his length, still concealed by his pants.

He climbed on the bed, propped on his elbow, inches from my center. His eyes were locked on my hand as he slid the fabric down and gripped his length, stroking it slowly. I could feel his breath fanning across my dampness and causing goosebumps to scatter across my flesh. I was so desperate to feel him there. I knew he wanted to be closer too, his tongue running over his lips.

I whimpered, my back arching. "Ryatt," I whimpered.

"Tell me what you want, Kitten."

"You," I begged, knowing he could pull away at any moment, like he had before. But I couldn't help myself. I wanted him. *Needed* him.

Ryatt's face was hard, his eyebrows pulled together before his willpower snapped, and he pushed forward, delving between my thighs, his tongue sliding up my damp slit. I cried out, my head falling back, lost in the sensation.

He spread me open, his tongue running against my sensitive bundle of nerves before dragging it lower and pushing inside of me.

My eyes went to where he still fisted his cock, stroking it with purpose now, groaning against my skin and causing a delicious vibration to ripple through my body.

I slid my fingers in his messy hair, gripping it and holding him right where I needed him. For someone who claimed they didn't need to reciprocate when it came to oral, he knew *exactly* what he was doing, and I was sure he was enjoying it every bit as much as I was.

"Ryatt," I whimpered as his assault slowed, becoming gentler, preventing my orgasm from cresting.

"Not yet." His hot breath against my wet mound caused me to shiver. He abandoned his own pleasure, turning so he could have a better angle and rubbing his fingers against my entrance as he sucked my clit between his lips. His other arm snaked under my thigh, gripping it to hold me in place.

"Ryatt," this time his name came out with an edge.

"I know," he whispered.

"I've never –"

"I *know*, Grace. I won't hurt you," he cut me off, pressing his lips softly against my mound before his tongue swirled around me again. "I want to feel you grip down on me as you come."

His words caused me to clench, and I felt my excitement drip from my body. He ran his fingers along my seam, collecting my juices before slowly pushing the tip of his finger inside of me.

"Eyes on me," he ordered. My gaze locked on his as he methodically pumped his finger in and out. My hips pushed back, meeting his thrusts, riding his hand as he watched me. "Such a good fucking girl." He slid it in further until he was met with resistance. I stilled, and he drew back, adding a second finger, causing me to tense; afraid it would hurt. "You can take it, Grace. Stretch for me."

My body burned around his intrusion as his mouth went back to my clit, licking and sucking until I was whimpering his name. He curved his fingers, pressing against a spot deep inside of me that nearly caused me to explode.

"Ryatt," I cried out. This time he didn't slow. His mouth was hot on my skin as he pressed the flat of his tongue against my clit. My body tightened around him, my fingers gripping his hair as waves of euphoria rocked through me.

Ryatt licked every last drop, even sucking his fingers clean of my juices.

"You taste so fucking good, Kitten." He climbed over my body, shoving my shirt up over my chest. "Take it off. Never hide yourself from me. It's a rule."

I quickly pulled my shirt over my head and tossed it on the floor, my body shaking with aftershocks from my release. Ryatt undid my skirt, tugging it off before he propped himself on his elbow beside my head, his other large palm gripping my hip below him. But his body wasn't touching mine as he stared down at me with lust-filled eyes. I put my hands against his muscular chest, sliding my fingers over his shoulders, my nails biting crescents into his flesh. His gaze lowered, raking down over me as I squirmed, wanting to be closer to him.

"Do you trust me yet?"

I nodded my head, causing a wicked smirk to play on his lips. "That's a mistake, sweetheart. I don't even trust myself," he replied as he lowered his hips. His hard length slid against my clit, and I gasped, my body wanting to push against him, but his grip on my hip tightened, keeping me firmly in place. I wanted to feel him everywhere. I stared down between us to where we touched, watching as Ryatt's hips rocked against me. It was the single most erotic thing I'd ever seen.

"If I can't be inside of you, I'm going to at least come all over you," he warned, rolling his hips again and again. The pressure was building all over, but I was at his mercy, unable to seek out my own release. "So warm and wet. Open your mouth for me, Grace."

My lips popped open like they had for him in the library, my tongue pushing out. He pursed his lips, and a bead of his saliva rolled over the lower one before dropping into my mouth and sliding over my tongue to the back of my throat. "*Fuck*. I want to be inside every part of you."

"I don't think you'd fit," I whispered, causing him to shudder, his fingers flexing on my side, tight enough to bruise.

"I promise you, Grace. I could, but I don't think I could be gentle once I am."

His hips continued to roll against me, and I could feel my excitement dripping down on the blanket below me.

"We could t-try." My voice was barely a whisper. Ryatt's eyes snapped to mine, he pushed harder against me, dragging his entire length along my aching center.

"Don't say that. Not when I'm having such a hard time controlling myself."

"Don't you want to?"

His forehead dropped against mine, his groans fanning over my face with every thrust. "Your pussy would be the death of me, Kitten."

I raised my chin, brushing my mouth against his. His teeth grabbed my lower lip, tugging it gently and eliciting a whimper from me. "*Fuck*," he groaned before his lips captured mine, hard, his tongue delving between them, swirling in time with his thrusts as a growl emanated from his chest. Even the way he kissed felt pornographic.

His body rocked forward with long slow strokes, the sensation almost unbearable. Instead of pressing me against the bed, he gripped me, pulling my body back against him, using me to pleasure himself.

"Ryatt," I moaned. "I'm going to come again."

He pushed himself up on his knees, both hands lifting my waist, his eyes watching as he dragged my pussy against him until I was shaking, soaking his length.

"Fuck, Grace," he growled, his hips stilling as he angled his cock down. Hot creamy liquid shot across my stomach and chest in thick ropes.

He held us there, his eyes dancing over my body as if trying to forever engrain this moment in his brain. I knew it was something I was never going to forget. I'd practically begged *Handsome Ransom* to take my virginity.

29

RYATT

I gripped the curve of her hips, unable to catch my breath as I stared down at her naked body, covered in my come, wishing I was able to get off inside of her. That thought alone should have worried me. I always pulled out. I didn't even blow my load down anyone's throat, except for Grace. The urge to *fill* her, *claim* her, *mark* her as mine was becoming overwhelming.

I knew it meant something to her as well. I was slowly collecting her firsts – watching her, touching her, tasting her. I was becoming greedy, wanting to steal all of them from her. You didn't take those sorts of things from someone as innocent as her, and not have them develop some sort of feelings. I saw the way she watched me. Every depraved desire was written all over her face and it was driving me fucking crazy.

Her punishment was supposed to scare her away. It was *supposed* to make her take a step back from me, so I could focus on what I needed to, keeping her safe. If anyone saw the way she watched me, she could be used as leverage against me. But it only made me want the real thing more.

My cock was still thick against her entrance, and I was struggling not to draw back and slam inside of her. I knew how tight she was, how snug her pussy would feel around my length, and how easy it would be to steal her virginity. But I couldn't take her innocence. That wasn't meant for me, even though every cell in my body right now screamed that she was *mine*.

"Grace," I rasped, struggling to keep the worst of my thoughts from the forefront of my mind. I pulled my gaze from between her legs to her face. "You need to tell me to stop."

"W-why?" she asked, her cheeks flushed, a thin sheen of sweat coating her milky skin.

"Because I went too far," I admitted. "And it wasn't even *close* to enough."

Grace shook her head, her hair splayed around her head like a dark halo. "I wanted you to –"

I swallowed hard. "It's not up to you."

"It's my decision," she whined. "I'm ready." Her hips pushed down against me, and my cock twitched from the pressure.

"Fuck," I groaned.

"I know you won't hurt me."

"I *want* to hurt you, Grace," I bit out. "I want to *fuck* you until you can't move." I thrust forward, pressing hard against her clit and causing her back to arch off the mattress. "I can't be your first. I'd fucking *wreck* you. And I'd enjoy every minute of it."

I forced myself to pull back from her body, covering my aching cock with my sweats, gritting my teeth at how the fabric brushed against me.

I grabbed Grace's panties and slowly tugged them up her legs. Picking up her shirt from the floor, I motioned for her to sit up before pulling it down over her head, concealing the sticky mess I'd made across her body. Something inside of me liked the idea of her sleeping covered in my come. I almost told her that, but I bit back the confession. I'd crossed too many lines.

"I'm sorry, Grace," I rasped.

She flinched, pushing from the bed and sliding past me.

That was beyond reckless. If my father no longer felt like Grace was useful to him, then she would suffer his wrath. Even as much as he despised *me*, I still had a purpose.

I hung my head and the glint of something silver caught my eye. "Grace," I reached out to grab her locket from the floor that must have come off when she took her shirt off. It was lying open and inside was a small black circle, something electronic. I turned around, my eyes going from the locket to Grace.

When she saw what I held, her eyes went wide, her face paling.

"What the fuck is this, Grace?"

"I-I don't –"

"You've been wearing a *wire*?"

30

GRACE

Ryatt's eyes were locked on mine, searching for answers. "What have you done, Grace?" The look of betrayal twisting his features caused my stomach to lurch. He pushed from the bed, grabbing his gun from the dresser.

I tried my best to shut off any feelings like he'd taught me. He shook his head, his large palm circling my throat as my back pressed against the wall. His weapon was pushing against my temple as my necklace dangled from his trigger finger.

"Don't do that. Don't hide from me. I want to see the fear in your eyes." His face was nearly touching mine, like only moments ago when I wanted nothing more than to have him closer. "I want to know that you understand what you've done."

"Are y-you going to hurt me?"

His eyes narrowed. "I haven't decided what I'm going to do with you yet."

I swallowed against his hand and his fingers flexed against my neck. "Please don't tell your dad," I begged as a tear fell from my lashes. Ryatt's thumb swiped over it, smearing it across my cheek.

"He will kill you, Grace."

"I know," my voice sounded so quiet, so small. "I didn't mean to hurt you."

"But you still did." He laughed sardonically. "What did you think was going to happen?"

"I don't know..."

"Jesus *Christ*, Kitten. I thought *I* was ruthless. But *you*..." he sneered, shaking his head, his grip tightening fractionally around my throat. He sounded too calm for the words he was saying, and it was unnerving. "You're fucking savage, Grace."

"How is it different from what you do to everyone? *Huh*?" I asked, thinking of the thousands of videos and images he uses for blackmail. "You destroy people on a whim." I struggled to keep myself from breaking down in front of him.

His forehead pressed against mine as his jaw clenched. "Everyone but *you*, Grace. I would *never* do this to *you*."

Ryatt took a step back from me, allowing his arms to fall to his sides. My hand went to my chest to fumble with my heart that he'd stolen. My gaze fell to his left hand, the necklace tangled in his fingers as he gripped his gun. I let my arm fall back to my side. Everything I'd done, all the danger, the humiliation, was all for nothing.

But none of it felt worse than the realization that I'd hurt Ryatt. He wasn't even a part of this when it all began. This was about his father. This was about avenging *my* father. And then I met *him*.

His eyes dragged up and down my body. "What was the plan?"

"He *killed* my *father.*"

Ryatt shrugged. "So, you wanted him to kill you *too*? Do you have *any* idea what he would do to you?"

"You *k-knew*?"

His eyes left mine as he bit out a curse. "I had a feeling. But I wasn't sure."

"I wanted revenge."

"What were you going to do? Turn him in? Take us *all* down? Did you think you'd blackmail me into doing it *for* you?"

"No!"

"*No?*"

"I d-didn't know that this would happen between us –"

"*Us*? There is no *us*, Grace," he bit out.

"If you're going to hurt me, can you just get it over with already?" My chin trembled as more tears slid down my cheeks.

"No. I think you're doing a good enough job at hurting *yourself.* I want you to suffer." He turned, storming out of the bedroom and slamming the door behind him. I'd almost preferred he would have hit me. A broken bone wouldn't hurt nearly as bad as a broken heart. *When had I let him in my heart?* I sank to the floor, wrapping my arms around my legs, sobbing, wishing I would have never met Ryatt Ransom.

***

When I finally emerged from the bedroom, Ryatt was sitting on the couch, his weapon still in hand. His eyes rose to meet mine, his face hard.

"I'm sorry –"

"Don't," he snapped. "Don't fucking lie to me."

"What would you do if someone killed *your* dad?" I asked, hoping he could understand where I was coming from.

"I'd buy him a fucking drink."

"Or *her...*"

His eyes met mine, his face hard. "Don't ever fucking say something like that again, Grace. Don't even fucking *think* it. Do you understand?"

"I deleted everything between us. I haven't shown anyone *anything.*"

"You can't use what you did to try to earn my trust back." He pushed from the couch, stalking toward the bedroom to grab a shirt.

"You hated me, Ryatt. You wanted to *ruin* me," I called out.

He emerged out of the room walking by me to the kitchen. He grabbed a bottle of liquor on the counter and drank back a swig. "Stop talking." He took another drink, shaking his head.

"I'm sorry –"

His hand was around my throat again, squeezing as my back hit the fridge. "*Shut* your *fucking* mouth, Grace, or I will shut it *for* you."

My eyes narrowed, tears spilling over my lashes. "So now you're back to hating me?"

"What makes you think I ever didn't, Kitten?" He turned, grabbing his keys and yanking open the front door. "Let's go. Get in the fucking car."

I followed him out into the cool night air, slipping into the passenger side of his car. When Ryatt got in, his stilled, his jaw clenched as he stared ahead out the windshield. "Where are the recordings?"

I unlocked my phone and pulled up the folder that held the files I had. He snatched it from my hand, selecting the files and airdropping them to himself before erasing them from my phone and tossing it back on my lap.

The car roared to life as I twisted the key in the ignition and took off toward the big house.

***

31

RYATT

Laying back in my chair, I stared up at the projector screen, watching Grace as she tossed and turned in her bed, while playing her audio recordings on my phone. Nothing she had amounted to anything more than petty bullshit. But these files would be more than enough for my father to decide she was a liability. I deleted them all.

At three in the morning, I waited to see if she'd sneak out and take a dip in the pool, but she never left her bed.

In fact, she didn't move until nearly lunch the next day, and that was just to use her bathroom in her room. Then she crawled back in her mass of covers and stared off at the television, her eyes unfocused.

I flipped through the different cameras on my phone before spotting Grace's mother in the kitchen. I made my way through the house to find her. Hope was sitting at the table, eating a salad and flipping through her wedding planning binder.

"Ryatt, I haven't seen you around much."

"I've been busy with school," I replied, grabbing a bottle of water from the fridge before turning to face her. "I think Grace hasn't been feeling well."

"Really?" her eyebrows pinched together like she forgot her daughter even existed, too focused on her own future plans.

"Maybe have the chef send up some soup or something," I suggested. "She likes lobster bisque."

"Alright," she replied before I walked out of the room, not wanting to have to spend any more time conversing with her.

***

32

GRACE

I lay across my bed, my eyes unfocused toward the television. It had been three days since I realized I was falling for Ryatt, at the very moment I'd destroyed everything. He walked away from me, taking my heart with him, and I hadn't been able to function since. Guilt sickened me, twisting my gut.

I hadn't seen him since he brought me back to the big house. He never spoke a word on the drive, and I honestly wasn't sure if he was going to take me out in the woods somewhere and abandon me. I actually was relieved to see the mansion come into view. But then I realized that I would probably never get to go back to the church again. To be alone with Ryatt, and play house, even if for a few hours, to escape our reality.

"You need to eat something," my mother called out, holding a glass of water in her hand. She sat it down on my dresser before coming to my side, putting her hand against my forehead to check for a fever.

"I'm not hungry," I muttered, gripping my blanket in my fists.

"You're not going to feel better if you don't get out of bed."

I rolled my eyes, turning to face the wall as fresh tears clouded my vision. "I just want to sleep."

My mother's hand rubbed over my hair a few times before she conceded. "You don't have to eat, but you need to come down for family dinner. It's been days."

My stomach lurched. I needed to get something in me, but the idea of sitting across from Ryatt was twisting my belly in knots. *What if he told Enzo?*

"Ten minutes, okay?" My mother's voice cut through my thoughts. I nodded, knowing I would have to face him eventually. And if I was honest, I wanted to see him. I hadn't gone this long without a word since we got closer.

I waited for my door to close before my mother before pushing from the bed and doing my best to make myself look presentable.

It was no use. I looked like I hadn't slept in days, my face pink and puffy from crying. I trudged down the hall and made my way to the dining room.

Enzo sat at the head of the table, my mother at his side. I let my eyes flit to Ryatt's empty seat, my chest feeling tight. My eyes began to cloud, and I swallowed against the lump in my throat. Then the front door slammed and the sound of his shoes against the marble made my breath hitch.

He circled the table, mumbling an apology for being late. I slowly raised my gaze to meet his angry glare, taking in the purple mark that marred the underside of his left eye, and the cut that sliced through his swollen lower lip. He was wearing slacks and a button-down. Leather straps circled his shoulders, holstering weapons against his ribs.

My eyes narrowed, wanting to ask him a million questions, but the scowl on his face warned me against opening my mouth.

"Nice of you to join us, son" Enzo rasped.

"I had some business to attend to," he replied. He picked up his glass of wine and I noticed red splatters on his sleeve. "I'll get you a list of places to send flowers," he added.

"Grace, how are you feeling?" Enzo's eyes were on me. "Your mother said you've been under the weather."

I nodded, my throat feeling tight. I wanted to run back to my room. "Better," I croaked out, my gaze falling to my plate.

"Good. I'd hate for you to be feeling ill during our trip to Italy."

Ryatt's eyes flashed with anger, his jaw tense. I wanted to ask him why he was so worried about the vacation, but he wasn't talking to me anymore. And I wasn't sure if I should even worry about Italy, when he held my very big secret in his hand. I touched my collar bone, instinctively, bristling when the locket was not there for me to fumble with.

"Son, I'm going to need your passport. You can bring it to me with Grace's after dinner."

"When do we leave?" Ryatt asked, his voice sounded gravely like maybe he hadn't been sleeping much lately.

Enzo was quiet for a beat. "Soon," he replied vaguely.

"Fine," was all Ryatt said before drinking down the rest of his wine. "Are we done?"

His father nodded once and Ryatt shoved from the table, stalking off across the room.

I waited a few more minutes before asking if I could be done too and sulking back to my room and curling up in my bed to cry some more.

***

"Why the fuck are you crying?" Ryatt asked, his voice void of emotion. I wiped my eyes, struggling to stifle my whimpers. "You did this to yourself, Grace. You did this to *me*."

"I know," I whispered, wiping the tears from my face.

"I need your passport."

I rolled over, knowing I must have looked like a mess, but I couldn't bring myself to care. And it was more than obvious Ryatt didn't. He would barely look at me as I pushed from my bed and pulled open my vanity drawer, my hand knocking around my various bottles of nail polish and makeup.

"It's... it's not here. This is where I left it." I glanced back at Ryatt, confused, but his face was impassive.

He shrugged. "Guess we will have to push off the trip until we can get you a new one."

He turned to leave as I spoke.

"You took it."

He stopped, turning back to look at me, his face void of emotion. "Why would I do that?"

I took a step closer to him before forcing myself to stop. "You tell me."

Ryatt rolled his eyes. "If there is something you want to ask, just ask it." He shoved his hands deep in the pockets of his slacks. My eyes roamed over the guns, the splatters of blood on his crisp Oxford. There were a million things I wanted to know but I wasn't sure he'd answer anything.

"You weren't happy when your dad said we were going to Italy. You didn't want me to go along. Why?"

"Women have no business in these meetings," he replied sounding bored.

"Am I in danger?"

His eyes searched mine before narrowing. "You should be more worried about me than anyone else right now, Grace."

"You haven't said anything," I noted. "Thank you."

"Don't do that. Don't thank me. I'm not doing you any favors. You fucked up everything and I'll be lucky if your bullshit doesn't get me killed."

"Why would it –"

"I'm supposed to be watching you. I should have known."

"I thought your job was to *protect* me."

Ryatt smirked but it didn't reach his eyes. "Who's going to protect you from *me*, Kitten?"

My heart felt like it sputtered and halted in my chest. He took in my expression and smiled, this time genuine. "There it is... now you understand how serious this is, don't you?"

"He killed my father," I snapped, tears springing to my eyes.

"I should have known. Girls with daddy issues always have the best pussy, but are so fucked in the head, aren't they?"

"Ryatt," I warned, my blood feeling like it was ice in my veins.

He reached out, his fingers ghosting along my jaw. "Don't worry, Gracie. I can keep a secret too. For a price."

33

RYATT

Her tongue ran over her lips, her fingers wringing together in front of her. "What price?"

"Open your mouth."

Her lips separated, her eyes studying mine. I grabbed her hair at the nape of her neck, holding her still as I raised my other hand to her mouth, slowly pushing two fingers inside. "Wider," I rasped, sinking my fingers deeper inside until she gagged.

"Shh..." I whispered as a tear rolled down over the apple of her cheek. "Relax your throat, Grace."

I pulled back before pushing forward again with a third digit. "That's my girl," I praised when she took me further. Her lips closed around them as her tongue ran along my skin. "That's it. Suck. Hollow out your cheeks. *Fuck*. Just like that." Her eyes were on mine, hooded. "Get on your knees, Kitten." I pulled my fingers free from her mouth before I guided her down, still gripping her hair. I sucked in a ragged breath as our eyes locked and she waited for me to tell her what to do. My cock was straining against my zipper. "Go ahead. Show me what you learned."

She reached up with shaky fingers, undoing the button of my pants and slowly lowering the zipper. Her eyes flitted to mine, and I clenched my jaw, nodding for her to keep going. Her eyes lowered, her plump bottom lip between her teeth as she pulled me free from the confines of my boxer briefs. I hissed at the feel of her skin against mine. I hadn't come since the last time we were together, and all the stress and built-up tension had me ready to explode. I didn't know how gentle I would be able to be with her. Part of me didn't want to be. I wasn't used to having to curb my needs for the women I normally entertained. And Grace was no different from them. In fact, she'd proven herself to be dangerous. Reckless. And she needed to learn who was in charge. I looked down at her, on her knees, stroking my cock as she waited for me to give her orders.

She needed to be punished. She didn't deserve my kindness after the danger she'd put us both in. But I also knew she was working alone. Those recordings she had didn't amount to much and they were stored on her phone. She wasn't reporting to law enforcement. And to her credit, she had deleted anything that incriminated me.

I got rid of the rest. She didn't need someone like my father coming after her.

"What are you waiting for?"

"For you to tell me what you want," she replied.

A menacing smile spread across my face. "I want you to suck my cock like it was what you were born to do, Kitten."

Grace wrapped her lips around the head of my dick, her tongue running against the slit, wiping away the salty drop of precum. I growled, my fingers fisting tighter in her hair. "More."

She took my length further into her mouth, her tongue running under the head and sliding back my shaft as her hand continued to stroke me. "Relax your throat," I reminded her, pushing myself deeper inside of her. "That's it. *Fuck.* That feels so fucking good." I gripped her hair with both hands, stilling her and rocking my hips forward, fucking her pretty little face. She took me deeper, and deeper, tears spilling from her lashes. "That's it, Grace. You can take it."

My stomach muscles coiled tight, and I began to rock faster, harder. "So perfect," I rasped. "I want you to take every drop." My hips stilled, my cock thickening as my come slid down her throat. She swallowed and I nearly doubled over at the sensation of her throat closing around me.

I released my grip on her hair, pulling my dick free from her mouth as she struggled to slow her breathing. I gripped her throat and she pushed to her feet, wobbling from sore knees. My fingers flexed around her neck, and I pulled her closer. "Who do you belong to, Kitten?" I asked, brushing the tears from her cheek with my other hand.

"You."

"Big girl words."

She swallowed against my hand and my dick twitched.

"I belong to *you*, Ryatt."

"You make a good little *fuck toy*, Kitten. Maybe you're worth keeping around for a little while."

I pressed my mouth hard against her swollen lips before releasing her and tucking my cock away.

"I'm not a toy."

"Yes, you are, Grace. You're *my* toy."

Her eyes narrowed. "Don't call me that."

"Is your pussy wet for me?"

"No."

"Such a little liar. Take off your panties."

Her eyes met mine and she shifted her weight from foot to foot.

"Take them off, Grace. *Now*."

Her hands went under her skirt, and she slowly tugged her purple silk underwear down her hips before stepping out of them.

I held out my hand for them and she reluctantly placed her damp underwear in my palm. I held them up to my nose, inhaling the sweet scent of her cunt. "Want to know what I think, Kitten?"

I took a step toward her and she took one backward.

"I'm not sure I do –"

"I think you like it when I tell you to do things because you can pretend you're innocent. A victim. But you know at any time, you can tell me to stop, and you don't. You like to be used, played with, defiled."

I reached up, running my thumb across her lower lip, and her eyes fluttered closed. "You *like* being my toy, don't you, Kitten?" Leaning closer, my lips brushed her ear. "Get on the bed and spread your legs for me, like a good girl."

I shoved her panties in my pocket as she crawled onto her bed, laying on her back with her knees bent. Wrapping my arms around her thighs, I tugged her pussy against my mouth, running my tongue along her wet slit, spreading her open. Grace cried out, pressing herself harder against me.

I groaned licking and sucking her sensitive flesh like she was my last fucking meal. And she might be if anyone catches me eating her out.

Sucking her clit between my teeth, I pushed two fingers against her entrance. She moaned as I fucked her, slowly with my hand, pumping in and out of her tight channel. My cock was rock solid, desperate to feel her pulse around me.

I added a third finger, hissing as she stilled, allowing me to stretch her. "Ride my hand, kitten. Show me how much you want my cock."

She pushed back against me, but I drew back, not wanting to break through her innocence. Her fingers slid through my hair, gripping it and holding my face against her.

"Ryatt," she panted, her hips rocking faster. I curved my fingers, rubbing against her g-spot. Her pussy gripped around my hand, coating me in her sweet nectar. I pulled my hand free, shoving my tongue inside of her and licking her clean of every last drop. "Oh my God," she sighed, her hands releasing my hair and dropping to her sides. I continued to run my tongue over her while she lay thighs splayed, her body languid. I brushed the pad of my thumb over her clit, rubbing it in slow circles.

"Give me one more, Kitten."

"Oh, God... Oh, God..." she moaned as her legs began to shake.

"You belong to me, Grace. You're mine to taste, to feel, and to use whenever and however I want." I pulled her hard against me, my tongue sliding against her little nub as she exploded, crying out my name loud enough to echo off the walls. My fingers gripped her thighs so tightly that I knew she would have bruises, unwilling to release her until she stopped quivering. I didn't care if security broke down her door, nothing was going to pull me away from her pussy.

"Ryatt," she whispered, her hips still undulating like she can't get enough. "Feels... so good..."

"Such a dirty little girl, getting her pussy eaten by her stepbrother," I chided, flicking my tongue over her clit before crawling over her, shoving her shirt up her chest to expose her perky little tits, nipples tight rosy buds, waiting to be sucked on. I took one in my mouth, rolling my tongue over it before doing the same to the other.

"You're not... my stepbrother," she shot back, her voice breathy.

"Not *yet*. Are you still going to ride my face when our parents get married, Kitten?" I asked, pulling my cock free. "Will you ride my cock too?"

I pressed the head of my dick against her entrance, sliding it between her lips as my eyes searched hers.

"Do it," she whispered, challenging me.

I pushed forward, just enough for the tip of my cock to slip inside of her. "If you say it again, I'm going to fuck you. And it will be the end of us both," I warned, hoping she had enough sense to tell me to stop, because God knows I didn't have the willpower to keep my hands off her.

"Ryatt..." she swallowed, my eyes watching as her throat bobbed. "We have to stop."

I clenched my jaw, my teeth feeling like they may crumble as I pulled back, shoving my cock back in my slacks and pushing from the bed. I slid my hand in my pocket, pulling out her necklace and tossing it on the bed for her. Then,

I stalked out of the room before I did something we both would regret.

***

34

GRACE

We sat in the car outside of school, my eyes dancing over the entrance. "Do you hate me?" I asked, glancing over at Ryatt. His jaw was tense as he stared ahead.

"It would make everything easier if I did," he replied.

"That's not an answer."

His eyes cut to mine, studying my face. "No," he bit out. "But that doesn't mean I'm not still fucking pissed at you."

"Why did you... touch me last night?"

"You didn't enjoy me making you come... *twice*?"

"I did... I just... I was surprised you didn't just call one of the other girls –"

"You'd rather I'd fuck them instead of you, Grace?"

"No," I shot back a little too quickly.

"Then when I want to come, you'll make me come. Be thankful I still find you useful."

I swallowed against the lump in my throat and pushed open the car door, stalking toward the building. I didn't wait for Ryatt but I knew he wasn't far behind. Even if he didn't like me right now, he wasn't going to let someone else hurt me. He still had a job to do.

"Grace." My head snapped up to take in Mr. Madden.

"Hi."

"I haven't heard from you for a few days. Is everything okay?"

"Um, yeah. Just wasn't feeling well." It was the truth. I didn't feel any better today about my situation, but I couldn't miss any more days. His palm gripped my shoulder as he leaned in closer. "If you need someone to talk to, I'm here for you." His eyes left mine as he looked behind me. I bristled, knowing he was staring at Ryatt.

"I know. Thank you. I'm okay," I replied as his arm fell to his side and Ryatt's heavy arm draped over my shoulder, pulling me into his side.

"She's *fine*," Ryatt snapped. "We're late for class."

Mr. Madden shoved his hands in the pockets of his slacks, forcing a smile. "I meant what I said, Grace. I'm always here for you."

Ryatt's arm flexed around my shoulders.

"I know," I replied. "Thanks, Liam."

Ryatt's body stiffened. "What the fuck did you just call him?" he asked. My body ran cold. The messages. At the church, when he'd taken my phone, he'd seen my messages with Liam.

"I-I –"

Ryatt shook his head, laughing humorlessly. "Liam is short for William. I guess you can't have students calling you Mr. Madden when you're trying to get in their panties."

"Ryatt, it's not what you –" I began as his arm left my shoulder, his palm pressing against my chest to move me back a step.

"Shut up, Grace," he bit out.

"Don't talk to her like that," Mr. Madden barked.

Ryatt took a step closer to him. "Don't tell me how to fucking talk to her, *Liam*."

"Isn't she going to be your *stepsister*?" Mr. Madden asked, his voice low. "You seem awfully jealous." My stomach lurched at the way he was speaking to Ryatt. Up until this point, I thought his intentions were just to help me out and make sure I was safe.

"Jealous?" Ryatt laughed. "She doesn't moan *your* name when I make her come."

"Ryatt," I screeched, my eyes searching the halls to see if anyone had heard him. A few students lingered a few classrooms away, their gaze on us as they whispered.

Mr. Madden scratched his eyebrow with his thumb, shaking his head before his eyes met mine. Ryatt stepped between us.

"Don't fucking look at her."

241

"Or what?" Mr. Madden asked.

Ryatt cocked back, swinging hard, his fist connecting with Mr. Maddens cheekbone. I screamed as they fell to the ground. Teachers and faculty came flying out of the classrooms and I was shoved back against the lockers as Ryatt continued to pummel him.

"Ryatt," I yelled over the crowd. "Ryatt, stop!"

After a few minutes Ryatt was pulled off Mr. Madden. His knuckles were bloodied, and his cheek bruised. I held my breath as I waited for Mr. Madden to stand, but he didn't. People shouted to call an ambulance.

My eyes met Ryatt's. He looked wild, feral. "Ryatt," I whispered.

"You've been a bad girl, Kitten. You're going to have to pay for that." His lips spread into a wicked smile, his hand reaching up and rubbing against my cheek, smearing Mr. Madden's blood across my skin. I hated myself for leaning into his touch. Seconds later a school security officer grabbed Ryatt's arm, pulling them behind his back as he barked orders at him. But I couldn't hear anything as I kept my eyes locked on Ryatt's. "Call my father," Ryatt ordered with a wink before he was pulled down the hall. He didn't resist and I was thankful he was cooperating with them.

I pulled my phone from my pocket and dialed Enzo. My voice wavered and I choked back a sob when he answered.

"Grace, what's wrong?"

"It's Ryatt. He's in trouble."

***

Hours later I was sitting in a police station, handing my phone over to an officer as they questioned me about my relationship with Liam. A lawyer sat at my side, even though I knew it wasn't necessary, but I wasn't going to question Enzo.

My head was spinning as words like *grooming* and *inappropriate contact* were being thrown around. All eyes were on me, looking at me with pity. I didn't deny it. Didn't argue. I knew if I said it wasn't what was going on, Ryatt would be in more trouble and even if he hated me right now, I didn't want anything to happen to him. He was defending me. *Right?* I still couldn't understand the way Mr. Madden had spoken to Ryatt. Maybe he really did have ulterior motives.

By the time we were on our way home, my stomach panged with guilt and hunger. Ryatt's eyes were on mine, his face hard.

"I'm sending you to see the twins in Sacramento," Enzo's gruff voice cut through the silence.

"Why?" Ryatt snapped.

"*Why?* You nearly killed your guidance counselor. He'll be pissing through a tube for months," his father replied, shaking his head.

243

"He deserved it," Ryatt replied, his eyes going to me before landing back on his dad.

"Be that as it may, you have become increasingly reckless. I can't deal with your bullshit right now. And the twins need some help."

Ryatt scoffed rolling his eyes. "Grace can't miss school."

"She won't. She's not going with you."

"For how long?" Ryatt asked, his nostrils flaring.

Enzo glanced out the window. "For as long as it takes."

***

35

RYATT

I watched Grace from the cameras on my phones, ignoring the slapping of skin and loud moans from the redhead the twins they were fucking. She was on her knees, sucking Ryker's cock as Ryder railed her from behind. I switched back to our text conversation, scrolling through the images she'd sent me from earlier in the day of her playing with herself. Our exchanges had gotten progressively dirtier as the days passed. Ironically, making us closer while so far apart.

What are you up to, Kitten? – I messaged.

Taking a nap – she replied.

Without me? – I typed.

Three little dots flashed on the screen before her next message came through – *Are you coming home soon?*

I hope so – I sent back.

"She's got another hole," Ryder called out as he slapped her ass. "She's an eager little beaver, aren't you, baby?"

"I'm good," I groaned, flipping through the different cams in my house before going back to Grace, on her bed, curled on her side.

My phone rang and my father's name flashed across the screen. *As long as it takes* turned out to be just shy of two weeks.

"Enjoying your vacation, son?" he asked just as the girl getting fucked by the twins cried out as she came.

I ignored his question. "What do you need?"

"I was just enjoying some home movies."

I tensed. I kept my hard drives at the church, but I moved files onto the theater room computer from time to time, and I may have left the surveillance of my father fucking a teenager on the drive when he ordered me to Sacramento. I was pissed, and I knew it wasn't smart, but I never thought clearly when it came to Grace. "I trust you haven't shown these to anyone."

I bit back a curse. "No. I wouldn't do that."

"Good. I'd hate to have to send flowers to my own fucking house," he replied with a laugh. "But we do have some things to discuss. Like your videos with Grace."

I ran my fingers through my hair, wondering which ones he'd seen, wishing I wasn't across the fucking state from her. "What about them?"

"Does she know you like to watch her? Live streaming her security cameras? I can't imagine your little sister would be too pleased to know you jerk off to her changing clothes."

"It's my job to watch her," I rasped, thankful that was all he'd seen. I must have left feed pulled up in the theater room.

"Are you ready to come home now?" My father's voice grated my nerves, and my heart began to thud against my sternum. He wasn't asking. Not really. This was a taunt. He had the power to keep me away for as long as he pleased. And nothing brought my father more joy than to inflict pain upon his only son.

"Things will be different this time," he added.

I rolled my eyes, resting my elbows on my knees. "What's changed?" I rasped, genuinely curious if he had something important to tell me.

"You've become hard. *Unpleasant*," he bit out. "Normally it would please me to know you were finally living up to your name. But your priorities have shifted."

"They haven't." It was the truth. I'd only ever had one goal, to destroy the man who created me.

My father let out a humorless chuckle. "You think I don't see what is happening? You thought you had the smoking gun, but you've only handed me more ammunition."

"Take your best shot," I bit out.

***

Six hours later I slipped inside the sprawling mansion, my eyes landing on Grace. I forced myself to look away from her and focus on my father.

"The prodigal son returns," he called out before taking a swig of his bourbon. "Aren't you going to greet your sister?" he asked with a smirk.

My eyes narrowed, but I didn't correct him. Instead, I forced a smile and closed the gap between us, pulling her into my arms before pressing a kiss to her temple. "How are you, *little sis*?" I took a step back from her, letting my arms fall to my side.

"Good," she whispered.

"How is school?"

"It's been okay," she replied.

"Turns out when you nearly kill a counselor and slap a cheerleader, people don't fuck with you," Enzo chimed in before taking another drink.

"Why did you bring me back?" I asked, pulling my eyes from Grace.

"You're not happy to be home?" he responded with the audacity to feign sadness.

"Why now?"

"Grace's new passport came in. We leave for Italy in the morning. Get packed."

I nodded, following after Grace as we made our way to the stairwell. When we hit the hallway, I grabbed her hips, turning her and pushing her up against the wall, pressing my throbbing cock against her. My lips were on hers, desperate to taste her. She moaned into my mouth, her fingers threading in my hair. I groaned as she tugged, holding me close.

"I've missed you, Kitten," I rasped as my lips trailed down her neck. "Is your pussy wet for me?"

"Always," she whispered, her head falling to the side, and I tugged down her top, sucking her nipple into my mouth until it peaked. Sinking to my knees, I pushed up her skirt and tugged down her panties. My tongue pressed against her clit, and she pushed her hips against my mouth.

"*Fuck*, I missed the taste of you," I groaned, spreading her open and licking up the juices that dripped from her cunt.

"You're not still mad at me?" she asked. I glanced up at her, watching as she worried her lip between her teeth.

"I can be angry and still eat you out, Kitten. It's called multitasking."

She giggled and I flicked my tongue against her clit, causing the sound to die in her throat. Her brows pinched together, and she rocked against my mouth. I gripped her hips, holding her tight as she struggled not to cry out when she came. I groaned against her mound, licking her clean before tugging her panties back up and pushing to my feet.

I kissed her again, slowly this time, letting her taste her juices on my tongue. "You've been a good girl?" I asked, and she nodded. "Why don't you show me how good of a girl you can be," I added, lifting her. She wrapped her legs around my waist as I took her toward her room.

Laying her in the center of her bed, I wasted no time peeling her clothing off her until she lay before me completely nude. Her pussy glistened as she squirmed under my stare. "Beautiful, Kitten," I rasped, before unbuttoning my shirt and dropping it to the floor. I toed off my shoes before undoing my pants. Grace pushed herself up, getting on her knees on the bed before me, gripping my cock and stroking it as her eyes locked on mine.

Leaning over, she sucked the head of my dick into her mouth, and I nearly came at how warm and wet her tongue was against me. I tangled my fingers in her hair, pulling her closer so my cock would slip back her throat. She offered no resistance, allowing me to fuck her face at a leisurely pace before pulling her back and causing my dick to spring free from her mouth.

36

GRACE

I looked up at Ryatt, wondering what I did to make him stop me from giving him head. "Did I do something wrong?" I asked as his knuckles ran along my cheek before his thumb brushed over my lower lip. He shook his head, and I exhaled the breath I'd been holding. "Then why?"

"Move over," he ordered, and I did before he laid down on my bed. "Come sit on my face, Kitten. I want you to ride my tongue."

I crawled over him, and he slapped my ass playfully. "Turn around so you can suck my cock, baby."

I put a thigh on either side of his face, and he grabbed my hips, yanking me down until my full weight was against him, his tongue delving inside of me like he was starving. I grabbed his cock, stroking it before lowering my mouth onto him. I moaned around his length, rocking my hips against his face. His fingers kneaded the thick flesh of my ass, holding me against him.

I opened my throat, sucking him back until my lips were against his pubic bone and he let out a low growl. If someone happened by the door, there was no way we could explain away the sounds we were making. But I couldn't bring myself to stop. I wanted to be closer to him.

Pleasure began to build inside of me, and my channel clenched, wishing his length was inside of me. I hollowed out my cheeks, sucking him with vigor as my orgasm crested. I cried around his thick intrusion feeling wetness roll down my thighs as he continued his assault with his mouth. Seconds later he exploded, hot come shooting back my throat. I swallowed every drop he gave me, licking him clean before climbing off him. I turned around, curling to his side. He wrapped his arms around me, tugging me flush against him as he pressed his lips to my forehead.

***

Hours later, after we woke up from our nap, I packed my bag for our trip as Ryatt watched me, a pensive expression on his face. "What are you thinking about?" I asked as I paused with a handful of panties in my hands.

"I don't want you to go on this trip."

"Why? You'll be with me."

I sank down on the bed beside him and he reached up, tucking my hair behind my ear. "I don't have a good feeling about it."

"You'll keep me safe. I trust you," I reassured him.

***

We were halfway through our fourteen-hour flight to Naples. Enzo and my mother had retired to his bedroom on the plane as Ryatt and I watched a movie, sharing a blanket as our eyes focused on the screen. His leg was pressed against mine and I couldn't focus on anything but the heat from his body.

"What's wrong, Kitten?"

"This movie is boring."

"Get some sleep," he suggested.

"I can't. I hate flying."

He glanced over at me before I felt his fingers slide across my thigh. "Need me to help you relax?"

"You think that's a good idea?" I nodded toward one of the security guards a few feet away, seated at a table facing away from us.

"He's wearing headphones," he reassured me as his fingers moved to the top of my sleep shorts, shoving down between the fabric and my skin. He rubbed the pads of his fingers against my clit, causing me to gasp. "Already wet for me." His fingers slid down. Spreading me open before he slowly shoved two fingers inside of me. The heel of his palm pressed against my clit and I rocked forward, chasing his touch.

Sliding my hand over his thigh, I pushed under the band of his sweatpants and gripped his hard cock, stroking it in time with his fingers. His mouth hung open, his panting blowing over my face as we fucked each other with our hands.

"It's taking everything in me not to pull you onto my lap and fuck you senseless."

"Do it," I whispered back. His eyes closed like he was fighting the urge before they locked back on mine.

"I'd have to slit his fucking throat," his eyes went to the security guy before meeting mine in a hard stare. "But it would be worth it to feel your tight cunt around my cock."

A shiver rolled through me, and I began to rock my hips faster. Ryatt was pumping into my hand, and I knew our ragged breathing was getting dangerously loud. My tongue ran over my lips and Ryatt pushed his mouth against mine, capturing my tongue. I cried out and he pulled back to watch my face. "*Fuck*, baby."

His words caused me to unravel and I came hard as his mouth slammed back against mine, capturing my cries of pleasure. His hips jerked up in my hand and my fingers were coated in warm come as his own orgasm rocked through his body.

The second the moment passed, we straightened ourselves, focusing on the screen. I watched Ryatt run his tongue against his fingers in my peripheral, his eyes falling closed and a low growl emanating from his chest.

He leaned closer, his lips to my ear. "I'll never get tired of the taste of you."

***

37

GRACE

We arrived at our villa around ten at night. Enzo sent a staff member to grab us dinner from Palazzo Petrucci in Piazza San Domenico Square and we called it an early night. Ryatt was in my room, eating lasagna with buffalo mozzarella while I stared at my shrimp in pea sauce.

"What's wrong?" he asked, taking another bite. I made a face and he smirked. "You want some of mine?"

"I think I'm just nervous about tomorrow."

Ryatt grabbed me around the waist and hauled me sideways onto his lap. "You don't have anything to be nervous about. No one is even going to look in our direction."

"Maybe we can site see while we're here. I'd like to explore the tunnels under the city."

"I'd like to explore *you*," he whispered before pulling me closer, his palm turning my face so his lips could capture mine. He was thick and hard beneath me, his hips pushing up to grind himself against my ass.

"Are you always this *ready*?" I asked, giggling against his mouth.

"When you're around, yes," he shot back before his tongue moved against mine again. I turned, climbing over his lap to straddle him. Ryatt grabbed my thighs, tugging me hard against him so he was pressed against my center.

"Can I ask you something?" His lips moved to my neck. "Why won't you... you know..."

He pulled back to look me over. "I *don't* know..."

I smacked against his chest playfully. "You know... go all the way with me."

"Why won't I *fuck* you?"

"Yes," I nodded, feeling my cheeks burn.

His mouth was back on mine. "Fill you with my come?"

"Yes," I whimpered.

"There is nothing I want more than to be inside of you, Grace. But you and I are on different paths in this family."

"What is that supposed to mean?"

"It means my future was planned long before you came along."

"I've seen you with other girls. It's not like you are celibate –"

"*Other* girls. If I knock up my fucking stepsister, I'll be castrated."

His mouth was against my neck again, his hands gripping my hips and pulling me against him. I was so close, but his phone vibrated against the table, and he stilled, his eyes dancing over the device.

"It's Enzo," he rasped. "I have to go."

He lifted me from his lap before pushing to his feet and gathering his things. "Lock your door. Don't answer for anyone but me."

I nodded as he leaned forward, pressing his lips against my forehead in a chaste kiss before disappearing out of my room.

***

I woke to the sun throwing streaks of light across my room, my skin warm from being tangled in my sheet. I grabbed my phone from beside the bed to check my messages. Ryatt had sent me one a few minutes ago, letting me know I should get ready. When I hadn't responded he sent another letting me know he was on his way to my room.

I sighed when there was a knock at my door. "I'm up," I called out, pulling open my door and startling when the person on the other side was not Ryatt. "C-can I help you?" I asked, angry at myself for not waiting to hear his voice before I opened it.

His lips twisted up in a smirk. He was a handsome man with dark hair and eyes, maybe around my age, but there was a wildness in his gaze. It caused my stomach to twist in a knot.

"Ciao, Bellissima. You must be Grace." His lips spread in a grin that caused my spine to straighten. "I'm Luca." He took my hand in his, raising it to his lips and pressing a kiss to my knuckles.

"Luca," Ryatt bit out and I pulled my hand free from Luca's hold.

"Ryatt," he called out, his smile friendly but it didn't reach his eyes.

"Get dressed, Grace," Ryatt ordered, his eyes never leaving Luca. "Can I help you with something?" he asked him, an edge to his tone.

"Just greeting my guest," Luca replied.

"She's not a part of this." Ryatt's eyes finally cut to mine. "Go *now*, Grace. Don't make me ask again."

I nodded, closing the door between us and hurrying to get ready for the day.

***

Within an hour I was ready, wearing a sundress Ryatt had bought for me and strappy leather sandals, just in case we were able to walk around the city later, I didn't want my feet to hurt. I kept my hair down, swiping on a little mascara. I didn't know what to expect throughout the day, but I knew there would be a dinner this evening with the family we had come to meet. It felt like there was some history between him and Luca and I was worried that tension would come to a head while we were here. I've never seen the *professional* side of Ryatt and how his father conducted his business. But

I'd seen him lose his temper. And how badly he could hurt someone who crossed him.

"Open up, Kitten," Ryatt growled, rapping his knuckles against my door. I pulled it open, taking in his hard stare.

"Sorry," I mumbled as I stepped to the side, letting him enter.

"Are you ready?"

I nodded.

His eyes took in my dress. "Let's go."

"Where?"

"I'm taking you to brunch," he replied, grabbing my hand and tugging me out the door behind him.

When we stepped out of the corridor, he dropped my hand, his eyes scanning the street as we stepped outside.

"Where are our parents?" I asked.

"My dad is *busy*, and your mother is shopping. We have a few hours and I thought maybe we could walk around."

"Do you come here a lot?" I asked as we slipped into a bar and slinked our way through the heavy crowd.

"I'm not much of a brunch kind of guy."

I laughed, shaking my head. "I meant Italy. Why are we in a bar?"

"This is where you get breakfast," he explained. "I've been here enough. I don't usually deal with Gio's business though," he explained before ordering us each an espresso and a cornetto.

We waited as he paid and when we collected our things before drinking back our shots. He left a coin on the counter for the barista, giving her thanks. We made our way back outside with our pastries in hand and walked further down the road.

And for a moment, it felt like we weren't ourselves. Just tourists, taking in a new country without a care. And I liked the idea of us being out alone in the world, together.

***

When I got back to my room, there was a white thigh length dress and nude heels laid out for me on my bed, along with gold jewelry. "My locket is silver. It won't match."

"Wear your necklace. None of this is important. It's going to be fine," Ryatt rasped, grabbing a peach from the fruit bowl on the table. He took a bite, sauntering toward me. He held it up to my mouth and I took a bite as well, a drop of juice rolling down my chin. He leaned in, licking the sweet nectar from my flesh. "Mmm... tastes even better on your skin."

My body felt hot and just that quickly, I forgot about what we were getting ready for.

"Yeah?" I unbuckled my sandals before gripping the hem of my sundress and tugging it over my head. His gaze fell to my panties, and I hooked my thumbs around the fabric and shoved them over my hips before stepping out of them. I was standing before him completely bare as I reached out, taking the peach from his hand and rubbing it over my breast. "What about here?"

Ryatt's lips curved into a wicked grin as he leaned in and ran his tongue against my flesh, causing my nipple to bud. I ran the peach over the other and he did the same, his eyes on mine. His fingers slid over mine, taking the peach from my hand and dragging it down my lower stomach and over my mound. I gasped as the sticky fruit rubbed against my clit.

"So fucking delicious," he groaned, sinking to his knees.

Ryatt's mouth was on me, hungrier now and causing me to cry out as he sucked my clit between his teeth. Hitching my leg over his shoulder, he continued to eat me out as he used the fruit to rub circles against my clit.

I bowed my back, feeling my juices dripping down my inner thighs. My fingers tangled in his hair as I cried out his name.

He pushed to his feet and took a bite of the peach. "I can't get enough of you, Kitten."

I reached out, fumbling with his slacks, but he grabbed my hand, stopping me. "You can thank me when we get back later." He winked, leaning forward, sucking my lower lip into his mouth. I could taste myself and the peach on his tongue as it slid into my mouth. "We'll have all night to ourselves."

***

38

GRACE

Ryatt and I sat next to each other at the massive ornately carved table in Gio's home. I tried to ignore how my thighs were still sticky from Ryatt, and how his fingers gripped me there under the table as some of the men around us talked. I couldn't focus on anything being said, just where he was touching me and the promise of more later. A man sat at a piano off in the corner as a woman sang a beautiful song in Italian. It would have felt romantic if I wasn't surrounded by some of the most powerful and dangerous men in the world.

All I could think about was after the meal, Ryatt was going to take me on another walk around the city, and what we would do afterword in my room.

Someone from the other end of the table said something in Italian, and Ryatt replied. My eyes widened, shocked that he understood them and was able to speak the language.

"Wow," I mouthed, taking a sip of my wine. He glanced over at me smirking, giving my thigh a squeeze. Luca, the guy who showed up at my room this morning was staring at me, his gaze unnerving. I tried my best to ignore him, smiling politely at the others around the table. Half of the guests were security, their faces hard even when the main guests where laughing. There were a few other women, like Gio's wife and some woman who was having a hard time keeping her hands off my soon to be stepfather. I wondered if that was the real reason my mother didn't come to dinner, and not an upset stomach from something she'd eaten earlier in the day.

The most important people at the meal were Enzo, Gio, Luca, and Ryatt from what I could tell.

The amount of food on the table was staggering. Enough to feed at least thirty people but I was too nervous to eat. Which made the two glasses of wine I'd consumed hit me a little harder than I'd liked. And I realized I had left my phone in my room, and I wanted to check in on my mother.

"I think I'd like to go lay down," I whispered to Ryatt. He nodded, wiping his mouth with his cloth napkin.

"I'll take you." He pushed from his seat and his father held up his hand.

"Where are you going?" Enzo asked as all eyes turned to us.

"Grace isn't feeling well. I'm going to take her back to her room so she can rest."

"Nonsense," his father replied with a wave of his hand. "We still have more courses coming."

"I'm really not hungry," I protested. "And I would like to check on my mother."

"Sit, Grace," Enzo ordered. "Ryatt will check on Hope for you."

Ryatt's eyes narrowed. "I'm not leaving Grace." His tone wasn't assertive, but I knew he was livid as he sank back down beside me, grabbing his glass of wine and drinking it back. His gaze was locked on his father in challenge. And to my surprise, Enzo just went back to his conversation, droning on the two families doing more business together before it turned more personal.

"The wedding will be soon," Enzo told Gio. "It will be great to have both families together again."

"I look forward to the celebration," Gio replied with a thick accent.

Ryatt leaned over, his voice low so only I could hear. "I'll take you back to your room when dinner is over. I promise."

I nodded, grabbing my glass of water and drinking it back as someone took my plate and replaced it with a clean one.

"Eat something," He encouraged me, looking at me like he was worried.

I agreed with a nod, and he took my plate, adding a little bit of pasta and salad, along with some bread before placing it back in front of me. His hand went back to my thigh, pushing my skirt up a few inches and rubbing back and forth across my skin with his thumb.

I ate a few bites and drank more water. By the time we had moved on to dessert I felt much better, warmth spreading from where he touched me, causing me to relax and finally begin to enjoy myself.

After the table was cleared, the men continued to drink or mill about the expansive room.

"Would you like to dance?" I turned to see Luca standing beside my chair and I glanced up at him before looking back to Ryatt.

"I'm about to take her back to her room. She's tired," Ryatt replied to him on my behalf.

Luca smiled, but it didn't reach his eyes. "I was asking *her*."

I licked my lips, my mouth feeling parched as my gaze met Enzo's. He was watching us with narrowed eyes.

I forced a smile and looked back to Luca. "Just one dance," I conceded as Ryatt's hand gripped my thigh painfully tight before releasing.

I immediately missed his touch as I pushed to my feet, sliding my hand in Luca's and allowing him to lead me toward the piano. I glanced back at Ryatt to see him drinking back his glass of wine as he watched us.

Luca rasped something in Italian as he gripped my hip. He leaned in close as we back to move. "You and Ryatt seem... close."

I cleared my throat. "We're family," I replied, trying to sound cheery.

"*Are* you?" He pulled back to look at me before leaning in again. "Because I've been watching you and I never touch my sister the way he touches you, *Kitten*."

My blood went cold and I stilled, pulling back but his hand gripped mine tight enough that I thought some of the bones might snap. My eyes went to Ryatt, wide with panic and he pushed from his seat, stalking toward us when Enzo put his hand on his sons chest, stopping him.

"I'd like to touch you like that," Luca added with nostrils flaring.

39

RYATT

"Take the night off, Ryatt," my father muttered. My eyes narrowed on him before looking to Luca.

"You told me to protect her. That's what I'm doing," I bit out.

"You've done good, son. But now you need to step away from her."

"Not a fucking chance."

"Excuse me?" My father moved toward me, his fists clenched at his sides. Grace was vibrating with fear, her eyes searching mine.

"I'm not throwing her to the wolves for you."

My father laughed, shaking his head. "*We're* the wolves, son." His eyes went to Grace. "And she's the sacrificial lamb."

Luca's eyes were wide, his pupils pinned. Whatever he was amped up on had him bouncing from foot to foot with anticipation.

"Don't do this."

"She's a good faith offering. And when I marry her mother, our families will be tied." My father's eyes narrowed. "I'm disappointed in you, Ryatt." He nodded to Luca's guards.

They pounced on me, grabbing my arms. "A soft heart is an easy target."

"No! Don't fucking do this. I swear on everything that if you hurt her, I will kill you all myself."

My father sneered at me before nodding to Luca. "Do it. Make him watch," he ordered before turning and walking away. Seconds later the door slammed behind him.

I struggled against the men who held me as Luca held Grace. Her eyes were locked on mine, swimming with unshed tears. "Ryatt," her voice trembled as the tears broke free, snaking down her cheeks.

"I'm so sorry, Kitten. I'm so sorry, forgive me, Grace," I choked out, my own vision blurring as I fought to free myself.

Luca placed his hand around her throat as a feral growl ripped from my chest.

"Get your fucking hands off her, you motherfucker," I snapped.

"Don't touch me!" Grace gripped his wrist, struggling to pry his hand from her neck. Two other men grabbed her, lowering her across the table and pinning her against it. Luca reached under her dress, tugging her panties down her legs as Grace kicked and fought against him.

Luca's smile widened. He was enjoying her struggle, and a sick fuck like him would enjoy causing her pain. I swallowed back the bile rising in my throat, trying to clear my head.

"Grace, baby, look at me. Look at me, Gracie."

Her wild eyes met mine, and her entire body coiled like a snake.

"Just look at me. That's it. Focus on me. Good girl."

I glanced at Luca, who was undoing his belt and freeing his cock from his slacks.

"Grace, I need you to shut it off. Can you do that for me, baby? It's a game. A mission."

Her chin quivered before her face screwed up in pain. "I can't, Ryatt," fresh tears ran from her eyes.

"It's a rule. You have to, Kitten. *Please*. I need you to just focus on me. I'm right here with you."

Her eyes squeezed closed before the tension seemed to slide from her face. When they focused on mine again, they looked vacant. Lost.

My eyes went to Luca again as he stroked himself. He was so fucking high that he was having trouble even getting hard.

"Luca, what is it you want? Anything you want, I will give you," I pleaded.

"I want to make her bleed," he shot back, laughing.

"You want to do business in California. That's what you want *right*?" I was panting, my skin torn and weeping blood from where his men struggled to keep their grips on me. "I have blackmail on half of the state. Politicians, cops, everybody. Take it, Gio. Take the entire Ransom fucking empire. It's yours. But you can't have *her*."

Gio stood up, holding up his hand to halt his son from his assault. "You belong to one of the most powerful families in your country. You'd give up everything for this girl?"

I shook my head. "I belong to *her*." My eyes went to Grace before focusing back on him. "I'd burn the fucking world for her," I rasped.

"*Al cuore non si comanda*." Gio's eyes widened fractionally, a slow smile spreading across his lips. "I might be interested in working with you in the future, Ryatt. When it's your time."

"If your son touches her, I will kill every last one of you. Starting with him."

"A blind man could see that you were in love with her. I don't know how your father didn't know."

"Because he's never loved anything in his life but himself."

"Or you're playing right into his hand. Maybe he's *offering* you a reason to stay." He eyed me a moment longer as the realization sank in that my father had put all of this into motion. He forced Grace into my life, made me stay by her side, and told me she was forbidden. He knew I'd defy him at every turn. I was fucking selfish. I was going to walk away from *everything* before she came into my life. "You sure she's what you want?"

I clenched my jaw, thinking over my options, but I wasn't going to walk away from Grace, no matter the cost.

"I want *her*."

"You know what you're agreeing to, son?" he asked, his eyes going to Grace before cutting back to me. I nodded, swallowing the bile rising in my throat. "Does she know?" He asked.

I slowly shook my head. "No."

"Luca," Gio barked. "Let her go."

"What?" Luca snapped.

"Let her *go*," he repeated.

The men who held Grace down released her, and she scurried from the table, slamming herself against my chest and wrapping her arms around my torso.

"I look forward to doing business with you, Ryatt." Gio nodded to the men who held me.

As soon as my arms were free, I wrapped them around Grace, crushing her against my body. My fingers tangled in her hair, inhaling the coconut scent that clung to her skin.

"Gio, wait," I called after him. Grace stiffened in my arms. "If we're going to join these families without a marriage, there needs to be bloodletting on *both* sides."

He stopped before turning back to me, his grin never wavering. "Go on."

I nodded toward Luca. "*Him*," I bit out. "I want five minutes alone with him."

His eyes went to his son who was practically salivating at the idea. "You sure you know what you're asking for?"

I stretched my neck to the side, cracking it. "No weapons. You can come back later to collect the pieces."

"What makes you think I'd let you walk into my home and threaten my son?"

"Because having me in your pocket is worth more than a psycho on a leash. One day he's going to break free, and not even you will be able to clean up the mess he leaves behind."

Gio glanced at his son before looking back to me. "Tempting. I'll keep you in mind if he ever bites the hand that feeds him," he replied before he left the room, his men and son following after him.

I pulled back from Grace holding her face in my palms as I looked over her tear-stained face. "I'm so sorry."

"You saved me, Ryatt."

I shook my head, brushing her hair back from her face. "I didn't save you, Grace. You have no idea what you are now a part of. What I've set in motion."

"What do y-you mean?" she asked, her fingers covering mine, pulling them from her face. I pressed my lips to her knuckles. "My fate was already decided. And it will be the same for the next generation. And the next –"

"I don't understand."

I swallowed back the bile rising in my throat. "When I first met you, I thought maybe, you were going to be the next. I hated the idea of being forced into something, then I couldn't stand the idea of having to share you –"

"Next *what*?"

"Offering."

***

40

GRACE

I held on to Ryatt as he ran his hand over my hair, holding me to him until every last rapture had rolled through my body, every tear had dried against my skin. Then he took me back to his room and put me to bed, never leaving my side.

I was too scared to ask him to explain what me staying with him meant, and he didn't offer more details. The look of horror on his face was enough to dissuade me. But it didn't matter, because whatever it was, I wouldn't leave him anyway. I had belonged to him since the moment we met, and now, he belonged to me too.

The terrifying ordeal offered me a different side of Ryatt I'd never seen. There was something there, hidden beneath the anger and disdain. I clung to it, to him, until the sun poured through the windows in the morning.

I stretched, blinking my eyes open. Ryatt's arm banded around me, pulling me flush against him with a groan.

"Too early," he rasped, rolling me on top of him so I could feel his hard length straining inside of his boxer briefs. I pressed my palm along the side of his neck. Feeling his heart pulse in his veins. I widened my hips, and he groaned as he rubbed against my center.

"I like waking up with you," I whispered, and his lips curved in a lopsided grin.

"You always woke up with me, Grace. I couldn't keep my eyes off you," he replied, his voice thick from sleep. His lips pressed against mine, his hands sliding under his t-shirt I was wearing, roaming over my back. "Some nights I would sit in the theater and watch you sleep for hours."

"I thought you hated me."

"Part of me did," he shot back with an eyebrow cocked. "Because I knew the last place you should be was in our home, but I was selfish enough to hope you didn't leave. I thought you'd make me weak."

"Did I?"

He shook his head, his throat bobbing as he swallowed. "No. Because of you, I'm going to be a very, very powerful man."

"Because of me, huh?" I asked, rocking my hips. "How does a *pawn* make a king powerful?"

"By becoming my queen." His mouth was on mine, his tongue sliding along the seam of my lips, kissing me slowly and leaving me breathless.

"When Gio said...he could tell you loved me, you didn't deny it."

The corner of his mouth turned up as his eyes searched mine. "Because it's true."

"Y-you love me?"

He nodded. "I love you, Grace." His mouth pressed against mine again. "And *you* love *me*."

"How can you be so sure?" I asked.

His hand slid to the center of my chest, pressing against my sternum. "Because your heart races whenever I touch you. It knows it belongs to me."

"It also races when I'm scared."

"You're not scared of me, Kitten."

"No, I'm not," I agreed.

"You love me."

"I do," I replied.

"Big girl words, Grace."

"I love you, Ryatt."

His lips spread in a devastating grin. "That's my fucking girl."

"Do you think anyone knows I didn't go to my room last night?"

"Doesn't matter anymore," he replied, pulling me against him harder. I whimpered, rocking again and again. He grabbed his shirt, tugging it. "Take this off," he rasped. I sat up, yanking it over my head. He grabbed my hips, rubbing me over his length.

I pressed my palms against his chest as we continued to move together.

"Fuck," he groaned. "I can't wait to bury my cock inside of you, Kitten."

"*Why* are we waiting again?" I asked, causing him to groan. He grabbed my hips harder, lifting me from him before shoving down his boxer briefs, freeing his thick length. He shoved my panties to the side and lowered me to slide against him skin to skin.

"Because I said so, Grace. And I make the rules," he rasped, leaning me forward to angle my clit against him. "The second I get inside of you, I'm never fucking leaving."

"Promise?"

"On my life," he ground me against him so hard I whimpered. I lowered myself closer to him, my hands on either side of his head, and his lips wrapped around one of my nipples, sucking it hard until it peaked against his tongue before he did the same with the other. I arched my back, rolling my hips against him, letting my eyes fall closed as I got lost in the sensation. His hips stilled, his fingers biting into me. "Eyes on me, Kitten."

My gaze locked on his and he slowly began to move against me again dragging me up and down his cock.

"I love watching your face as you come," he growled.

My body began to shake, my muscles tightening as waves of pleasure rolled through me. I cried out, sweat slicking our skin. I crawled down his body, taking his length in my hand, and stroking him slowly before sucking the tip of his cock into my mouth. His hands tangled in my hair, hissing before biting out a few curses under his breath. I sucked back his length, and he came as soon as he hit the back of my throat. "*Fuck*, baby. You're so fucking perfect."

He pulled me up against him, wrapping his arms round me and held me as I pressed my face against his chest listening to the steady thumping of his heart against my ear.

Twenty minutes later, there was a knocking at the door, but he didn't move, or loosen his hold on me. Instead, his fingers brushed my hair from my face.

The knock rang out again and this time he stiffened before exhaling loudly. His lips pressed against the top of my head. "Stay in bed. I'm not done with you yet."

I crawled off him, tugging the sheet around my body.

Ryatt pulled open the door revealing his father who stood in his suit, looking as menacing as ever.

"Plane leaves in two hours," he rasped, his eyes going to me before going back to his son. "I trust you're following the rules."

"That's all you have to say?" Ryatt spat back at him.

"If you're wanting an apology, you need to lower your expectations, son. You threatened to leave the business. I protected my assets."

"She's a human fucking being, not a bargaining chip."

"She's your future wife," his father's eyes were back on me, and I stiffened. Ryatt and I just finally admitted we didn't hate each other and now his father was calling me his *future wife*?

"That wasn't your decision to make."

Enzo shook his head. "I didn't make it, Ryatt. *You* did."

"What was I supposed to do? Let you give her to Luca? Let that fucking psycho rape her?"

"You and I both knew that you would stop him. You could have had her gone a long time ago. She's here because of *you*. You have two hours. Tell her the truth. If she agrees you'll both be on the plane. If she doesn't leave her here."

41

RYATT

I slammed the door, turning back to face Grace, her eyes wide and filled with fear once again. "Fuck," I growled, picking up the stand by the door and throwing it against the wall.

"Ryatt," Grace yelled as she pushed from the bed, clutching the sheet to her chest. "It doesn't matter what it is. I'm going with *you*."

"It won't be any better for you there," I rasped, hating myself for not ignoring her and pushing her away. Her palm pressed against my chest and I took a step back from her.

"How wouldn't it be? I'll be with you."

I crossed the room, sinking down on the edge of the bed, my elbows propped on my knees as I hung my head, unable to look her in the eye. "Do you know anything about my mother?"

"No," she replied, sinking down next to me.

"She met my dad when she was seventeen. Enzo had just taken over for his father who was battling cancer. He was only twenty. But he couldn't wait to become a monster like my grandfather. His plan was to consolidate power, control the entire state of California."

"Where is she now?"

He shrugged. "She lives in France but, she hasn't been herself for years. There's no light behind her eyes." My gaze met hers. "My father did that to her. He took everything from her, and she let him, because she was young and in love."

"There had to be something good about him if she stayed."

I shook my head. "There wasn't. Once she fell for him, she discovered who he really was. By then it was too late. He wouldn't let her go. And then after she became pregnant for the first time, she just gave up. Did whatever he wanted. Because she wanted to keep her kid safe."

"The first time? You...you have siblings?"

I nodded. "Three brothers."

"What? Ryatt, where are they?"

"One is in Fresno. He's the oldest at twenty-five. And the twins are twenty-two. They're in Sacramento."

"The twins? That's where Enzo sent you after the Mr. Madden thing."

I nodded.

"How have I not heard about them?"

"Because I didn't want you to know them. We're not one big happy family, Grace. We have the same mother, but that's all we have in common."

"I don't understand. If your mother met Enzo at seventeen and stayed with him, how did she have kids that are older than you with other men?"

I laid back on the bed and Grace laid back beside me. "My dad used her like he used everyone, to grow his empire. She was an *offering* to Marco Grayson and Arlo Cross. Now, when we take over, the entire state will be held by the four of us. But for now, my father controls us by controlling her."

"I'm so sorry."

"He wants me to do the same to you."

"What do you mean?" she asked, propping on her side. I grabbed the silver heart dangling from her chest.

"If I marry you, you would be my wife, but you would belong to all of us."

"What?" She sat back up before pushing to her feet. "I'd have to have children with –"

"Sons," I clarified. "But no. We're already related. California is a family business now. But it's a sign of good faith."

"So, your brothers won't marry?"

I shrugged sitting up. "They can do whatever they want. But you would still be there, whenever they...*fuck*. I can't do this. I can't ask you to do this." I pushed from the bed, pacing the room as I ran my fingers through my hair.

Grace placed her palm against my stomach, stopping me. "What other choice do we have?"

I thought that over. "I could kill Luca...Gio..."

"We're in their territory, Ryatt. We wouldn't make it out of the country, *if* you could even make it out of his home."

"Then we go back to California. I take care of my father. Once I'm in charge, I make the rules."

"And your brothers wouldn't have a problem with that? *Their* fathers?"

"*Fuck*," I growled, slamming my fist into the wall.

"You can't just kill everyone."

"And I can't make you do this. You'll resent me. You'll hate me, and you'll end up just like my mother."

"*You're* not making me do anything. This is your father."

"My father." I laughed sardonically, shaking my head. "He's a monster and I'm next in line to be just like him. I don't want that for you."

Grace slid her hand along my cheek. "You're *not* him, Ryatt. And I'm *not* your mother. I can do whatever it is we need to do for us to be together."

"You don't know what you're saying."

"*Why*? Because I didn't grow up with a criminal for a father?"

"Men like him don't take no for an answer."

"I know. That's why my dad is dead."

I gripped her wrist, pulling her hand from my face. "Why *did* he go after your dad, Grace? What could he possibly have against a mechanic?" Grace's pulse raced under my fingertips.

"He wasn't a mechanic, Ryatt. He was in witness protection."

42

GRACE

Ryatt's eyes were blazing, his grip on my wrist tightening as his eyes searched mine. "Pack your shit, Kitten. We have a plane to catch." He released me, turning to leave my room and slamming the door behind him.

***

Two hours later we were in the Ransom private jet, flying back to the United States. Enzo and my mother were on the other side of the table from us, enjoying their meal. Enzo's eyes met mine as he took a drink from his glass. "We have dinner next week with your brothers," he spoke to Ryatt.

"Brothers?" my mother asked, her brows pinched together in confusion. Enzo didn't even look at her as he replied.

"Ryatt is one of four."

"You have *four* sons?" she asked.

"No. I have *one*," he shot back before turning his attention back to Ryatt. "They're coming to meet Grace and we can discuss the wedding plans."

"Everything is already planned," my mother replied with a laugh.

"Grace needs to get a dress," he corrected her.

"She's had a maid of honor dress for weeks now. It's perfect."

"I appreciate you planning out the wedding. I will take it from here." Enzo rolled his eyes. "Grace is marrying Ryatt."

"W-what? They will be stepsiblings," she laughed as her face pinched in confusion. My skin grew hot and Ryatt grabbed my hand, giving it a squeeze.

"No, they won't. You and I aren't getting married," he corrected her.

"Grace?" she asked, her eyes searching mine. I swallowed against the lump in my throat. "What is going on?"

Enzo took another sip of his drink. "I already have a wife, Hope."

My mother's eyes went wide, glistening with unshed tears before she pushed from her seat and stormed to the bedroom in the back of the plane.

**

I sighed as I stared over the scattered papers between us. "Well, obviously you can't cheat on me." His eyes met mine, his jaw hard.

"That applies to you as well," he shot back.

"You know *I'm* not like that." I felt my face heat. I had no intention of sleeping with anyone else, but I knew Ryatt had a sordid past. There was also the issue of his brothers hanging thick in the air around us.

The muscles ticked in his jaw, taking my defense as a personal dig.

"I want you to fuck me, Kitten," he bit out, causing my eyes to go wide.

"Now?" My heart jack-hammered against my chest.

"Every day. Twice a day."

"I can't put that in here," I let out a nervous laugh. "Your father will read it."

"He's a man. He knows what men do with their wives."

"Ryatt," I chided. "This is a prenup. Not a bill of sale. I'm not your property."

"Because you already belong to me, Grace." Ryatt's lips twisted up in a wicked grin.

"And *you* belong to *me*," I replied.

"I want to be able to eat your pussy whenever I want. Night or day."

I looked down at where I knotted my fingers together on my lap, unable to look him in the eye. His fingers gripped my chin, raising my face to meet his hooded gaze. "I want you right now."

"The wedding is in six weeks."

"No penetration," he conceded as he reached over, rubbing my thigh with his thumb. "What? Because we're getting married, I can't touch you now? You're going to make me wait?"

"You touch me all the time."

"It's not enough. It will *never* be *enough*, Kitten."

I held all the cards. Including my v-card. And something like that was very tempting to a man like Ryatt. He didn't want to keep being the deviant he had been in the past. He wanted to be a better man – for me. For us. But it didn't change the fact that I was an offering, and Ryatt was going to be taking his father's place at the head of the Ransom empire.

I pressed my teeth into my bottom lip, not wanting to actually have this conversation. Instead, I gave him a small nod. Ryatt pushed himself closer. His fingers running through my hair as he pressed his lips softly to mine, slowly lowering me back on the couch as the papers crumpled under us. He settled himself between my legs, and I gasped as his hard length nestled between my legs. My skirt bunched at my hips and thin cotton pressed against his jeans' rough fabric. He groaned, his hips rocking forward. I gripped his shirt, fisting it at his sides.

"Ryatt," I whimpered as his mouth kissed along my jaw, down the length of my throat. He gripped his shirt from behind his neck, pulling it over his head. My fingers explored the taut skin over his ribs, gliding over his muscular shoulders as he kissed his way down the center of my chest.

His gaze met mine and he slowly shoved my shirt up my body. His fingers pushed my bra cup down as his mouth explored my flesh. I gasped as the flat of his tongue ran over my nipple, drawing it to a peak before sucking it into his mouth.

His lips continued their downward assault as he lapped and licked at my body like it was his final feast. When he reached the edge of my skirt, he gripped it at my hips and slowly dragged the fabric, along with my panties down over my hips. My hands slid to my center, covering myself as he sat back on his knees, admiring me.

"Don't break the rules," he rasped, his fingers wrapping around my wrist and slowly pulling my hand away. His gaze left mine, skating down under he reached the apex of my thighs. A deep sound emanated from his chest as his palm ran up my inner thigh, pushing my legs wide. He lowered his body and I heard the sound of him inhaling before his breath blew over my freshly waxed mound, causing my hips to rise, desperate for his touch.

"Fuck, you're so beautiful," he rasped, the tip of his finger sliding against the crease of my thigh. I felt his lips follow. "Always so wet for me." His tongue ran against my slit and I cried out, my back arching from the cushions. His hands circled my thighs, holding me down and splayed before him as he circled my clit with his tongue.

It took all of thirty seconds until my entire body clenched, pleasure rippling through my body as I gripped onto Ryatt's hair. Holding him against me until every last shudder subsided.

Ryatt pressed a gentle kiss to my inner thigh before he rasped, "I can't wait six more weeks. Pack a bag for Vegas. We'll sneak off after the dinner with my brothers."

***

43

GRACE

I stood in front of my mirror in my bedroom, smoothing my hands over the front of my dress as Ryatt came up behind, wrapping his arms around my waist.

"Nervous?" he asked, pressing his lips to my neck.

"This whole thing is just...weird."

He turned me around to face him, his hands sliding along my hips. "Don't worry about them."

"How can I *not* worry when you told me I'm going to have to *sleep* with them."

"*We* haven't even fucked yet, Grace. Don't think about the future. Focus on now." His hand slid up my inner thigh, hitching up my skirt as he rubbed his fingers along the center of my cotton panties. I let my eyes fall closed, lost in the sensation. "Look at me," he rasped, sliding my underwear to the side and slowly pushing two fingers inside of me.

My eyes met his, my breath hitching as he pumped his digits slowly in and out of me. I gripped his shoulders, my nails biting into his skin.

"Turn around," he ordered, pulling his hand free from between my legs.

I did as I was told and Ryatt sank down on his knees in front of me, tugging my panties down my legs before his mouth was against my clit.

I looked at our reflection in the mirror. *Handsome Ransom* was on his knees for me, giving me pleasure. And even though my entire life felt out of control, I also felt powerful. He belonged to me. He loved me.

"Ryatt..." I threaded my fingers in his hair, rocking against his mouth. My pussy throbbed as I unraveled, coating his tongue with my arousal. He groaned against me, sending a delicious vibration through my core. I shuddered, tugging at his hair. He pushed to his feet, his mouth on mine, kissing me deeply. Grabbing the back of my thighs, he lifted me and I wrapped my legs around his waist, rocking against his hard length as he pressed against my center. He walked us to my bed, laying me on my back before standing and tugging his cock free from his slacks. He pressed the head of himself against my entrance and I arched my back. His lips moved against mine as he stroked himself. He slipped the head of himself inside of me and groaned as my pussy still pulsed from my release.

"*Fuck*, Kitten," he rasped, pumping himself faster as his lips trained down my neck, his tongue hot and wet against my skin. "I want to come inside of you."

I spread my legs wider, my hands slipping under his shirt, raking my nails along his back. "Do it," I whimpered. "*Please...*"

"Look at us," he groaned. I pushed up on my elbows, looking down between us where his cock pressed against my entrance. "It's taking everything in me not to slam inside of you."

My tongue ran over my lips before I reached down between us, grabbing his thick length and stroking him. His eyes went from my hand to my face, his eyebrows pinching together. I watched as his muscles of his stomach tightened and pulled. I was in awe of watching Ryatt fuck my hand. He looked so hard yet vulnerable as he let me give him pleasure. I squeezed him tighter, speeding up my strokes.

"*Fuck*," he muttered. "*Fuck, fuck*, I *fucking* love you," he growled as his body stilled, shooting warmth inside of me as a rapture of pleasure rolled through him.

"Jesus, Christ, Kitten." He grabbed his dick rubbing it against my clit as his come dripped down my ass crack onto the bed below. "Look how pretty your pussy is, dripping with my come."

My eyes went to the mirror to take in my splayed leg, milky fluid coating my center. He pushed to his feet, shoving his cock back in his slacks before grabbing my panties and tugging them up my thighs.

"Let's go."

"I have to shower," I told him as I pushed up on my elbows.

"No time. My brothers are here. And I like the idea of you dripping all over your panties."

"They're here?"

He nodded, holding out his hand for me to take. I slid my fingers over his and let him pull me to my feet.

"How do I look?"

"Fucking perfect," he groaned, lacing our fingers together. "Let's go."

We made our way to the dining room. I took in the two men standing in front of Enzo with their backs to me. Ryatt's father said something, and they both turned around, taking me in. Their lips twisted up in heart stopping identical smiles. Their hair was dark like Ryatt's eyes the same ocean blue with swaths of gray as if an angry storm was brewing.

"Grace, this is Ryder and Ryker Cross," Ryatt introduced us. I nodded, giving them a polite smile. One of them held out a tattooed hand, his eyes dragging down my body.

"I'm Ryder," he greeted as he took my hand. Ryker slapped his palm against his brother's chest and wrapped his arms around me in a hug.

"We're family," he rasped, his hands sliding down my back as he pulled me flush against his muscular frame.

"Get the fuck off of her," Ryatt growled but he didn't sound angry, just annoyed. Ryker released me, standing to his full height. The twins were maybe an inch shorter than Ryatt, their hair had a wave to it, making it look messy, but still effortlessly styled.

"So, how am I supposed to tell you guys apart?"

Ryder and Ryker exchanged a look, a mischievous glint in their eyes. "We could show you, but I think Ryatt would get pissed."

My eyebrows knitted together in confusion as I looked at Ryatt who was shaking his head. "Keep your dicks in your pants."

"She asked," one of them shot back. I studied them, trying to see if I could spot any difference. Even the tattoos that crept up their necks and down their fingers were the same. Their sleeves were rolled up their forearms, their slacks slate gray. Even the drinks in their hands were the same amber color.

"Can I get you a drink," one of them asked me.

"Sure," I replied.

Ryatt stalked over to the bar. "I got it."

Enzo continued their conversation where he had let off as Ryatt brought me over a drink he'd mixed. I thanked him taking a tentative sip of the fruity concoction.

The front door opened, and all eyes turned to the large man who stepped inside. His beard was thick and as dark as the hair that brushed the top of his shoulders. His suit was immaculately tailored to fit his large muscular frame. When he took off his sunglasses, his eyes landing on mine with a devastating grin, the cup I was holding slipped from my fingers, splattering the red drink up my white dress.

***

44

RYATT

Grace dropped to the ground and began to pick up the shards of glass from her cup.

"Leave it," I told her, nodding to one of the staff to get the mess cleaned up.

"Ouch," she hissed, sucking her fingertip into her mouth.

I helped her to her feet and took her to the kitchen to get her cut cleaned up and bandaged.

"Sorry," she whispered.

"Don't be sorry, Kitten." I took her finger into my mouth, sucking the fresh drop of blood from the tip before holding it over the sink and dumping some peroxide over the wound. After a bandage, she was good as new. "Go get changed."

Grace nodded, pressing her lips against mine.

I watched her walk away before going back to greet Relic.

"Fuck her yet?" he asked as he pulled me in for a quick hug.

"Jesus Christ," I muttered rolling my eyes. "I didn't break the rules."

Relic took a drink from his glass, eyeing me. "So, when's the wedding?"

"I haven't even proposed to her."

He shrugged. "That shit doesn't matter. Balls in motion."

"Five weeks," Enzo clarified.

"Are you wanting to congratulate me or wanting to stick your dick in her?" I asked Relic.

"Can I answer that?" Ryder asked and I shot him a death glare as he in Ryker laughed. "Because we'd like to be second in line."

"Watch your fucking mouths," I spat.

"That's enough," Enzo warned.

Grace came back and we all fell silent as all eyes were trained on her. "Am I...interrupting?"

"Of course not," I assured her, pressing a kiss to her cheek.

"Let's eat," my father called out. We made our way to the grand dining room. I sat next to Grace, the twins took seats across from her and Relic sat on her other side. My father took his place at the head of the table.

"Aren't Arlo and Marco coming?" I asked.

"Marco is in France and Arlo had a prior engagement. But they will be at the wedding," he explained.

My hand fell to Grace's thigh, squeezing it as the staff placed the first course in front of us. The chef was at their side, explaining the meal.

I nodded to one of the helpers, pointing to our wine glasses and they were quickly filled. Grace whispered thanks before taking a large sip.

"Grace, you graduate this year, correct?" Relic asked her and she nodded.

"Yes. Ryatt and I have classes together."

"Convenient," he replied, and I rolled my eyes.

"You gonna go to college at Cali Sate?" Ryder asked.

"Yeah, you could stay with us," Ryker added.

"Um... I haven't really thought about it," Grace replied, drinking back more of her wine.

"She'll be too busy," Enzo added, his eyes meeting mine.

"It's up to her," I shot back, my eyes scanning the men around the table.

"Actually, it's up to *you*," my father corrected me.

"No, It's not. I'm not you and she's not my mother," I snapped.

Enzo let out a humorless chuckle as he wiped his mouth with his cloth napkin.

"Speaking of which, why is Marco in France?" I asked, my gaze on Relic.

"Visiting our mother," he replied, annoyance in his tone. Relic hated his father nearly as much as I hated my own.

"No doubt, making sure I *comply*."

"Ryatt," Enzo warned, and Relic cleared his throat, raising his glass.

"I for one, am very happy for you two," he toasted.

"I'm happy for *all* of us," Ryker added as he and his brother laughed.

Grace shoved her chair back and pushed to her feet. "I'm going to use the restroom."

The staff removed our plates and replaced them with the next course.

"That's enough," I bit out, my gaze locked on Rykers. "Do you want her to fucking *hate* you?" I asked. "Because it's up to her if she goes through with this. *Not* me, *not* Enzo," I gave my father a pointed glare. "Fucking *none* of us."

"She'll do it," Enzo rasped, taking a drink from his glass. "Because she loves you. She'll do anything for you. Just like your mother would for me."

"But you never loved her back," I snapped. "That's the difference between us. I would do *anything* for *her*. Fucking *try* me." I shoved to my feet, gripping my steak knife in my palm.

"Ryatt?" Grace came back into the room, her eyes scanning all of us before she hurried to my side.

"It's fine." I let my knife clatter to my plate, my eyes on her.

"*Anything*, uh?" she whispered, her eyebrow cocked and a mischievous grin playing on her lips. Her fingers laced with mine and she pressed her mouth to my cheek before her lips were next to my ear. "I'm going to see about that after dinner." My cock thickened at her words, my focus now on her and all the things I wanted to do to her.

Her attention turned to the rest of the table. "Thank you all for coming to celebrate our... future." Here eyes met mine. "To *us*." She grabbed her wine glass, raising it in the air. The others did the same before drinking. I drained the contents of my glass, slamming it back onto the table before placing a palm on each of Grace's cheeks and pulling her in to press my lips against hers. Her body melted against me, and I reluctantly pulled back to look her in the eye.

She gave me a small smile and I sighed, sinking back into my seat. Ryker and Ryder's eyes were both on me, their brows pinched together in confusion.

"What?" I asked as I picked up my silverware and took a bite of my food.

"Nothing," Ryder replied with a shrug.

"We've just never seen you calm down so fast," Ryker clarified. "She's good for you."

"She's good for all of us," Enzo added. "To bringing our families together. Salut." He drank from his glass again.

***

The second dinner was over I was in my room, packing a back for Vegas as Grace sat on my bed, her eyes heavy from the wine she'd indulged in.

"Your dad's gonna be mad," she warned. My eyes cut to her before shoving more clothes in my bag.

"I don't give a fuck."

She sighed, laying back against my pillow. "What's the plan?"

We fly to Vegas, get married, fulfil the viewing, and then I finally get to fuck you whenever I want."

"Viewing?" she asked, pushing up on her elbows.

I groaned, looking up at the ceiling before my eyes settled on her. "My brother's will need to verify that you are a virgin."

"W-what? How?" Her face paled, eyes growing wide with panic. I shook my head, swallowing against the lump in my throat.

"We don't' have to do this, Grace. I can find somewhere for you to go."

"*Me*? Like *alone*?"

I nodded.

"Ryatt, I'm not leaving you. But I need to know what to expect. I don't want to be shocked when we get in bed together on our wedding night."

"My brothers will be there with us. They'll verify your virginity and watch us consummate the marriage."

"*Watch* us?"

"The watching isn't the part that bothers me."

Her eyebrows knitted together.

"They need to verify with their hand."

Grace pushed from the bed, stalking toward me. "You're telling me your brothers are going to *finger* me on our wedding night?"

"They can technically do a lot of things. That will be up to us."

She winced, shaking her head.

"It's not too late to walk away," I reassured her, unable to keep the disappointment from my voice. I hated that I was pushing her to do this. If it's not her, it would be someone else and I couldn't imagine spending my life with anyone but Grace.

"Yes, it is," she replied, closing the gap between us and wrapping her arms around my waist. I crushed her against me, inhaling the scent of her hair before pressing my lips to the top of her head.

***

45

GRACE

We stood in the chapel, our eyes locked as we said our *I do's*. Ryatt slid a ring band onto my finger, to go with the princess cut diamond ring we'd picked out earlier in the evening. I looked down at it, taking in the four inlayed diamonds against the silver, representing all of the brothers. My gaze went to the twins and Relic who stood beside my husband. They were as much a part of this ceremony as Ryatt. But this wedding was merely a steppingstone to why we were really here. The full ceremony would still take place in a few weeks, with all the major families and business associates in attendance.

This was a way for us to control our future ourselves. Only the other brothers needed to attend the viewing. But anyone could be welcomed into the room to witness our consummation, and that was the last thing Ryatt or I wanted. And to be honest, getting drunk on the plane with all of Ryatt's brothers actually made me feel more comfortable around them.

And I knew if he was allowing this to go forward, he trusted them with me, even if he didn't particularly like them.

We drank champagne in the limo on our way back to the hotel in an attempt to loosen up. But my nerves had me on edge, knowing what lay ahead for us.

"Slow down, *wife*. You need to be coherent when we get back to our suite," Ryatt chided me as all the guys drank back their alcohol.

My cheeks heated at hearing him call me his wife for the first time, and my lips twisted up into a smirk. But as the limo slowed to a stop, my nerves got the better of me again.

One of the twins placed their hand on my knee, giving it a squeeze. "It's not going to be as bad as it sounds. You may actually enjoy it," he rasped with a wink, his tongue running out over his lower lip. "And you now have four men who will never let *anything* happen to you," he added, his face going serious. "We aren't like our fathers."

I nodded, thankful he was trying to comfort me. But nothing was going to make this moment easier. Ryatt stepped out of the car and held out his hand for me to take. I slipped out of the vehicle, my eyes dancing over the front of the hotel as the other guys got out behind me.

All eyes were on us as we stepped inside of the building and made our way to the private elevator for our suite.

Ryatt wrapped his arms around me from behind pulling me back against his chest, his lips against my ear. "I love you, wife," he whispered.

"I love you, husband," I replied as the doors sprung open.

Ryatt lifted me in his arms and carried me into the room. He didn't stop until we were in front of the large ornate bed before lowering me to my feet.

Relic grabbed a bottle of champagne and opened it, filling a glass for each of us. Ryatt handed one to me and I smiled, thanking him as I drank it back.

One of the twins pulled a white eye mask from his pocket and held it up between his fingers.

"What's that for?" I asked, my eyes flitting between all of them.

"We thought it might make it easier for you," The other twin replied. I nodded, taking another drink from my glass.

Ryatt turned on the sound system, filling the room with music before sauntering back over to me, long pieces of silk in his hand. As if reading my mind he explained, "To tie you to the bed so we can have our way with you." His voice was thick with lust, causing my stomach to clench.

Relic took my glass from my hand and one of the twins put the mask over my eyes. Ryatt's voice was at my ear, his lips moving against my skin. "Are you ready?"

I nodded, my tongue running over my lips.

"Big girl words, Kitten."

"I'm ready," I breathed as a hand went to my back, unzipping my white sundress before pushing the straps from my shoulder and causing the fabric to pool at my feet.

A hand was around my calf, and I lifted my leg, allowing them to pull off my heel before doing the same to the other.

Someone unsnapped my bra, slowly sliding it down my arms and I felt my nipples bud at the sudden rush of cold air against my skin.

The music grew louder, and I was thankful I couldn't hear them or there was no awkward silence. I was lost in the song, my head swimming from the champagne.

I was led around the bed, Ryatt's mouth was near me again, "Climb on."

I felt around before me, gripping the comforter on the bed before climbing into the center. Simultaneously, my limbs were grabbed and spread, pulling arms wide and legs splayed as soft fabric was looped around them and secured in place.

"You want to come for us, Kitten?" Ryatt asked, his heavy palm sliding up my inner thigh.

"Yes," I breathed as I felt a mouth press against my stomach, slowly trailing its way to my mound. My belly tightened as Ryatt's mouth moved over my clit, slow at first. He groaned and I felt it reverberate through every nerve ending in my body.

My lips popped open, and I shuddered as he spread me open, his tongue running against my entrance. My back arched, forgetting that there were other eyes on me besides Ryatt's. His mouth peppered kisses down the inside of my thigh and I let out a whimper, desperate to have him back at my center. But as I finger pressed inside of me, I gasped. The digit slowly pumped in and out of me before a second was added, stretching me.

And then lips circled my clit again, sucking on it before teeth slid against my aching nub. The fingers curved, hitting me just where I needed them and I pushed back against the intrusion, riding his hand, my muscles tensing as my orgasm neared.

Just as I was about to tumble over the edge, the mouth pulled back and fingers were in their place. And a mouth was closing around one of my nipples. I stilled. There was no denying it now. With a hand inside of me, one on my clit and I mouth on my breast, I knew it wasn't just Ryatt touching me.

My lower lip was pulled between someone's teeth before they sucked on the sensitive flesh. I moaned as I tongue rolled against mine. Their kiss was slow at first but soon became deeper.

My pussy was empty again, but not for long. Soon thick fingers pushed inside of me.

Two.

Then three.

My tight channel burned. Then a tongue was on my other nipples. My body writhed in pleasure, overwhelmed by the sensation of having so many mouths and hands on my body.

Then something thick nudged my entrance and I tensed. A mouth was at my ear whispering for me to relax. It was one of the twins.

"Take it like a good girl, Grace," he rasped.

Someone's fingers began to rub circles against my clit, nearly bringing me to my peak as Ryatt slammed inside of me to the hilt. I cried out but my protests were swallowed as a tongue was in my mouth again. I could tell from the beard it was Relic, his heavy palm around my throat, squeezing the sides.

Ryatt stilled, giving me time to adjust to his harsh intrusion, but the pressure on my clit made it impossible for me not to move. I pushed my hips against them, taking Ryatt deeper.

His hips began to move, slowly pumping himself in and out of me. "Good girl, Kitten," Ryatt groaned, his praise causing my pussy to pulse around him. "*Fuck*." A growl ripped from his chest as he stilled, thickening inside of me. And then I felt him fill me as my body continued to grip down, milking him of every drop he had to give me.

But the fingers on my clit kept rubbing against me, drawing out my pleasure as Ryatt pulled out of me with a hiss.

"Now leave us so I can continue fucking my wife," Ryatt ordered. After a few seconds I heard the sound of the elevator doors open and close before Ryatt pulled the mask from my eyes.

"Are you okay?" he asked. "Did I hurt you?"

"No," I reassured him. "I'm fine."

His lips pressed against mine, tenderly as his hand slipped between us and he rubbed my pussy, causing pleasure to build inside of me again. My body shook under his touch, but he didn't relent until I was shaking, coming against his fingers.

***

46

RYATT

"Next round is on me," I called out to Avery, holding up my beer. She smiled, nodding her head as she disappeared behind the bar. Relic had his gaze fixed on her ass before draining the contents of his bottle.

"I wish I had your kind of pull," he joked.

"Nah," I waved away his comment. "I'm a one-woman man." I glanced down at my wedding band.

"Hell, I don't blame ya'. Grace is some piece of ass," he quipped, raking his fingers through his coal-black hair.

"That's my wife you're talking about, man."

"I'm just sayin'. You're a lucky guy."

"Come on. Women love this whole mountain man thing you have going on." Relic has only been in charge of his crew in Fresno for a few months after his father died in a questionable boating accident. He was the oldest of my brothers at twenty-five, and the most ruthless. I'd watched him cut off a man's hand just for slapping a waitress's ass once.

The world didn't reward good deeds and hard work. We'd learned that early. Sometimes, you had to take what you wanted. It was survival. And having a man like Relic on my side came in handy over the years.

It had been nine months since the wedding in Vegas. Since then Grace and I moved into the church, and after graduation we opened our own gym in town.

When Relic came in to celebrate our opening, he brought damn near his entire crew with him, ensuring it was a success, and the perfect cover for whatever side jobs me and my brothers had going on behind the scenes. *Was It morally questionable?* Yes. But they were *mostly* victimless crimes. Underground poker nights were their favorite pastime.

"Hey, I'm not sayin' I don't get laid. But... quality over quantity," he explained. I couldn't help but laugh. I'd watched him fuck half his town, including the mayor's wife, just because he didn't like his politics.

"I hear that." I tipped the neck of my bottle toward him as Avery returned with our drinks, her tits spilling out over her crop top.

"Remember that little redhead at the fair? You were what? Fifteen?"

I barked out a laugh, picturing her on her knees behind the haunted house. "We were fucking wild."

"I still am. You're the one who grew up."

"Says the *mob boss*."

"Hey," he shushed me with a laugh. "Don't be a narc." We both chuckled before Relic cleared his throat, scraping his lip with his thumbnail. "Have you given any more thought to that thing we talked about?"

I leaned back in my seat, exhaling. "I don't know, man. I'm trying to be on the up and up now."

"Don't forget how you got there," his voice was low. "It wasn't because you played by the rules. You wouldn't have that pretty little wife and successful business without us. And it's time to fulfill your end of the agreement."

My eyes met his as I clenched my jaw. "And you'll never let me forget that you like to have your hand in *everything*."

"That's right, brother. Soon I'll be in your wife."

***

47

GRACE

I rubbed the sleep from my eyes, desperate to hang on to a few more minutes of slumber. But Ryatt had woken up in the night, like he always did, and couldn't keep his hands off me. His fingers were inside of me, slowly pumping in and out as his mouth circled my clit.

"Ryatt," I groaned. "I'm too tired."

"Go back to sleep," he rasped. "I just wanted to taste you."

I moaned as his fingers curved, rubbing against my g-spot. "How am I supposed to sleep when you're doing that?"

He chuckled, his breath blowing over my wet pussy and causing me to shiver. "I *need* you, Grace," he protested.

"Can't you jerk off like a normal guy?" I asked.

"I do jerk off, *wife*. But it's not enough." His fingers continued teasing me as he added a third. "How can you expect me to ignore you when all you have on is those sexy panties?"

"I don't sleep with more clothes on because you would just take them off me anyway," I groaned, squeezing my eyes closed as he swiped his tongue against my clit.

"If I had it my way, you'd never wear *anything*."

"If you had it your way, I'd be chained to the bed for you to use whenever you want."

He moaned against my mound, the vibration causing me to clench around his fingers. "That would be fucking *perfect*," he rasped.

"I'm more than just a vagina."

"I know, baby. You also have that sexy fucking mouth I love to shove my cock in," he teased, his fingers pumping faster. "And that cute little ass."

"Ryatt," I meant to say his name in protest, but it came out as I whimper. I watched his lips curve into a smile against my skin.

"You ready to come for me, Kitten?"

My body began to shake, waves of euphoria rippling through me as Ryatt devoured me. He didn't stop until my body was exhausted and sated.

He smirked up at me as he crawled over me, pressing the head of his length against my entrance.

"You do that just so I won't fight you when you want to have sex," I joked.

"I do it because I love the taste of your pussy," he groaned, slowly sinking inside of me. And I love those little sounds you make when you come. And I promise you, I wouldn't mind it at all if you fought me," he added with a wink.

I narrowed my eyes as he drew back, just as slowly before slamming into me to the hilt. My back bowed at the sudden aggressive intrusion.

"You need help," I taunted as he did it again.

"No, Mrs. Ransom. I just need you."

His mouth captured mine and the taste of my excitement coated my tongue.

***

I stifled a yawn as I waited in line to order my coffee.

"You look tired," Relic called from behind me.

I startled, turning to face him. "Gee, thanks. Are you following me now?"

"I am." He replied, his eyes dancing over my face. "I didn't mean it like that."

I took in his crisp white button-down, the top few buttons left open. His shoulder length hair was tied back at the nape of his neck.

"Ryatt keeping you up at night?"

My eyes widened, causing him to chuckle.

"Can't say I blame him," he added, his gaze narrowing. I felt my cheeks heat and I shook my head, causing my long chocolate hair to fall around my face. "If I spent all day around those gym bunnies, my cock would always be hard."

I screwed up my face in disgust. "I trust Ryatt."

"I know," he replied. "I'm just saying, he's only a man."

"Are you trying to make me jealous?" I asked, folding my arms across my chest.

"If I wanted to make you jealous," he replied, lowering his voice as he leaned in closer. "I'd show you my cock."

I turned to face the counter, rolling my eyes. "I have my fill of that thank you very much," my face burning when I realized how that sounded.

"I bet you do," he quipped.

I turned, smacking him playfully across his hard stomach before stepping forward to place my order. Relic held up his hand, speaking to the barista. "We'll have a vanilla latte and a venti coffee, black."

When I glanced up at him he shot me a wink as he pulled out his wallet to pay. We moved to the end of the counter to wait for our beverages.

"I can buy my own drink, you know."

"I know," he replied, clearing his throat. "But it's our job to spoil you."

My eyes cut to him as I chewed my lip. "It's Ryatt's job. He's my husband."

"You never told him, did you." It wasn't a question, but I shook my head anyway.

"Nothing to tell, Mr. Grayson."

"We both know that's not true." A slow smile spread across his lips, and I was thankful when the barista sat our drinks in front of us.

***

48

RYATT

Emma lay on her back, her legs raised, ankles crossed. I ignored the way the bottom of her ass cheeks peaked out from under her tight workout shorts that were nothing more than glorified underwear. Her hair sat in a chocolate messy bun on top her head with loose strands framing her narrow face.

"Activate your core," I instructed, putting my palm against her lower stomach to feel her muscles flex and pull as she did a crunch. "That's it. Good girl," I praised her as she blew out an exhale. "Five more."

"I'm not going to be able to move if I keep going," she joked, her skin flushed.

"Don't stop." I pressed against her belly as her body began to tremble.

Her ragged breath was coming out in shallow pants now. "I think... I'm..."

A whimper escaped her, her body vibrating beneath my touch as her eyes pierced mine.

She came. She just fucking *came*. I'd heard of it happening. They call it a coregasm. But this was the first time I'd witnessed it in the gym. And my hand was on her body. My hand is *still* on her body as she lays on the mat, her skin shimmering with a sheen of sweat. The flush of her cheeks and her lips glistened after her tongue ran out slowly to wet them. Her nipples pulled taut under her sports bra's thin blue stretchy fabric. It was causing my cock to stiffen. And there was no way for me to hide it.

"I didn't..." her voice trailed off.

I wasn't sure if I should acknowledge what had happened or pretend I didn't notice. But it was impossible to ignore the small damp spot between her still-raised legs.

I decided to be professional. "It's completely natural." I slid my hand from her soft skin and pushed to my feet.

I held out my hand for her to take, and she did, allowing me to pull her up.

"Now I get why so many women love to work out."

I let out a laugh, turning away from her and desperately trying to will my cock to relax. I'd seen Emma around school before but she had been a junior last year and I was preoccupied with Grace, so we'd never interacted before.

"Can't wait to find out what a runner's high is," she added.

"I run every day. You're welcome to join me sometime if you want."

"Thanks," she replied as I turned back to face her. "Are you sure I didn't make this weird?"

"It's not really something you had any control over."

"It just sort of... happened," she explained, and I wished she'd quit talking about it so my dick could relax. "If I'm honest it's never been that easy."

I ran my hand through my messy hair, wishing I could wear my ring when I worked out, but I hadn't wanted to risk getting caught on something.

I grabbed my shirt I'd hung over the treadmill and tugged it over my body. I shouldn't know how hard it is for her to achieve an orgasm. And I shouldn't know how her body trembles when it happens.

I just hoped she didn't think it was my intention to make her get off. I was as shocked as she was when it happened.

***

"A coregasm?" Relic repeated with a laugh. "Jesus Christ."

"It wasn't intentional," I reiterated.

"Bet it was still hot as fuck." He took a long pull from his beer as we both stared off at the bonfire. "Back in the day, you would have railed her on the elliptical."

I didn't reply. All I could picture was Emma's face and the way her eyes locked onto mine.

"You gonna fuck her?"

"What? No. I'm married. I love my wife."

"What's not to love? But what you could do with that gym bunny isn't about up here," he pointed to his heart.

"You think I'm going to get distracted? Huh? Let you fuck my wife?"

"No. I'm going to *fuck* your *wife* because that is the rule. She's an *offering*, Ryatt. And that is the only reason she isn't chained to Luca's bed right now. She belongs to *all* of us. Would it kill you to think with your cock every once and a while? Might make this a little easier on yourself."

I rolled my eyes before smiling at Grace as she came out of the back door with fresh beers, her oversized shirt nearly swallowing her shorts. I took in her long-tanned legs, wanting to have them wrapped around my shoulders.

"I do. That's why I have Grace," I shot back as she approached, before pulling her onto my lap and pressing a kiss to the side of her neck.

She let out a giggle, wiggling her ass against my lap. I gripped her hips, tugging back over my length, concealed by my gray sweatpants.

"Why do you *have* me?" she asked, causing Relic to chuckle.

"So, I can fuck you whenever I want," I whispered in her ear. Her laughter echoed off the trees. "Are you *drunk*, Kitten?" I asked her, my fingers sliding along her ribs, slipping under her threadbare vintage Doors t-shirt. My thumb ran along the underside of her breast as a shiver rolled through her.

"Maybe."

"She's wasted," Relic taunted, earning him a glare.

"Careful, *wife*," my lips brushed against her ear. "Someone may take advantage of you." I dragged my hand down her stomach, teasing the edge of her sleep shorts with my fingertips. I followed her gaze and glanced through the flames of the fire, my eyes landing on Relic who was watching us intently as he took another drink of his beer. She was the first woman I'd ever had that I didn't let him take a shot at. And he resented me for it. My brothers shared everything. And now that it was required of me, I couldn't bring myself to do it.

"He can't see my hand under this shirt," I reassured her as I slipped my fingers under the elastic band of her bottoms, brushing over the top of her mound and causing her to inhale sharply. Her hips pressed back, rocking against my length.

Her chest was rising and falling rapidly, nipples tenting the fabric.

"Spread your legs a little wider for me, baby."

She slid her bare toes across the dirt, her back pressing against my chest.

"Good girl." I moved my hand lower, brushing the pad of my finger across her clit.

"We have a guest," she whispered, louder than intended in her inebriated state. "He can see us."

"Is that why your pussy is so wet?"

Her cheeks darkened. I nuzzled against her neck, sucking the thin skin between my teeth as I slowly rubbed circles against her nub.

"I know you like to be watched."

Relic moved his palm against the front of his dark slacks as he watched Grace fuck my hand, beneath her pajamas.

"You do this shit just to make me jealous," he groaned, and Grace's lips twisted up in a smirk.

"Stop being such a player and you could get laid whenever you want," she teased. "I'm sure there is no shortage of women wanting to wed *Relic Grayson*."

"Or Ryatt could learn to share," he snapped back, an edge to his tone.

I rolled my eyes, spreading Grace's pussy open with my fingers before teasing her entrance. I shoved two fingers inside her, rubbing the heel of my hand against her clit and causing her to whimper. Her hips began to rock, stroking my straining cock with her ass.

"Grace doesn't want to fuck you," I replied to Relic as her pussy began to clench around my digits. "Do you, *Grace?*"

"No." She shook her head, her mouth open as she tumbled over the edge, her juices coating my fingers.

Relic flinched at her words, his jaw ticking. He was pissed. *Good.* He needed to be reminded that he doesn't always get what he wants.

***

I couldn't sleep. My eyes flitted to the alarm clock that read two thirty in the morning. My cock was stiff from a dream I'd had of Emma at the gym, her body shaking as she came undone beneath me, but in my subconscious it was Grace coming for me on the floor of our gym.

I pictured my fingers rubbing the damp spot on her shorts, telling her to keep going. Wanting to make her come again.

I slid my hand under the sheet and gripped my cock as I glanced over at Grace. The sheet was tugged down from tossing and turning, causing her right breast to be exposed. I knew if I pulled it lower, she'd only be wearing her panties.

I tightened my grip on myself and slowly pulled my length. My hand drifted lower, cupping my balls before I pushed the sheet down and reaching over and rubbing my fingers over Grace's panties. She groaned as I settled myself between her legs, pressing my lips against the damp fabric.

"Mmm... what are you doing?" she asked, her voice rough from sleep.

"I want to eat your pussy," I replied, tugging down her underwear to expose her bare mound.

Grace's fingers knotted through my hair as I licked her clit.

"It's the middle of the night."

"You're my wife. I can fuck you whenever I want." I tugged her underwear down her legs and tossed them on the floor before spreading her thighs wide. "You're so fucking pretty," I praised her as I spread her lower lips, rubbing my thumb over her little bundle of nerves. Her back bowed as she pushed back against my touch, letting out a needy whimper.

"Do you think it will always be like this?" she asked as my tongue ran against her slit. "We'll never get tired of fucking each other?"

"How could I get tired of *this*?" I asked, sucking her clit into my mouth. "You taste so sweet."

"God, I love your mouth," she whispered.

"Come here." I pushed to my knees to climb beside her. "I want you to ride my face."

Grace raked her teeth over her lower lip as she got on her knees. I knew she was shy when it came to sex, but she didn't need to be. Her body was fucking perfect. Her tits filled my hand and were perky with pale pink nipples I loved to suck on. And her cunt was tight and milked my cock every time I made her come.

I laid on my back, rubbing the inside of Grace's thigh. "Come on, baby. I want your pussy on my mouth."

Her cheeks darkened, her brown hair falling over her face as she slowly placed a leg on the other side of my shoulder. I grabbed her thighs, tugging her down and causing her to yelp as my tongue delved into her tight cunt.

"Oh..." she gasped.

"Grab the headboard," I ordered.

Grace did as she was told, gripping the top of the bed as I moved her hips, latching onto her clit. My eyes stared up at her tits, her nipples hard and begging to be touched. Like she could read my mind one of her hands gripped onto her breast, kneading it as she began to ride my face.

"Don't stop," she whimpered, like it was even an option.

"I want you to come on my tongue," I rasped.

Her tight body began to quiver. I gripped her thighs bruisingly as her hips continued to rock.

"Please." Her fingers threaded into my hair as her hips bucked. "Ryatt," she moaned, coating my tongue in her juices.

***

49

GRACE

I rubbed my temple, my head throbbing from drinking too much last night. I could still feel the warmth of the fire on my skin, the heat from Relic's gaze as he watched us. Humiliation flooded me. I knew before I met Ryatt, he and Relic did a lot of questionable things together. And sometimes that included women. Something about that disgusted and intrigued me at the same time. Everyone wanted them and would take them any way they could have them. But I didn't want to share him, or myself with anyone.

Ryatt wanted what he couldn't have. And eventually, he changed for me. But every once and awhile, we danced along that line of right and wrong. He never pushed me farther than I was willing to go. But lately, that line feels like it's blurring.

Ryatt's hand slid across my belly from behind as he pressed a kiss to the back of my head. "Good morning, wife."

"Good morning," I croaked, gripping the edge of the counter.

"Sleep well?"

I spun in his arms, smirking. "You mean when I wasn't riding your face in the middle of the night?"

His eyebrow cocked as he leaned in closer, his lips brushing mine. "Are you saying you didn't enjoy it?"

"No. I'm saying it's hard to function on three hours of sleep with a hangover."

The corners of his mouth twisted up in a smirk. "You did drink a lot last night."

"Yeah," I agreed. "*Way* too much."

"Gotta admit. Drunk Grace is a fun one." Ryatt ran his fingers through his dark hair, causing it to stick up haphazardly.

"Yeah. I *bet* you enjoyed it. So did *Relic*."

His eyes snapped to mine as he grabbed the coffee pot to pour himself a mug. "I seem to remember you enjoying yourself as well." His eyes narrowed as he took a tentative sip of his beverage.

"I-I did," I shook my head. "But stuff like that can't keep happening." I looked at my hands, where my fingers tangled together.

Ryatt stepped closer, grabbing my wrist and pressing my palm against his sweatpants. His length was thick and hard beneath my touch. "I'm not mad, baby. I don't mind if you like to have a little fun." He tucked a long dark strand of my hair behind my ear. "You forget how different this is for me."

"Trust me, I don't forget how you used to be. But that's not *me*. That's not *us*."

"Are you trying to remind *me*, or *yourself*?" he bit out as he leaned back against the counter, taking another sip of his coffee. My eyes roamed over his bare chest to the v-muscles that disappeared behind the low-slung waistband of his sweats. My gaze settled on the very prominent length below the fabric.

"I just feel like it's *never* enough for you. *I'm* never enough –"

Ryatt sat down his mug and closed the gap between us in two large strides. Grabbing my ass, he lifted me effortlessly into his arms. I wrapped my legs around him as my back was pressed against the fridge. His hips surged forward, and I groaned as he rubbed against my center.

"You're right," his eyes searched mine. "I can never get enough of you. All I think about is being inside of you, tasting you, making you moan my fucking name with those sexy fucking lips." He rocked against me again, slowly, deliberately. "*That*," his hand slid along my cheek. "That look in your eye right now. I don't want you to ever look at another human being the way you look at me."

"Never," I whispered against his lips before his tongue slowly delved inside my mouth. I pushed back against him, desperate to have him inside of me again.

"But that doesn't mean I can't enjoy you in every sick and depraved way my dirty mind can think of, right?" He asked with a low laugh.

I smacked against his chest playfully, shaking my head. "Way to ruin the moment."

He lowered me to the ground, rolling his eyes. "If you got to fuck something as beautiful as you, would you be able to keep your hands to yourself?" he asked, causing my cheeks to heat.

"*You're* beautiful too, Mr. Ransom," I shot back, "But so was Lucifer."

That comment earned me a heart-stopping lopsided grin. "Did you just compare me to the *Devil*?"

"Maybe."

"Afraid I'm gonna fall from *Grace*?" he asked.

I shook my head. "I'm afraid you'll pull me down with you."

***

50

RYATT

I'd just gotten done doing pull-ups as my eyes locked on Emma's. She smiled, giving me a little wave before disappearing into the locker room. A few minutes later she was making her way to my side.

I tugged my earbud from my ear, giving her a chaste hello.

"You look like you're working up a sweat."

I smirked. "That's the general idea," I quipped, causing her to let out a little giggle.

"I was thinking, maybe you could help me again. I really want to develop a workout routine for my body."

With her words my eyes drifted over her, taking in her subtle curves.

"Are you looking to lose weight, bulk up, tone, or maintain?"

"I'm not sure." She turned around, looking at herself in the mirror, and giving me an unobstructed view of her ass in too little shorts. "What do you think? Do I need to work on my butt?"

I shook my head, clearing my throat. "I think that should be up to you. Don't change yourself for someone else." My words rang hollow from the advice I didn't take myself.

She eyed me for a moment. "If you have a minute, I'd like to knock out a set of crunches."

My gaze went to the other people in the gym. It was relatively empty this time of day. No one was paying attention to me or my inner turmoil over helping this patron. I quickly nodded and followed her to the mats in the far-right corner.

"I really appreciate it," she added, lowering herself to her back. "I just want to make sure I'm doing it right."

"It's no problem." My mouth was suddenly parched, remembering the last time she was in this position. "I help anyone who needs it," I added, so she didn't think I was giving her special treatment. "Lift your legs and cross your ankles. I pressed against the back of her thigh to raise her higher.

She locked her hands behind her head, her gaze on me.

"Look up at the ceiling. Make sure you're not straining your neck. Good girl."

She pulled herself up, exhaling.

"Perfect. Tighten," I ordered, placing my hand on her stomach, my fingers on the slick material of her shorts. "That's it. Squeeze your muscles."

"Like that?" she asked, her eyes finding mine. I clenched my jaw, rubbing my hand over her lower stomach.

"You feel it. Right here?" I asked.

"Yes," she sighed.

"Perfect." I pressed my free palm back against the underside of her thigh, helping her keep in the correct position. "Just like that." Her muscles quivered beneath my touch. "Don't quit," I warned, watching as her brows pulled together.

"But –"

My eyes cut to hers. "Don't stop, Emma. Not until your body is shaking."

She licked her lips, her muscles pulling and tightening before a gasp escaped her, followed by a whimper. I gripped the back of her thigh tighter. "Another."

She did as she was told, doing four more before she collapsed on her back, a sated look on her face as her arms fell to her sides, her thighs splaying. Her body continued to tremble, and I waited until the last rapture passed through her before pulling my hands from her hot skin.

"Good girl. You did six more than last time," I smiled down at her as I shot her a wink.

"Maybe I should *come* more often," she joked, and my body tensed from her words, glancing around to make sure no one had heard her.

"It's important not to overwhelm yourself. Twice a week is a good place to start."

Emma pushed herself up on her elbows, a bead of sweat rolling down her chest and disappearing between her tits.

The sound of loud chatter by the door grabbed my attention. I glanced over, giving Relic a nod. He'd brought two other friends with him, ready to work out. His eyes went to Emma, a smirk on his lips as he took her in.

I stood to my full height, holding out a hand for her. She took it and yelped as I pulled her to her feet.

"Friends of yours?" she asked, her smile broadening. I nodded in their direction. "Yeah. Something like that," I replied, rubbing my palm against the back of my neck as Relic approached.

"Hey, Ryatt. Working up a sweat?" he asked, his eyes raking over Emma's tits.

"What the hell are you doing here, man? I thought you had a meeting."

He shook his head, pulling his shirt over his head. Emma's eyes widened, taking in his tattooed chest. Relic was built, his shoulders wider than mine, his muscles thick. Judging by her reaction, she was impressed.

"This is Emma," I introduced. "Emma, this is Relic, my brother."

"I see the resemblance," she replied, holding out her hand for him. He took it, pressing his lips to the back of it, and I stifled a laugh.

"Do you come here often?" she chirped, pushing her tits out.

"Probably not as often as you," he quipped, his eyes flitting to me.

I narrowed my gaze at him. "I'm gonna make sure machines are wiped down," I told him, clapping my hand on his shoulder. "Behave, man."

***

An hour later Relic was leaning on the desk by the entrance, covered in sweat. "There is no way you aren't fucking that."

My eyes went to Emma across the room, catching her watching me, before I shook my head. "I'm not."

"Mind if I take a shot at her?"

"I do, actually."

Relic's eyebrows pulled together. "You can't have them both."

"I don't want them both." Even if I did find her attractive, I wasn't going to act on it. And things between Relic and I had been strained since I settled down. I didn't want him having another reason to spend more time in my territory.

Relic smirked, looking over his shoulder at Emma. "Awfully possessive of a girl you don't want."

I rolled my eyes. "Don't you have a business to run?"

He nodded. "I'll see you later, Ryatt. Tell Grace I said hello."

***

51

GRACE

The front door closed, just as I pulled the meatloaf from the oven. "I wasn't sure you were coming home for dinner," I quipped.

"Sorry. Long day," Ryatt groaned, pressing a kiss to my temple. "Relic brought some friends in today."

"It's good for business." I replied, thinking of the picture he'd sent me of the girl flirting with Ryatt at the gym. I tried not to let it bother me. Ryatt was sexy and powerful. Women would always want him. But I'd be lying if I said I wasn't insecure.

"All I could think about was coming home to you," he murmured as his lips pressed against my shoulder, his fingers skimming along where my dress fell against my thigh. I let my eyes fall closed, relishing in his touch.

"Maybe we can get away. Our first anniversary is coming up," I glanced over at him, hopeful. Ryatt smirked against my skin. "What's the point when you know we won't leave the bed anyway?" His hand snaked behind me, grabbing my ass and causing me to yelp.

"Come on, Ryatt. We could make love on the beach or in a cabin in the woods."

"The woods?" he pulled back, his face screwed up in disgust. "What about snakes and ticks? And I don't even want to think about where you'll get sand if we fuck on the beach."

"Fine," I let out a frustrated sigh as I swatted his hand from my ass. "What about a cruise?"

Ryatt gripped my legs, lifting me onto the counter before settling between my parted thighs. "How about here in our kitchen?" His lips found my neck, sucking and licking the flesh below my ear. He pushed the strap of my sundress from my shoulder, pressing his lips against me before tugging it lower to free my left breast. I gasped, my fingers threading in his hair as he sucked my nipple into his mouth, drawing it into a peak before doing the same to the other.

I let my head fall back, closing my eyes as he pushed my skirt up to my waist, gripping my panties. "I can't get enough of you, Kitten," he groaned, his lips moving against my inner thigh. I let him push my legs apart. He tugged me closer to the edge, and I had to brace myself on the counter as his hot breath blew against the apex of my thighs.

"You can have me wherever you want me, Ryatt," I replied as his tongue ran along the thin fabric, pressing against my clit.

Ryatt stood, towering over me as he tugged my panties down my hips and tossed them to the floor.

"How about I just eat you for dinner?" He sank down, running the flat of his tongue against my slit, causing me to let out a moan.

348

"So, I take this as you forgot your dad was coming by to discuss expanding the business to San Diego."

His head snapped up. "Shit," He groaned.

"You need to get ready. Wear that blue button-down I got you. It matches your eyes."

"Why? I'm not trying to fuck my dad."

I rolled my eyes. "And we need to show him you're not some deviant who spends all day trying to get inside of his *almost* stepdaughter."

"Wow, that was *oddly* fucking hot," he muttered.

"You need therapy."

"I need your pussy." He leaned forward, swirling my tongue around my clit.

"Ryatt," I protested, pushing against his shoulders. "You worked hard for this."

"I am hard," He groaned, spreading my legs wider.

"No," I giggled. "*Worked* hard."

"I did. I earned this hot little cunt against my mouth."

"And you can have it. *After* the meeting."

He pushed to his feet, running his tongue over his lower lip, swiping away my juices. "I'm going to make you pay later for making me wait." He warned me and I felt my cheeks go hot but gave him a nod because if we kept arguing he was going to get his way.

"Whatever you want," I placated.

His eyes went dark as he leaned in closer to me. "You couldn't handle the things I want to do to you," he bit out before turning and stalking toward our room to get ready.

***

His father arrived an hour later, a perpetual scowl on his face, followed by Relic and the twins.

"Enzo," I greeted him with the biggest smile I could muster for someone I hated. "It's good to see you."

"How have you been?" he asked, smiling back.

"Things have been great. The gym is doing amazing," I replied, giving each of the brothers a friendly hug.

"Where is Ryatt?"

Ryatt turned the corner, his face hardening as he took in his brothers, nodding to them.

"I made meatloaf," I told them, hoping to ease some of the tension.

Enzo's eyes danced around the room.

"Would you guys like a drink?" I asked, holding up a bottle of scotch.

"Hell, yeah," one of the twins called out, pressing a kiss to my cheek as the other twin lifted the bottle from my hand.

"Make yourselves at home," I groaned, rolling my eyes as I turned to the cabinets and pulled out glasses.

"I'll take wine," Enzo replied, following Ryatt and Relic into the dining room.

I snatched the bottle of liquor back from the twins. "This isn't a frat house," I warned, eyeing their nearly full glasses. "Which one are you?" I asked, my eyes drifting to the twin leaning back against the counter, drinking his alcohol as if it was water.

"Ryder," he replied with a panty melting smirk.

"It's actually really easy to tell us apart," Ryker chimed in. "We could show you."

I narrowed my eyes, taking Ryder's glass and drinking back a sip of the harsh liquid. "I don't think Enzo would enjoy your guys having a *you know what* measuring contest at the dinner table."

"*You know what*?" Ryder laughed, taking a step closer so I could smell the spice of the scotch on his breath. "We've had our tongues inside of you, Princess. No need to be shy now."

"And it's not the size that's different. It's the piercings," Ryker clarified.

I rolled my eyes, feeling my cheeks heat. "Can you two please behave. Just for like an hour? Two hours tops?"

They looked at each other before their eyes landed back on me as I poured a glass of wine for Enzo. "Fine. You get two hours. But after that, we're getting drunk," Ryder conceded.

***

52

GRACE

Two and a half hours later I was pouring drinks for all of us as we sat around the table, playing cards in hand.

I had no idea what I was doing and the drinks didn't help. Ryder was at my side, trying to explain the rules of the game and Relic and Ryatt discussed business. Ryker was across from me, a mischievous smirk on his face as he laid down his hand.

Ryder let out a string of expletives, taking my cards from my hand and tossing them on the pile in the center of the table. "Fuck this. You cheat," he scolded his brother.

"I didn't cheat. You just suck," Ryker snapped back before taking a drink from his glass.

"She sucks," Ryder clarified, pointing to me.

"Hey," I yelled, hitting him playfully across the stomach with the back of my hand. "I do, actually. Very well."

That got Ryatt's attention and he shot me a wink. "Very true."

"Prove it," Ryker teased, his eyes narrowing on me.

My face grew hot under his stare, and I shook my head.

"Never have I ever... had a threesome," Ryker called out, holding up his glass. All four men took a drink. My eyes went to Ryatt's, my stomach churning. "Don't worry princess. Your times coming," Ryker added.

"Never have I ever... had a piercing," Ryder called out and he and his twin drank again. So did I, pointing to my earlobes. "That doesn't count," he groaned.

"Fine. Whatever," I replied. "My turn." My eyes danced around the table. The twins were making me feel like a prude and it was grating my nerves. "Never have I ever... made a girl come."

They chuckled, taking a drink before I picked up my glass and took a healthy swig, causing their jaws to drop.

"You're kidding," Relic called out over the twin's laughter.

"Yourself doesn't count," Ryker teased. I rolled my eyes.

"Are you serious, Kitten?" Ryatt rasped, his eyes narrowed.

I shrugged. "I went to an all-girls school."

"I want details." Ryder slid closer to me.

"It was n-nothing," I stammered. "We were just messing around."

"Come on, Princess. Are we talking fingers, mouths, tribbing?" Ryder's tongue slid out over his lower lip.

"I'm not talking about this," I pushed from my seat and made my way to the kitchen.

"You brought it up," Ryker called after me.

I grabbed a charcuterie tray I'd purchased earlier from the fridge, when arms snaked around my waist, pulling me back against their hard chest. "I want details," Ryatt rasped against my ear, his length thick against my ass. I laughed, wiggling out of his arms and making my way back to the table, setting the food down for the boys.

Ryker's hand grabbed my wrist before I could turn away, and his eyes locked on mine. "Truth or dare, Princess."

"Truth." My heart was racing, and I knew he could feel it under the thin skin of my wrist. He didn't release me.

"Did you enjoy your wedding night with us?" he asked.

My eyes danced around the room. They already knew the answer to that question. "Obviously," I muttered.

"So, when are we going to get to do it again?" Ryder asked. I shrugged as Ryatt pulled me down on his lap, his arm banded around my waist.

"The year isn't up yet," Ryatt reminded them.

"Soon," Relic replied, taking a pull from his beer.

"Grace will fulfill her duties as offering," Ryatt growled, his arm tightening around my middle.

"Maybe she doesn't have it in her," Ryder added, egging them on. "I'm not sure you could handle us, Princess," his gaze slid down my body as he struggled to suppress a smirk.

Their tones were getting more serious, and I wanted to diffuse the situation. "Truth or dare?" I asked Ryker.

"Dare," his eyebrow rose.

"I dare you..." I thought over my options. "To show me your piercings."

Relic choked on his drink, and Ryder cheered, "Fuck yeah."

Ryker's eyes narrowed. "You gotta make me hard first," he shot back.

I licked my lips, my heart racing. "My friend and I were having a sleepover, watching a really *intense* movie. And we were talking about it, and what we thought we would like." All eyes were locked on mine. "And then...we showed each other how we like to touch ourselves. And then we did it to each other." My face felt like it was on fire.

"Were you naked?" Ryker asked.

"Panties and a t-shirt," I replied.

"Did she touch you like this?" Ryatt's grip remained tight around me, seatbelting me against him. But his fingers slid up my inner thigh, pushing my skirt up until the pads of his fingers rubbed over my center. My lips popped open with a gasp as he pressed against me in small circle motions. "Your panties are damp, Kitten," he groaned against my ear as he thickened beneath my ass. His fingers pushed the fabric to the side, sliding the pad of his finger against my slit before circling my clit again. One thing I could count on was Ryatt never passing up the opportunity to watch or be watched. And judging by the way he was pushing his cock against me from behind, he was no longer upset about his brothers. His only concern was getting me off. He pushed two fingers inside of me, slowly pumping them in and out.

Ryker pushed to his feet, standing in front of me as he undid his slacks, pulling out his cock that rivaled my husband's. He stroked himself, a cocky smirk on his lips as I took him in, counting the barbells that lined the underside of his thick length. There were four maybe more.

"What do you think, Princess? Imagine how good this is going to feel inside of you," Ryker rasped.

"Clear the table," Ryatt ordered, and his brothers did so without protest. His arm released me, his fingers pulling free from my center as he grabbed my hips and stood me up. "Lay down," he rasped.

53

GRACE

Relic grabbed my hips, hoisting me up onto the wooden surface. Ryatt reached under my skirt, tugging my panties down before handing them to Ryder who held them up to his nose, inhaling my scent. Ryatt shoved my knees wide, kissing his way down my inner thigh before his mouth was on my pussy, licking up my juices. I watched as Ryder pulled out his cock, pierced at the tip as well as a few barbells like his brother. He wrapped my panties around his length and began to stroke himself. His gaze was on my lips, his brothers between my thighs.

"I thought you didn't want to share me?" My voice was thick with lust.

"He doesn't care about that. He just wants to be a part of it," one of the twins chimed in.

"We used to share all the time," the other twin added.

"Grace is different," Ryatt rasped.

"Is she?" Relic asked. "Her pussy is wet for us. She wants us. Why deny her the pleasure?"

Relic unzipped my skirt at the hip and slid it off, so my mound was exposed to them, his view unobstructed. Then he pushed my shirt up over my tits, palming one of them before tugging the fabric over my head.

I lay before them, legs splayed, completely nude as I had on our wedding night. But this time. I wasn't blindfolded or tied in place. Ryatt's fingers pushed back inside of me, and I arched my back, pushing my chest in the air. Ryder groaned, taking my nipple into his mouth, swirling his tongue against my flesh until it budded.

"You want to come for my brothers, Kitten?" Ryatt asked. I nodded, overcome with need. "Big girl words, baby."

"I want to come for you," I moaned as Relic pulled out his cock, stroking himself as his free hand rubbed my clit. Ryatt wasted no time, pulling out his own dick, pressing the head of himself against my entrance.

One of the twins captured my mouth, their tongue swirling against mine and leaving my breathless before the pulled back. Ryker was staring down at me with lust filled eyes, his teeth pushing into his lower lip as the tip of his cock brushed against my mouth. My tongue ran out, brushing away the bead of precum on his skin and he hissed. "Fuck, Princess," he bit out as he slipped himself into my mouth. I circled my lips around him, sucking.

Before I knew what was happening a large hand grabbed my wrist, wrapping my fingers around their cock, guiding me to stroke them slowly. Then a cock was in my other hand, my palm gliding against cool metal and thick flesh. I was completely consumed by them, my pussy pulsing. Ryatt pulled himself free from me before his mouth was on my cunt again. I tried to cry out, but the sound was muffled as Ryker came down my throat, hissing as I swallowed back everything he gave me.

"Fuck, Princess," he rasped, pulling his length from me before his lips pressed against mine again, fucking my mouth slowly with his tongue.

Relic released my hand and settled between my legs, his beard tickling my thighs as he latched his lips around my clit, sucking it into his mouth.

"Oh," I cried out, rutting against his face as Ryder nudged my lips with the head of his cock, the cold metal sliding over my tongue as I took his length back into my throat. Tears ran down my temples as he fucked my mouth hard and fast, his fingers tangled in my hair and holding me still as his hips moved.

Relic shoved two fingers inside of me and my pussy pulsed around them. "How many times do you think we can make her come?" One of the twins asked.

"We have all night to find out," the other replied.

My body shook and moaned around Ryder's cock, causing him to come as I unraveled against Relic's face. He licked me clean before rounding the table and holding his length next to my face. I took it without protest. He was thick and I wasn't sure I would be able to accommodate him, but he went slowly, gentle even. It was in complete contrast to his appearance. He was the type of guy you would think would through you over his shoulder and fuck you until your couldn't walk. "That's it, Grace. Take it like a good girl," he rasped as Ryatt's cock pushed back inside of my pussy. His fingers bit into my hips and he fucked me hard. Slamming into me to the hilt. Relic's eyes never left mine, watching as I sucked him back further, stretching my throat around him. His fingers stroked the side of my neck, feather soft as if I might break beneath him. "Shh..." he whispered as I let out a whimper. "That's it, sweetheart. Take me all the way."

I relaxed my throat, wanting to please him, to please all of them.

"Fuck, she's a natural," I heard one of the twins say.

Ryatt stilled, his cock thickening before I felt him release, pumping warm liquid inside of me. He came so much I could feel it dripping down my ass to the table below. He pulled himself free, his fingers running over my sticky slit before rubbing my clit again.

"That's it. That's it," Relic rasped. "Just like that, baby. So fucking good," he groaned, coming against my tongue before pulling his cock from my throat and pressing his lips softly against my forehead.

I struggled to slow my breathing, splayed across the table as the men gathered my clothing, dressing me as if I was a doll, praising me for taking them so well and how they couldn't wait to do more things to me in the future.

I found myself wanting more of them too. No longer worried they would hurt or take advantage of me. Ryatt clearly had rules in place and not once did someone cross a line he'd drawn.

Once my clothing was back in place, Ryatt lifted me in his arms and carried me to our bedroom. I nuzzled against his chest, listening to the steady thudding of his heart, my eyes falling closed. He laid me on our bed, pressing his lips against my temple. "Get some rest, Kitten. I'll wake you later for some more fun."

***

54

RYATT

"This is an easy trail," I informed Emma, tugging my foot to the back of my thigh, stretching. We'd been working out together for nearly three weeks now. She finally decided to take me up on the offer to run with me.

"I think I can handle it." She shot back, pulling her hair up into a high ponytail.

I smirked. "If you need to stop just let me know. I usually go for a few miles."

She nodded and we began to jog at a leisurely pace to get warmed up. "So, have you always been this into working out?" she asked.

"My wife and I own the gym, actually."

"Wife?" Her gaze fell to my hand.

"I don't wear my ring when I work out. Not safe with all the equipment."

She nodded as I began to pick up the pace. "How about you? Any boyfriend? Fiancé?"

"No. Just me. Perpetually alone."

I chuckled. "What's that mean?"

Emma shrugged her ponytail swaying from side to side with each step, perspiration starting to cause her skin to glisten in the sunshine that filtered through the trees. "Um... I'm just not good at focusing all my attention on someone else. You know? I can barely take care of myself."

"Maybe you need someone who can take care of *you*."

"Do guys like that even exist?" she asked, smiling over at me. "All the ones I've met think I'm their mother." She made a face, and I chuckled. "They can't cook, make their own appointments..."

"Maybe you're not looking in the right places. They're out there," I reassured her.

"Like your brother? What's his name? Relic?"

I barked out a laugh. "Relic is good for a lot of things, but I don't think he's what you're looking for."

"Why not?"

I glanced over at her, not sure if I wanted to elaborate. "He likes to indulge in certain things."

"Like *drugs*?"

I laughed again. "No. Women. Lots of women."

She shrugged, scrunching up her button nose.

"But if you're not looking for a commitment, I can hook you guys up." I cocked an eyebrow, glancing over at her. "I mean, you two met at my gym so I'd feel kind of responsible if I didn't at least warn you..."

"Warn me?"

"Relic isn't the type of guy to buy you flowers and have a romantic evening if you know what I mean."

"He likes to fuck," she shot back. "I mean, what guy doesn't?"

I shrugged in agreement. "Just don't take it out on my business if he breaks your heart. The gym is not responsible for your sex life. We only try to help improve how you look naked," I joked.

"Well, I mean, I have gotten off in the gym more than I have at home in the last month," she whispered, giving me a devilish smirk. My eyes lingered on her lips for a beat.

"I kind of already have my eye on someone," she added.

"No kidding," I muttered, trying to focus on my pacing and not her.

"Ouch," she cried out, slowing to a stop.

"What's wrong? Twist an ankle?"

"No. It's a cramp. Oh, my God," she groaned, grabbing the back of her thigh.

"Here." I tugged my t-shirt over my head and laid it on the trail. "Lay on your back. I'll help you."

Emma gingerly lowered herself to the ground. I sank down to my knees, straightening her left leg before raising the right, looping it over my shoulder. "This is going to hurt. I'm going to stretch you out." I warned as I pushed forward. She hissed, her hands going to my shoulders, her nails biting crescents into my skin.

"Relax," I groaned, rocking forward again as my fingers kneaded the back of her thigh. Her chest was rising and falling rapidly as she panted. My eyes roamed over her face, trying to pretend I didn't notice how her hooded eyes flitted to my mouth, her tongue darting out to wet her own lips. "How's that feel?" I asked.

"It hurts," she exhaled. I continued to massage her, rocking further forward, careful to keep from touching her anywhere else.

"If someone saw us, they'd get the wrong idea," she whispered.

"What idea is that?" I asked.

"That maybe you were cheating on your wife." Her eyebrow rose.

"I wouldn't do that." I pulled back, releasing the tension in her thigh muscle.

"She's a lucky woman."

I pushed to my feet, holding out my hand for her to take. Her soft fingers slid against my palm, and I tugged her to her feet before grabbing my shirt and shaking the dirt and leaves from the fabric.

"I'm the lucky one."

Her nose scrunched as the corners of her lips twisted up in a smirk. "I don't know about that. You're the first man that could make me come without ever getting into my pants." My jaw tensed before she let out a giggle. "You should see your face."

I groaned as I fought a smirk, letting my shoulders fall as I shook my head.

"Don't worry. Our secret is safe with me," she shot over her shoulder as she began to jog again.

I stalked after her, falling into a steady rhythm.

"I don't like to keep secrets from my wife," I called out. Emma glanced back over her shoulder at me, her eyes sparkling mischievously.

"So, you told her about it?" she asked.

"No." I cleared my throat, regretting going off into the woods with her. Emma came to a stop, her hands on her hips as she turned to face me. My eyes fell to her hardened nipples beneath her sports bra before I yanked my gaze back to hers. "Emma, I know you're just having fun and joking around, but if someone overheard you, it could destroy my life."

She took a step toward me, craning her neck to meet my gaze. "I have no intention of telling your wife that you can make me wet just by telling me I'm a good girl," she continued to tease. I set my jaw, the muscle jumping beneath the skin as I tried to find a delicate way to tell Emma that her behavior needed to change.

"Right now, you're being a very *bad* girl," I replied, my eyes narrowing.

She pressed her teeth into her lower lip. "Oh, I think I like that too," she replied, her breasts pushing against my chest as she inhaled. "You gonna punish me now?"

I grabbed her shoulders, pushing her back a step before letting my hands fall to my sides, regretting touching her at all.

"Emma, I like you. You're funny and willing to take on challenges. But this," I motioned between us. "Can't go anywhere. Do you understand?"

She nodded. "Does that mean you won't be making me come anymore?"

I pinched the bridge of my nose, shaking my head.

"Fine," she replied with a shrug, her fingers sliding down over her taut stomach.

"What are you doing?"

"If you won't make me come, I'll have to do it myself." Her fingers slid below the elastic waistband of her shorts, tugging them down as her fingers found her clit. *Fuck.*

"Emma," I groaned, unable to look away from her hand as she rubbed circles against her pussy. "I won't do this."

"You're not doing this. I am," she shot back as she leaned against a tree, her gaze dropping to the front of my shorts where I knew my cock was straining against the fabric. I palmed my length to conceal myself, but just that little touch caused my body to jerk. I pushed against my dick as Emma tugged her shorts to midthigh, baring her smooth mound to me as she spread her lips open, revealing her bubblegum pink cunt.

"You like it?" she asked, her voice thick with lust. "I know you like to watch."

"What the fuck did you just say?" I asked, my voice echoing through the trees. "Who put you up to this?"

"Does it matter?" she whispered before her plump teeth pressed into her lower lip. I closed the space between us, gripping her chin in my hand.

"I asked you a fucking question. Unless you want to end up on a missing person poster, I suggest you fucking answer me."

Her eyebrows pinched together, confused by how I'd suddenly gone from the nice guy next door to threatening her life.

"You're b-brother."

I sneered, gripping her face tighter. "How much did he pay you?"

"A grand." Her hand stilled and I glanced down to her exposed pussy.

"Then you better finish. I want his money's worth."

I pressed my palm on the tree over her head, leaning in closer to her. Her chin lifted in my palm so her pants and whimpers blew over my face. I didn't look down between us. I had no desire to watch her come. I just wanted her to feel like the cheap whore she was.

Her muscles tensed, and I could smell her pussy as she got off, crying out in pleasure.

"Tell my brother it takes more than *you* to get me to give up Grace." I turned, stalking away.

"You're just going to leave me like this?" she called after me.

"That's what you wanted, isn't it?" I yelled over my shoulder. "To be *used*?"

"I didn't want you to leave."

I turned to face her, taking in her still half-naked body. "That's what I do, Emma. I throw away my toys when I'm done playing with them." My eyes narrowed.

Her chin wobbled as she stared at me in disbelief.

"I tried to warn you." I turned to continue back down the trail. "Quit pouting. You earned your pay."

***

"You're my fucking hero," Relic clapped his hand on my shoulder. "Get this man a beer," he yelled toward the bar. "I can't believe you made her beg for it and you still didn't give in."

I leaned in, lowering my voice. "I don't need you to pay women to fuck me," I bit out. "If I wanted to cheat on my wife, I could."

Relic shrugged, drinking from his beer bottle. "When did you become such a pussy?"

"I'm happy with my wife," I shot back, taking a long pull from my drink.

"Come on, man. It's not like Grace is going to find out. No one gets hurt. No crime."

I rolled my eyes. "I should get home. I've been spending too much time at work lately. Grace is getting annoyed. Wants to take a vacation."

"So, take her somewhere and fuck her brains out. We can all go. Fulfill our obligations. Everyone wins."

"That's my fucking wife, asshole. I'm looking into buying a second location. And I haven't trained anyone else to manage the gym while I'm gone."

"I don't know how you ever leave the house with such a hot piece of ass at home." He shook his head. "I'd be balls deep inside of her every chance I get."

I pushed from my stool, pulling out a stack of bills and slapping them on the bar top. "That's what I'm going to go do," I shot back.

"Can I watch?" he asked as I walked away.

***

I dropped my keys on the stand next to the front door, wandering into the kitchen to look for Grace. There was a note on the table that read – *Dinner is in the fridge.*

I tossed it in the trash before making my way upstairs. Water whined through the pipes in the wall. She was in the shower. I peeled off my shirt, shoved my shorts down, and toed off my sneakers. My cock was hard at the thought of watching her soapy wet body.

I pressed against the door, catching her reflection in the mirror as she rubbed her hands over her skin, oblivious that I was watching. I grabbed my cock, stroking it slowly as I watched her rub her bath scrunchie over her tits, causing her nipples to harden.

Music played over a wireless speaker, and she hummed along, dipping her hand between her legs. As she turned around to rinse herself under the spray of water, she jumped, letting out a sting of cusswords. "You scared me!"

I smiled, sauntering toward her, my thick cock in my hand as I continued to stroke myself. "You looked so good, I didn't want to disturb you."

Grace slid the glass door open, inviting me in.

"Need help rinsing off?"

Her cheeks darkened at my words. I loved how innocent my little Grace was. We'd married only nine months ago, but she was only nineteen, and I was the only experience she had when it came to sex. Besides the two encounters with my brothers. I was the first and only man inside of her beautiful cunt. I didn't want that to change. Offering or not.

I pulled the shower sprayer from its holster, twisting the head to make the water come out in a pulse. Her teeth bit down on her lip as I sprayed across her tits, using my free hand to grope her, rubbing my thumb across her nipples to cause them to harden. I sucked one in my mouth, scraping my teeth across her delicate flesh and causing her to whimper. I lowered the water, spraying the bubbles from her skin before holding it in front of her pussy. She gasped as it pulsed water against her clit.

"Spread your pussy for me, baby," I rasped, kissing along her throat. She did as she was told, using her fingers to open herself wide for me so I could get an unobstructed view of her cunt. I pressed the head of my cock against her tight hole, groaning as it stretched around me to take my large size. "Now, hold on to me, sweetheart." Her hands wrapped around my neck and I lifted her, pressing her back against the wall. With one arm around her waist, I used the other to spray her clit again. She moaned, sinking deeper onto my cock.

"You're so fucking tight," I rasped as she clenched down on me. I knew the water pressure was probably too strong for her sensitive bundle of nerves, but I wanted her to come hard for me. I didn't want to take it easy.

Maybe I was still pissed about what had happened earlier in the day. But I'd deal with my brother another time.

Grace mewled, riding my cock as water ran between us. "That's it, baby. Fuck me just like that," I praised her. Her shoulders leaned against the shower wall, pushing her tits up. I watched as they bounced with each thrust of our hips. A feral growl emanated from my chest as her pussy pulsed around me, milking my cock. I filled her, loving that my come would be dripping down her thighs all night. "Good fucking girl," I groaned, lowering her to her toes.

"You always make me blush," she whispered, turning away from me. I grabbed her chin, forcing her to look me in the eye.

"I love the way you blush when I fuck you. Don't ever try to hide it from me. You know it's against the rules."

"I think you have an addiction."

"I do. And if I go with my cock buried inside of you, I'll die a happy man."

She fought against a smirk as she pushed up on her toes, pressing her lips against mine. I slid my tongue against the seam of her lips, pushing between them and kissing her deeply.

When I finally released her she was breathless, her hair nearly dry as it stuck against her face. I turned off the water and lifted her like a baby, carrying her to our bed as I wondered if could ever really change who I was. I could barely control my anger today and the things I wanted to do to Emma when I found out my brother paid her would take more than *sending flowers* to fix. I laid Grace down, her damp hair fanning out on the bed. She drew her legs up to press her knees together. I pushed her milky thighs apart, shaking my head as I leaned over her, running the tip of my tongue over her cunt before sucking her clit into my mouth.

She whimpered as I crawled over her, pressing another kiss to her lips. "Good night, Mr. Ransom."

"It certainly is, Mrs. Ransom."

***

55

GRACE

I groaned, pushing my hips back against Ryatt's mouth, not ready to open my eyes for the day.

"I can't get enough of your sweet pussy," he rasped, spreading me wide and delving his tongue inside of me. "Always so wet and ready for me."

I threaded my fingers through his hair, rocking my hips against his mouth. "This is quite a good morning kiss," I joked as he sucked my clit between his teeth. "Oh, just like that."

Ryatt's tongue flicked against my nub, his fingers gripping my thighs and holding me against his face.

"I'm going to come," I panted.

His tongue never slowed as he slid two fingers inside of me, slowly pumping them in and out before curling them and rubbing over my g-spot.

"Oh, God, Ryatt," I moaned, feeling my body grip down on his digits as a flood of pleasure released from me. Ryatt's tongue lapped up every drop of my excitement before pressing a final kiss against my clit.

I felt like I could sleep again for a million hours, but as Ryatt pushed up on his knees, hovering over me, his thick cock was in his hand. "Roll over." He grabbed my hips, flipping me over before tugging my hips up in the air. He pressed his large palm between my shoulder blades, pressing my head back against the bed. "I love how your cunt drips for me, Kitten," he rasped, lining the head of his cock against my entrance. I gripped the covers in my fists as he slowly shoved forward, filling me to the hilt. His heavy sac rocked against my clit as he drew back and slammed inside me hard. His hands held my hips in place as he began to fuck me, hard and fast, my already sensitive pussy still fluttering from coming against his tongue.

"I can never get enough of this," he groaned. "Your body was made for me."

"Only you," I whimpered. His pace quickened, his thrusts becoming sloppier before he stilled, buried deep inside of me and filling me with his seed.

***

"I don't need to work out today after that," Ryatt joked, tugging his shirt over his still damp hair from his shower.

I smiled, sliding his eggs on his plate with a slice of ham. He kissed my cheek as he took it from me before settling into his seat at the kitchen table.

"What's that?" he asked, pointing to the television. I grabbed the remote turning up the volume.

"The woman's body was found undressed just outside of Coffer Trail. Her identity has not been released, but she appears to be in her early twenties. Police are asking for any information, no matter how insignificant. They're also asking citizens to avoid the area at this time."

"You run that trail," I watched in disbelief as police cars lined the street of our small community. "I hope it wasn't someone you know."

"Why would it be someone *I* know?"

"Because it's so close to the gym," I pointed out as I sank down in my chair at the kitchen table to eat my food. "Maybe I'll call Relic later. See if he knows anything."

Ryatt glared over at me. "You call *Relic* now?" he asked, his tone accusatory.

"I mean, he's our family –"

"He's *my* family, Grace."

I jerked back. "I know."

"And he wants to *fuck* you." Ryatt pushed back his chair, grabbing his plate.

"Fine. I won't call him." I threw up my hands, leaning back in my seat. "Okay?"

"No. It's not okay. How often do the two of you speak behind my back?" he asked, scraping his food in the trash before his plate clattered in the sink.

"What is *wrong* with you? You literally let him go down on me in front of you, now you're acting like I can't even *speak* to him?" I shoved my chair back, pushing to my feet. Ryatt straightened his back, towering over me. At his full height of six foot three, I had to crane my neck to meet his gaze.

"Do whatever you want," he bit out before walking out the front door.

***

56

RYATT

I paced the lobby of the gym, wiping my hand across my jaw, with my cell pressed to my ear.

"Relic, why the fuck have you been ignoring my calls?"

"I'm busy," he groaned, stifling a yawn. A woman murmured through the phone, and I rolled my eyes.

"We have a serious fucking problem."

"Let me guess? Another beautiful woman wants to fuck you, and you only have one cock to go around."

"No, you prick. There was a body found on the trail where I left Emma yesterday. The girl you fucking paid to try to sleep with me."

"You left her *on* the trail?" he repeated, sounding more awake now. "Fuck, baby, we need to finish this later," he groaned to his guest.

I raked my fingers through my hair. "I need you to see if it's her, man. I'm losing my fucking mind."

"Calm down. I'll see what I can find out."

"I'll close down the gym and head back home."

"No," Relic snapped. "Go about your day as usual. I'll be in touch." The call disconnected.

Go about my day as usual? I fucking left her standing in the woods alone. And now Emma may be dead because of it – because of me.

***

Fifty-six minutes later Relic was stepping into the gym.

"Who is it? Is it Emma?"

"Not sure. Body was pretty banged up. Someone really did a number on her."

I sank down on my haunches, my head in my hands as my gut wrenched. "I didn't do anything to her. I swear." But that was a lie. I could have made sure she made it out of the woods safely. I could have protected her. I deserved whatever happened to me because of that. But if Grace found out I was alone with her, I didn't know if she'd believe I didn't touch her.

Relic nodded, scratching his cheek as his eyes danced around the room. "There's not much I can do for you here, Ryatt. Maybe we should call your father."

I pushed back to my feet, stalking toward him. "You'd fucking love that, wouldn't you? All everyone has been trying to do is get me back in that fucking mansion."

Relic held up his palms. "Calm down. I said I *should*. For now, nothing is pointing to you. We need to keep it that way. But I'm not gonna lie, this is a really fucked up situation you've gotten yourself into. Did anyone see you with her yesterday?"

"No one was really paying attention when she was working out."

"Good. That's good."

"We walked out separately after I closed."

"Did she say anything to you? Make you believe she may be in some sort of trouble?"

I shrugged, my head swimming. "Just that you paid her so she would try to fuck me."

Relic's eyes narrowed. "She already wanted to fuck you."

"I'm not going to say this again. Stop getting in the middle of my marriage or we're going to have a much bigger problem than some dead girl in the woods."

Relic smiled his lip twitching like he was enjoying bringing this side out of me. "I'm going to see what else I can find out. I'll come by tonight. We can cook out on the grill or something."

I nodded, clapping my hand on his shoulder. "Thank you, *brother*."

Relic nodded once before stepping back out into the blinding sun.

***

Every minute of the day dragged by. I couldn't think, couldn't work out. I just paced the floor, waiting for the moment I could lock up and get home.

I drove to my house at breakneck speed, barely stopping at the stop signs. I just needed a strong drink. Grace was setting up the grill when I arrived. I kissed her on the cheek and went upstairs to run through the shower. By the time Relic showed up, I'd already had four generous shots of whiskey –drowning my regret. If it weren't for Relic, she'd still be alive. I shook the thought from my head. It might not even be her.

"Can you talk to him?" I heard Grace whisper to Relic as I tipped my glass to my lips, watching the flames dance in the fire pit. Relic murmured something back to her that I couldn't decipher and it caused her to giggle. I clenched my jaw, pouring another shot into my glass as Grace disappeared inside to get ready for dinner.

Relic trudged over, sinking down into the chair next to me with a groan. "No news," he said, staring off at the fire. "No missing persons fitting the victim's description." I drank back more of the amber liquid. "You might want to slow down."

"No," my eyes cut to him. "I might not."

"Grace knows somethings wrong. You want her to worry?"

I laughed sardonically. "She always has your shoulder to cry on, doesn't she?"

"What's that supposed to mean?"

I shook my head, pouring another drink. "Nothing."

"Look, I'm trying to help you here. Neither of us wants Grace to get hurt."

My mind went to Emma. She shouldn't have been hurt either. "I appreciate your concern for my *wife*."

The muscles in Relic's jaw jumped as he shook his head. "Maybe she *should* know."

My head snapped to the back door before my narrowed gaze settled back on him. "You'd tell her, just to get a chance at getting in her panties?" I bit out. "You were the one pushing me to fuck Emma."

Relic's lip twisted up and he shrugged. "You're being awfully ungrateful for all I'm doing for you, Ryatt. I was offering you a *distraction*. I'm going to *fuck* Grace, whether you want me to or not. So will the twins. There is no other option."

"I can walk away. Take her somewhere else and leave all this behind."

"You can't walk away, Ryatt. Your father will never let you. And Grace is the offering, with or without you."

"Anything so you can take your shot at Grace. Even if it means fucking over your own brother."

"I already had my shot at Grace," he snapped.

"What?"

The backdoor opened and slammed shut as she made her way outback, holding a bowl of potato salad.

"We'll talk more about this later," I warned, pushing from my chair to help my wife set up for the barbecue.

***

I couldn't stop glaring at Grace and Relic, who chatted happily as they ate their steaks.

"What do you think?" Grace's eyes met mine, looking at me expectantly. I hadn't heard a word she'd said, my thoughts spinning as I wondered what Relic meant when he said he'd had his shot with her. Then my thoughts went to Emma.

"About what?" I asked.

She forced a smile, tucking her hair behind her ear. "About going to Relic's cabin for our anniversary. We could ski during the day. The twins could come too. Make it a family vacation –"

"Relic does enough for us already," I replied. Grace's smile faltered, and Relic laid his palm on her thigh, his gaze never leaving mine.

"We can talk about it when you're sober."

"No, we don't need to talk about it later. I said no." I replied, taking another drink from my glass.

"I'll get the apple pie," Grace pushed from the bench of the picnic table and hurried inside. I didn't miss the way her eyes glossed over.

"She knows something is wrong with you. Why are you trying to hurt her?"

"Hurt her? Because I don't want to go to a cabin with you for our anniversary?" I scoffed.

"You've been ignoring her all night."

"Good thing she has you to comfort her."

"Yeah, it is."

Grace came back outside, a smile on her face that didn't reach her eyes as she set the pie on the table. "Dessert?" she asked, looking between us.

Relic's lips twisted up in a smirk. "You know I can't resist tasting your pie, Grace."

***

57

GRACE

I felt the tension rising between Relic and Ryatt. Something was wrong. He'd never gone this long without touching me. He usually couldn't keep his hands off my body. I worried my lip, wishing I could get Relic alone to ask him what was going on. I took another shot, wincing at the harsh taste. But after the night I was having a good buzz wouldn't hurt.

My body swayed as I grabbed a bag of marshmallows and perched myself on Ryatt's lap. His hands didn't wrap around me, and I relaxed back against him, holding up the bag. "Do you want to roast one?" I asked. He shook his head, his eyes glazed as he stared at the flames.

"Are you mad at me?" I asked, trying to keep my voice at a whisper as tears pricked my eyes. I leaned to the side so I could look at him.

"Why would I be mad at you?" His eyes slid to mine, his tone cold.

"I-I don't know," I muttered, my gaze drifting to Relic, worried he might have said something to Ryatt about our past.

"Don't worry about him, sweetheart. He's just drunk," Relic reassured me, taking a long pull from his bottle of beer, draining its contents before tossing it on the ground with the rest of his collection.

"That's right, Grace. He didn't spill your secrets *yet*."

"Ryatt," Relic barked. "If you want to talk about this, man to man, we can do that. Leave her alone."

"Yeah?" he asked, grabbing my waist and lifting me up, so I could stand. Ryatt pushed to his feet, and Relic did the same. I put my body between them, pressing a palm against their chests to separate them.

Ryatt grabbed his shirt behind his neck, pulling it over his head and tossing it into the grass. "What the fuck happened between you and my wife?" he barked, and my skin grew cold as their muscles flexed beneath my fingers.

"Nothing happened," I croaked, my eyes brimming with unshed tears. I'd never seen Ryatt this pissed off before.

"Don't pretend you care about her now," Relic goaded, an evil smirk twisting on his lips.

"What's that supposed to mean?" I asked, searching Relic's face but he didn't take his eyes off Ryatt.

"What's it mean, Ryatt?" Relic asked, flashing his teeth as his grin widened.

Ryatt put his arm against my chest, pushing me out of the way as he swung, his fist connected with the left side of Relic's jaw. "Ryatt!" I screeched. Relic touched his lip before pulling back and inspecting the smattering of blood on the pads of his fingers before his tongue ran out over his busted lip.

"Go," I yelled, shoving against Ryatt's chest. He stumbled back a few steps as his nostrils flared before turning and stalking off into the house. I turned to Relic, taking his face delicately in my hands to inspect the damage.

"I'm fine," Relic bit out as he grabbed my wrist, pulling my hand gently from his face. "We're fine," he reiterated. "Just had a few too many."

"What the hell is going on between you two?" I asked, my pulse hammering under his touch.

"Nothing for you to worry about. I promise."

My eyes searched his, my chin wobbling. "What did you tell him?"

"He doesn't know." His free hand came up, pushing a strand of hair from my face, his eyes searching mine.

"I'm going to tell him," I decided. "It was only a meeting. Nothing happened between us." I swallowed against the lump forming in my throat.

"Nothing?" he asked, his gaze falling to my lips as the column of his throat bobbed. I pulled my hand free from his hold. As his other hand trailed down the side of my neck. "It should have been *us*," he confessed.

I took a step back from him. "You didn't want *me*, remember?"

"That's not true." He shook his head. "You were too good for me."

"I wasn't –"

He pressed his fingers against my lips to silence me. "I didn't want to dirty you; use you like I used everyone else. I wanted you to have the life you deserved with a husband who wouldn't need to defile or share you. And then you were offered to Ryatt." He said his brother's name like it was a curse as his hand fell to his side. "And by the time I realized the mistake I made, it was too late. You already loved him. And now I'm forced to watch as he gets what I want because I can't walk away. Being near you is better than not having you at all."

I shook my head, wiping a wayward tear from my cheek. "Relic," I said his name as I exhaled.

"I had to watch him shove his fingers inside of you, knowing he was doing it to make me jealous because he sees how I look at you."

"How do you look at me?" I asked, my voice barely a whisper.

His hand slid against my cheek, his thumb rubbing gently across my skin, setting it on fire. "Like it should have been us."

"But it wasn't," Ryatt called out from behind us. I spun around to face him. "She was *offered* to you?" he asked, looking past me to his brother.

"She was," Relic bit out.

Ryatt's eyes narrowed as he shook his head, his jaw tense.

"You can't keep her to yourself forever, brother," Relic added. "She was meant for *all* of us."

"You're right." Ryatt's eyes went to me. "Pack a bag, Kitten. We're going to see the twins."

TO BE CONTINUED...

Don't miss out!

Visit the website below and you can sign up to receive emails whenever Teresa Mummert publishes a new book. There's no charge and no obligation.

https://books2read.com/r/B-A-BVD-CFZLC

BOOKS 2 READ

Connecting independent readers to independent writers.

Did you love *Savage Grace*? Then you should read *Girl Gone Bad*[1] by Teresa Mummert!

[2]

Life hasn't been easy for Beatrice "Birdie" Harper. Every man she's known has let her down. Her father was no exception. She spent years struggling to distance herself from the monster who raised her. His betrayal catapulted her onto a path to discover if evil is born or created – nature versus nurture. And ultimately, if her struggle to be a good person will be in vain. Navigating life as an adult has become a gauntlet of lies and infidelity. When all hope for a normal existence seems lost, Birdie meets the man of her dreams –

1. https://books2read.com/u/bz1KZG

2. https://books2read.com/u/bz1KZG

sexy, charismatic, and covered in tattoos. But figuring out which secrets to expose and which to bury will be the difference between Birdie finally getting her happily ever after or paying the ultimate price.

Read more at www.TeresaMummert.com.

Also by Teresa Mummert

Hollow Point Series
Hollow

Honor Series
Honor Student
Honor Thy Teacher
Honor and Obey
Honor and Betray

How to Date a Dead Guy
How to Date a Dead Guy

Shame On You
Shameless

Twisted Tales
Breaking Beauty

Standalone
The Note
Safe Word
Bleed Ink: A Self-Publishing Guide
Perfect Lie
Pretty Little Things
Rellik
The Good Girls
Something Wicked
Heathens
Crave
Something in the Water
The Choking Kind
Girl Gone Bad
Savage Grace

Watch for more at www.TeresaMummert.com.

About the Author

TERESA MUMMERT is a New York Times and USA Today bestselling author. Her work includes word-of-mouth bestselling, White Trash Trilogy, which landed her a three-book publishing deal with Simon & Schuster. She is also the author of the wildly popular Honor Series which chronicles the taboo romance between a student and her college professor. To date, she's written over twenty-five novels and plans for many more releases in the future.

Read more at www.TeresaMummert.com.

Milton Keynes UK
Ingram Content Group UK Ltd.
UKHW020738040823
426331UK00015B/737